BLACK REIGN PUBLISHING
PRESENTS

SOUL of a MENACE

A Thug Life Story

By. Ty Robinson

D1510618

Copyright © 2020 Black Reign Publishing

All rights reserved. Without limiting the rights under copyright reserved. No part of this book may be reproduced, stored, copied and or introduced into a retrieval system, to transmitted in any form, or by any means (Electronic, mechanical, photocopying, recording, or otherwise), without prior written consent from both the author and the publisher, except for the brief quotes that are used in literary reviews.

This is a work of fiction. It is not meant to depict, portray or represent any particular real persons. All the characters, incidents and dialogues are the product of the author's imagination and are not to be construed as real. Any references or similarities to actual events, entities, real people (living or dead) or to real locales and/or to any particular places of locations are only intended to give this story a sense of realism. Any similarity in names, characters, entities, and incidents are coincidental.

*"In the same reality of slaves, no black male is born a thug. Just like slaves, thugs were, and are still being **created**. Thugs are manufactured. Black boys and men are not America's nightmare. We're just denied the fruits of the American dream and societal conditions nurture many of us to co-exist with a nightmare of a lie. That we're the greatest threat to a peaceful life, public safety, and the pursuit of happiness in society. A thug in the streets of America's hoods are the same as a monster. Created, then feared by its creator."*

BASED ON REAL LIFE EVENTS

PROLOGUE

I ain't been about no bitch ass shit for the thirty-one years I been on this earth and I ain't about start now. It's far too late in the game for me to act like a pussy. As I watched rural America pass by as I sit on this prison bus, I'm like, FUCK IT. It is what it is. The only sound around me was the noise of the bus itself. Twenty-two dudes plus myself in orange jumpsuits, handcuffs, and shackles. Heading for a federal prison in the middle of nowhere Missouri. This bus ride was the same as the federal prisoner flight from New York. Silent. Unlike the state level Department of Corrections transports; Federal inmates are forbidden to speak. These U.S. Marshalls were no joke. Most of them were jacked up white boys with tough guy attitudes and had no problem "tuning" a motherfucker up. We weren't allowed to speak because they didn't want us planning shit on them, but mostly it was about power & control. We were Federal property now and they had the "power" to "control" everything in our reality.

Though I wasn't allowed to talk, that didn't stop me from observing my surroundings and the other convicted dudes I was travelling with. Twenty-three of us in all. Half of my group were black, the other quarter were white dudes, and the rest were a small mix of Hispanics and two Asians. This wasn't my first time being transported to a prison and I learned years ago how to tell the difference. Between an inmate and a convict. Yeah! There's a difference. I studied the dudes I been travelling with since I was transported from the Federal Detention Center in Brooklyn to JFK airport. Most of them were inmates. Bitch made motherfuckers that looked hard as a rock but were soft as baby shit on the inside. I knew from the door that four of them were straight from P.C. Protective Custody. I never saw any of them in general population or anywhere else for that matter. The rest of us, myself included, were convicts.

Real motherfuckin' criminals. Thugs. Gangsters. Gladiators. Killers. It was the expression on their faces and the look in their eyes. The inmates among us were trying to put on their war face. That hard, *"ain't afraid to die"* look. That shit was window dressing though. I saw right through it. Those dudes were food, and once the wolves caught a whiff of their scent when they got to their home jail; they were going to get eaten

5

alive! The convicts like myself though were predators lying in wait. A few caught me sizing them up and our non-verbal exchange spoke louder than any words would have. Their expression was the same as mine. Calm. Blank. No emotions. Our eyes were the same too. Steady. Ruthless. Lethal. One dude, a Haitian from the Bronx, son and I were on the same page. When I peeped me analyzing him, dude held my stare for a second, then nodded. I sent the nod back, then returned my attention to watching nothing through my window as the bus rolled on the Missouri interstate.

Twenty-five miles into the middle of nowhere and over ten miles from anything that resembled civilization was FCI-Harrisonville. The newest medium security facility in the Federal prison system. It's been six hours since we landed in Missouri. We had to drop fourteen motherfuckers off at FCC-Independence before heading off to Harrisonville. Independence was a minimum-security facility. All of the non-violent and white-collar crime inmates were delivered to their new home before I was taken to mine. Harrisonville was for a Class-A II Federal prisoners. Offenders with extensive violent records, have done state time, and were classified by the Federal Bureau of Prisons as HIGH-RISK inmates. Plus, all of us being sent to Harrisonville had no less than a minimum of five years with a maximum of fifteen years. I was in for ten on this ride. Not long after the bus was driven through a triple set of razor wire topped fences, it was time to go through the bullshit once again.

Intake & reception. Strip & cavity search, shower & decontamination, medical evaluation, blood draw & urine collection, paperwork with a staff member, and then uniform & linens issue. For my first two weeks, I wasn't "permitted" to wear civilian clothing. Until I was "cleared", I had to wear a two-piece khaki uniform and those corny ass white skippy shoes. Me and the eight others I arrived with were escorted to the classification unit. A dormitory like cell block for new inmates. I was assigned to cell #10 with an older black dude. He was six-one like me, dark skinned, but skinny as fuck with graying dreads and a thick beard. When I entered the cell, O.G. was chilling on his bunk across from mine. Smoking a cigarette and reading a book. Dude looked up, studied me for a moment, then muttered in a deep raspy voice,
"Let me give you some privacy, youngblood."

O.G. stubbed his menthol out, saved his place in his book, and took it with him as he strolled pass me to exit the cell. Before I got settled in, I sat my shit down on my unmade bunk and sat on it. I went into my box of property and took out my Newports with a book of matches. I fired up my cig and smoked in silence. I had three months in on a ten-year sentence, but I wasn't worried about shit. The feds routinely let niggas out early for good behavior, but that was predicated on me exhibiting good behavior. Easier said than done. The one thing I knew all too well about prison was that doin' time without the temptation to push a niggas shit back was all but impossible. If motherfuckers didn't try me, I was more than willing to stay in my lane and serve out this sentence. Without fuckin' a nigga up or sheddin' someone's blood. However, it was reality in prison with all the real & wannabe tough guys, so called gangsters, and motherfuckers that think they're killers testing me. Forcing me to show their ass what was up and why I had a Cobra head tatted on my chest. Over my heart.

As I smoked in my cell for the time being, I stared at the barred-up window. Allowing myself to think about things that I wasn't going to see for a long time. Home. The streets. My hood. I grinned to myself as I took a pull on my port. I thought about my life from ten years old to right now at thirty-one. I mentally reminisced about being an angry young pup that became a vicious ass wolf. I thought about the terror years of my youth. Fist fights at the playground and on corners, skippin' school, stealing cars, and then getting into the game. I smiled as I remembered running from the cops, the times I got caught and was sent to juvenile detention, and then when I really got deep in the streets. I put my cigarette out in the toilet, returned to my bunk and sat with my back against the wall, staring at the opposite one with my arms crossed. Still on memory lane. I thought about the first time I got some pussy. How good that shit felt. I remembered the first time I had sold a bag of coke, the first time I smoked weed, that time I got rolled on & stomped out by the police, and the first time I held a gun in my hand. The power I felt as I gripped that steel.

The streets and a life of crime was all that I knew. My world was about money, sex, guns, & mayhem. That's it. I was born and bred for the streets. I did it all. I sold dope, robbed niggas, banked more cash than I knew what to do with, slid dick up in bad bitches, and as quiet as kept, I was a player in the murder game. If the police and Feds played hard with me; I'd be stuck in the box for the rest of my natural life. Unlike a lot of niggas that claim to live that THUG LIFE; I did. I didn't need a gun to send a nigga to meet his maker, I was about my money, I fear nothing, I don't regret shit, and I live by a code. I never snitch, my word is my bond, and if I have to body a motherfucker; I'm more than willing to

7

walk right up on their ass and see their white of their eyes as I put a hot one in their cranium. Niggas talk about being a thug; I live it. I got a ten-year stretch hanging over my head. If shit goes smooth, I'll keep a clean slate and be out in five. I can do five years like it ain't shit. Yet, if any of these dudes in here wanna test me, it is what it is. Whether it's in the streets or here in prison; I am who I am and will do what I gotta do. I've never been a punk, pussy, coward, or bitch. Anybody who want it, can get it. I don't give a fuck a niggas rep, where he's from, or what he's done. I am who the fuck I am and I'll step to anybody! Anytime! Anywhere! With no fear, hesitation, or mercy. I didn't choose the Thug Life.

The Thug Life chose me.

CHAPTER ONE

"Born a sin, playing to win, 100 coffins for the death of 99 men."

Thirty-one years before I was sentenced to Ten-years in the Feds, I was born in Queens, but raised up in Rochester, New York. My moms was from Staten Island and my pops hailed from the Southside of the Bronx. They met at an afterparty following a concert and never separated. From the stories I was told as a youngin', my parents were on some next level shit in the mid-eighties. Half black power-militant revolutionaries, half gangster ass hustlers that were serious about their money. A few years before I came along, my mom and dad were on that Bonnie & Clyde shit. Selling dope and pulling robberies when not fighting the power. I knew everything about my parents. One minutes they were at Black Conscious meetings and protesting against the system; the next, they were hustlin' product or hittin' a lick. Robbing Jewish diamond dealers, check cash spots, or travelling outside of metro NYC to hit an unsuspecting suburban bank in a quiet town.

Having a child didn't slow my moms and pops down for a second. My mom did take a break during her pregnancy with me, or after she brought me into this world. They named me Sharif Amir Watkins, but I was rarely, if ever referred to by my given name. I was always Sha or Reef. By the time I was five, we moved from out of the projects in Queens to Rochester. We went from a high rise in an infamous housing projects apartment to a big ass row house in a relatively crime free, mostly black neighborhood in a new city. Five hours away from the Big Apple. I didn't know until later on why we moved so far away from Queens. My pops had leveled up his criminal game. He went from buying product to sell in our hood from some Dominicans in Manhattan, to being supplied by someone in Canada. The move to Rochester was business. Relocating there put my pops closer to Buffalo where he met with his suppliers for his dope, and Rochester was prime real-estate for a takeover back then.

My father and his connect saw the city and surrounding towns as a gold mine. It was 1994, America was a decade into the crack era, and certain parts of the country were considered an untapped source of big-time drug money. The flame of the drug game was getting hotter in Rochester, so my pops and his connect decided to heat that shit up. Not long after we moved and got settled in, my dad got to work. He went back to Queens and recruited a bunch of niggas from all five boroughs. Niggas that he knew and hustlers with solid reps that he knew of arrived in Rochester to join his new crew. My moms played the part of the stay at wife, but she was just as deep in the business as my father was. Yeah, she put on a show of being a home maker, took me to & from school, and seemed to be a nice and sweet law-abiding woman; but it was all a façade. An act. My moms was a good wife and mother, but just like my pops; she was a gangster. He dealt with the connect, ran the crew, and handled business in the streets. My mom handled the money and infrastructure.

Pops was the CEO of the company, moms was the CFO. Chief Financial Officer. She and a couple of chicks she put on cleaned cash by hand, pressed and banded the bills, she dealt with the accountants, and had bank accounts all over the place. While I was in school and being a kid, my parents were building something real. Their own empire. After a year in Rochester, they had shit on lock. Mad niggas from NYC had relocated, they took over a projects, ran local hustlers off their corners, and spread out like a virus. My father had the game on smash. Whether it was weed, dope, or coke; Karim Watkins was that nigga! My parents were smart hustlers though. It wasn't about driving around in expensive cars, dipped in gold and Gucci, throwing money around like they were in a fuckin' rap video. My parents put up the image of black entrepreneurs. They dressed casually, we were cool with all most of our neighbors, and they invested in the hood. They were drug trafficking gangsters hiding in plain sight.

While my pops inner circle niggas from the city ran shit on the streets for him, like a VP of a corporation, he controlled the ebb & flow of the business from the shadows of anonymity. Rochester knew Karim and Joi Watkins as a loving couple that were business partners. My mom funneled their drug money into local businesses, forming deals with the owners, and turning their endeavors into profitable ones. Around the time I was in 4th grade, my parents had as much legit business ventures as they did illegal action. They were partners in a hot spot barbershop / salon, a nail shop, clothing-sneaker-and corner stores, three laundromats, a restaurant, sports bar, a night club, and a very popular strip joint. Yo! The shit was crazy! We had stupid money, everybody loved & respected my parents, I had mad friends, and I was a fly young nigga. I had more clothes, sneakers, and video games than I knew what to do with. The

Watkins changed Rochester. I would learn later on in my life that my parents altered the city in a big way.

On one side of the fence, their connect supplied them with so much product, high quality product, that they dominated the drug scene. My pops ran his crew like a mafia army. Niggas revered him like he was Frank Lucas, his soldiers were vicious but disciplined, and they were serious about their money and making sure business ran smoothly. Problems were dealt with violently, but silently. If motherfuckers became an issue that threatened the empire, or did some foul shit such as rob one of my pops dealers; it was black magic time. POOF! Niggas disappeared. Without a trace. The police always made noise with their murder investigations and whatever, but they never came knockin' on our door with a warrant. I figured out much later that the law must have been on the payroll. Because there was no doubt that my father had them niggas murked. Over the years I lived in Rochester, my pops organization transformed the environment. The hoods became just as treacherous as any in Brooklyn or the Bronx, while the safer neighborhoods were elevated.

That was my mothers work. My moms was the benevolent Black Queen and diplomat. She showed love and charity to the women of Rochester. Most of them were young black single mothers. She helped them move into better apartments, pulled strings for good jobs, and assisted them with anything they needed. Moms even put up the cash for home remodels, renovations, back to school shopping, and neighborhood clean-up crews. That was the other side of the fence. My parents were both destroyers and builders. The gift and the curse in the city. Outside of being the King and Queen of Rochester, they were the best parents I could have ever asked for. My mother taught me how to dress, to keep myself clean & groomed, and for eleven years, she imparted the ways of a gentleman in me. My mom loved three things in her world. Me, her husband, and her money. Pops molded me to be a man long before I turned eighteen. From the time I could walk, he schooled me in the art of boxing. Though he never boxed professionally or even as amateur; his hands were deadly.

Starting at four, me and my dad practiced boxing. He taught me how to hold my hands, position my feet, and how to throw punches. We hit the bag, he worked on my speed and precision with the mitts, and we sparred all the time. By six I was sharp, I hit hard, I was nice defensively, and I wasn't afraid to get hit. The older I got, the more aggressive my pops was with me when we trained. Though he would tag me with hard shots, he never let me cry or act like wounded punk. MAN UP! He would bark at me. MAN THE FUCK UP! I first thought my pops was being cruel, but I learned that he wasn't. After our sparring sessions, he would kneel down, wipe the blood from my nose or the corner of my lip, grin, and then give it to me real. Explaining to me that I couldn't be weak in the world. That I was a warrior and there is no place for softness in a warriors' life. Society preys on the weak, soft, and tender hearted. He further explained that it was his job to prepare me for the world. That despite our money and all of our comforts; I wasn't no spoiled rich kid. I was cut from thoroughbred cloth and that I was to never act like I was a sheep. I was a wolf and wolves don't cry, run, or bow down to anyone. EVER!

Even before I was ten years old, my father was grooming me to become a man. Every Saturday morning, he took me with him to the barber shop for us to get out hair cut together. It was cool as fuck kicking it with my dad. After I was done, I sat in the shop as he got his hair cut. My pops rocked the same style. A one and half with the grain that made his waves flow like an ocean, a close fade, and a razor-sharp squared shape up. His barber always put a hot towel on his face for a while, then would give him a straight razor shave, followed by lining up his perfectly groomed GO-T. We always spent like two and a half hours in the barbershop. My father was like an exalted politician. I watched him hold court with the barbers, dudes getting a cut, and motherfuckers that just hung out at the shop. They cracked jokes, engaged in heated discussions, laughed, and talked sports. Before we left, I always watched my pops pass off two hundred-dollar bills to our barber, they shook hands, and then we left.

Saturday was father and son day for us. After leaving the barber shop, we went to get something to eat at my favorite spot. Southern Joe's Chicken. Joe's was ten times better than KFC and Popeyes. Mr. Joe was from North Carolina and his fried chicken was fire! Me and my pops got down and then we rolled over to the ave. My parents had enough money to buy me whatever I wanted, but as I was taught; I wasn't no rich kid that got whatever he wanted just because. I was expected to keep my grades up and do what I was told. I did, and my father rewarded me. I was a sneaker fanatic, so after we got our hair cut and then left the restaurant, it was time to pick out my next pair of kicks. Nike was the top brand in the 90's. Air Force One's, Air Max's, and Air Jordan's. I picked out a pair of Black on white Air Force's, Royal blue on white Air Max's, and I decided to go with a fresh ass pair of Reeboks. It was 1999 and Allen Iverson's signature "The Answer" sneakers had just hit the market. I got those with a matching Iverson jersey, 76ers cap, and shorts to go with them.

As always, when we arrived home, my mother was chillin' on the couch in the living room. She had went to get her hair and nails done while we were out having our father & son time. When we walked through the door, she was relaxing on the couch watching TV and enjoying a glass of wine. She checked out my hair cut, happily told me that she like the new part style I had, and then I showed her my new shit. My pops sat next to her. Once I was done showing her my stuff, I took my shit up to my room, and fired up my PlayStation while my parents chilled downstairs to do adult shit. Later on, I watched a college football game with my dad while my mom was out socializing with her business partners. I was eleven years old and that night, my dad allowed me to have some of his beer for the first time. He laughed at my facial reaction, then rubbed my head before he kissed it. I got to stay up to eleven with him, then I was sent to bed. That night, both my parents told me they loved me. My dad when I went up to my room, then an hour or so later when my mother returned home. I didn't know what I was going to be when I grew up, but I was certain of one thing. I had a mother and father that loved me. More than they loved the streets.

****

Three months later, the walls of Jericho came crashing down. My pops was always cautious about the law. He did everything he could to insulate himself, us, and the empire from being infiltrated by the cops or feds. I knew what my parents were, just as I knew that their main concern was the rats. Snitches and confidential informants. People from my dad's crew went to jail all the time, but they were always taken care of. They went to court with high priced lawyers, they received money as they did their time, their people were looked out for, and they never came home to nothing. My father believed in that old school gangster code. Take care of your people and your people will take care of you. My parents were so on alert for threats from the outside, that they were blind from threats within the family. Niggas that my pops made rich and respected turned on him. It wasn't the police or FBI that crushed the Kingdom. It was traitorous ass motherfuckers within its walls.

I was going on twelve when life as I knew it was forever changed. As school let out, I was eager to leave. It was a Friday. Me and my parents were heading down to NY for the weekend. I wanted to see my aunts, uncles, and cousins; but that's not why I was so excited. My pops got us tickets to the boxing title fight at Madison Square Garden on Saturday night. Roy Jones Jr was fighting for the belt and we both wanted to see him rumble. We loved Roy. I had been looking forward to going to the fight with my dad all week long. When the bell sounded to end the school day, I was out! I didn't even link up with my homies as we did at the end of the day. I grabbed my book bag and was gone. I exited the building with everyone else expecting to see my mom's white Audi. I didn't see it in the mixture of other parent's vehicles and buses. I was still looking for my moms' car when I saw a familiar face heading towards me. My pops right hand man. Tone. Uncle T.

For as far back as I could remember, Uncle Tone was a major part of my life. He and my dad were childhood friends, they played football together, started hustling together, and they built the empire side by side. Uncle T was like a second father to me. He didn't have any kids of his own, but he treated me like I was his natural born son. He walked up on me, placed his hand on my shoulder, and in a low voice, he told me to come with him. I went with him to his car, we got in, and he pulled off. I was confused, but I didn't say anything. Uncle T didn't speak either. His eyes were focused on the road as he drove. I was even more confused when we began to leave Rochester. Heading south. A few miles outside of the city, as I was about to ask him where were we going and where were my parents; he answered both questions that I had yet to ask.

Subtly was not my uncles' way. He was direct and blunt. Without taking his off the road, he shattered my world. By telling me that my mom and dad were gone. That they were dead. I stared at him as he went on to say that someone shot and killed both of them in my dad's car. They were supposed to be meeting with some people about business when someone on a motorcycle pulled up next to them at a red light and murdered them before speeding off. I felt my heart starting to beat faster, my throat and chest got all tight, I could hear myself breathing, and my eyes filled up with tears. However, something in me kept them from falling. I just stared at my uncle as he shared with me that my father had planned for this day. He had what I needed and that he was taking me somewhere safe. A place where no one in New York will know where I am and that I was going with someone that my parents trusted without question to take care of me. I sat back in my seat and looked out the window. Wanting to cry my soul out, but for some reason, I was unable to.

We drove for nearly six hours and it was dark when we finally stopped. In front of a row house in the city of Newark, Delaware. Uncle T went to the trunk and took out a medium sized gym bag as I climbed out of the passenger seat. With his hand on my shoulder, he walked with me towards the house. Standing behind the screen door was someone I knew; but not very well. My pops sister. Vanessa. She was in her 40's, but looked like she was 25. My aunt was one of those bad ass chicks in the hood that aged like fine wine and looked like a movie star. She had long hair, a pretty face, and built like a brick house. She looked mean, but when she saw me, her eyes softened and she hugged me. In a soft voice, she told me to go on in the house and have a seat. From her leather sofa, I heard her and Uncle T talking on the porch. He told her that there was money in the bag, along with my birth certificate, social security card, and guardianship papers. He instructed her to wait a few days then contact the lawyer on the papers and the attorney will make sure to finesse the custody shit for me. Before he left, Uncle T came in, hugged me, told me to listen to my aunt, and when he can, he will check in on me. With that, he exited the house and drove away. Leaving me in Delaware.

My aunt lived alone until I arrived. Her house was nice as fuck and looked expensive. My bedroom was down from hers at the end of the hall. That first night, after she showed me where my room was, I went in and closed the door. I sat on my new bed and stared at nothing. I hadn't said shit since my Uncle Tone told me that my moms and pops were dead. Now I was six hours away from home, my parents were in the morgue, and for the time being; all I had was my aunt. I felt a venomous anger growing inside. I stared at the wall across the room as I balled my hands into tight fists. I saw my mothers' beautiful chocolate brown face and that smooth half smile she always did. I bit into my bottom lip and started breathing hard through my nose as my pops face replaced my mothers. I felt the tears coming as I saw my father standing in front of me. The mitts on his hands, giving me instructions as I hit them with the punch combinations that he had taught me. I recalled dancing with my mom in the living room as she sipped her wine. I saw my pop sitting in the chair getting his fade touched up as he laughed and joked with his barber.

I tried to fight them off, remembering that my father told me that I was warrior. And warriors don't cry. I heard his voice in my head telling me to *MAN UP! You ain't no punk, Sha! So don't cry like one!* I fought so hard not to let tears go that I started shaking. Then I remembered my moms hugging me and kissing me on my forehead every day when she dropped me off at school. I heard her voice too. Telling me that I was her little King, to focus on my school work, and that she loved me. With that sunrise like smile on her face. That's when I gave in. I stared at the wall a few feet away from me and silently cried. I allowed my tears to fall as I stopped trying to force my parents faces from my mind. Inside, I was a hurricane though. A biblical storm of pain, sadness, and furious anger. The hurt was cold, but my anger...my rage...was hot. Hot as the sun. I felt more anger than anything else. The pain was for my father, while my rage was from losing my mother. I cried for a long fuckin' time that night. I decided right then and there to get it all out. My pops told me that I couldn't go through life weak. So right there in my new bedroom, I let all that sad shit flow out of my eyes. Swearing that once I was dry, I'll never cry again. NEVER!

****

Two weeks went by before my aunt was able to get me registered me for school. In that time, she got me settled in. With the money in the gym bag that arrived with me, my auntie was able to take me shopping for everything I was going to need. My aunt didn't seem big on conversation, but she was cool with me. She told me that since I was old enough to dress myself, I was old enough to pick out my own wardrobe. In two weeks, I filled my closet and dresser with clothes and sneakers. My aunt didn't object to or suggest anything while we were out shopping. I selected what I wanted, she paid for it, and we left the store. She let me pick out what kind of TV and video game I wanted for my room, and went to the grocery store to stock up on food. Mostly microwave shit because Aunt Vanessa made it known early on. She was not a housewife slaving in the kitchen, but she will make sure that there was food in it. Once she got things handled with the lawyer my Uncle connected her with, she signed me up for school, went with me on my first day, and our life together officially began.

I figured out quickly that my aunt was not a normal type of chick. She was bad, she slept in a lot, her dress style was top notch, and she took care of herself. Her hair and nails were on point, she drove a Lexus, and she was paid out the ass. She always had money. Every morning before I left for school, she had put $30 on the dining room table. A twenty and a ten. She told me that was to pay for my breakfast & lunch at school, and to do whatever what I wanted with the rest after school. Like clockwork, every morning when I came down stairs, there was thirty bucks on the table. The only time my aunt went with me to school was on my first day. To meet the principal and my teachers. She also had to fill out my emergency contact and shit. After that, I went by myself. I caught the bus with the other kids two blocks down from the house. I didn't know anyone in Newark, and given the fire burning inside me; I wasn't interested in getting know anyone either. I was the new kid on the block, but my presence let all of them know that fuckin' with me, was a bad move.

I had the ice grill on every single day. I didn't smile, I didn't laugh, I didn't talk to anyone, and I never unscrewed my face. Some of my teachers tried that happy go lucky shit with me, but quickly stopped when I didn't crack anything that even looked like a smile. The other boys in my class were on that normal kid shit. Joking around, being class clowns, hype, and loud. The girls were into their little cliques, looking cute, and just as silly as the boys were. Then, there was me. The stone-faced black cloud that sat in the back of the classroom. Never speaking, laughing, or even raising my hand to answer one of the teachers' questions. I did my school work though. Through my anguish and anger, I remembered what my parents expected of me. Pops was big on my education. Though I had wanted to be a professional boxer when I grew up, my father told me to educate my mind though. He dropped a jewel on me when I was nine. The greatest fighters are the smartest fighters. Any nigga can learn how to box, but the masters of the ring are intelligent. Not just violent.

Thus, I did all of my assignments in class and completed my homework as required. Other than that, I didn't do shit else at school. I didn't kick it with anyone, I sat by myself at breakfast and lunch, I didn't participate in any of the gym activities, and I didn't do shit during recess. While my classmates ran around playing ball or chillin', I sat on bench. Alone. Far away from everyone. Quietly watching everything going on with uncaring eyes. Even when some of the girls that thought I was cute would stroll by smiling at me and shit; all they got back was a brief stare of indifference. It didn't take long for them to stop flirting with me and none of young dudes fucked with me. That was cool with me. I didn't want to fuck with their happy and goofy asses anyway. The only thing I looked forward to each day was going home. I had asked my aunt for a freestanding heavy bag for basement and she took me to Dick's Sporting Goods to get one. Every day after school, as soon as I got in the house, I went down to the basement, put my gloves on, and started hitting the bag. Like I use to do with my pops.

It was a good thing my father taught me how to box and I kept up with it in Newark. As it goes when you're the new dude in a new city; someone was going to fuck with you. I was the new kid at school, and it was only a matter of time before a motherfucker tried me. It took a month before I was on a young niggas radar to bully and fuck with. My pops prepared me for this. He told me that one day, someone was going to come at me to punk me out. Intimidate me. Establish dominance. My father told me that when that day comes and a motherfucker step to me; do what I gotta do. Let no one put fear in my heart, stand my ground, and if need be; bang it out with him. My pops looked me dead in my eyes and gave it to me raw. If a dude step to me on some bully shit, make it crystal clear the moment he crossed the line. Show em' exactly who I am, what I'm made of, and make a hard statement to him, and everyone the fuck else!

Ain't no bitch in Sharif Watkins!

CHAPTER TWO

"The streets is an ocean and black boys are turned into sharks."

I hadn't yet developed a killer instinct, but I was my father's son. My eyes were always open because I inherited my pops sharp sense of being aware of my surroundings. It was second nature for me to know who was around me and size people up. It was ingrained in me since I was a lil' nigga not to fuck with strangers. I didn't speak to motherfuckers that I didn't know. Adult or dudes my age. That mindset was still active now that I was in Delaware. At school, I didn't have words. For anyone. Mostly because I was angry twenty-four hours a day, but for two other reasons. I was raised to keep my mouth shut and observe and I thought the other kids I went to school with were corny as fuck! Loud mouth ass boys, giddy-chit chatty ass girls, class clowns, diva's in training, goody-too-shoes, and the phony tough. I didn't really pay the females no mind, no matter how cute they were, but it was most of the boys at my school that irked my nerves. Particularly the ones that thought they were thugs.

One of the things I was grateful to my father for was the knowledge he consistently dropped on me. I had just turned eight and had gotten into a fight at school. The kid I rumbled with had said something foul to me at lunch, so I got up and busted him in his nose. We fought and both us got suspended. When I told my pops what happened, just like my mom, he wasn't even mad. However, there was something that I needed to learn. My pops and I hopped in his car and went for a drive. We rolled around Rochester as he opened to eyes to the kind of motherfuckers I was going to face in the world. My dads' philosophy was that there are three types of men in the world. Lions, Wolves, and Hyenas.

A man with the heart of a Lion is an extremely mentally and physically strong individual, but has a good heart and only uses violence out of necessity. The wolf is similar to the Lion in being strong in mind and body, but the difference is the wolf does not have a good heart. The wolf is built for violence, because it's a true hunter. A wolf lives for the thrill of the kill, but there's no cowardice in a wolf. A wolf will come right at you; looking you right in the eyes as it comes for your life. There's no fear, mercy, or weakness in a wolf.

Then, there was the Hyena my pops explained to me. The Hyena was just as strong as the Lion and wolf; with one vast difference. That strength was only physical. A Hyena is a scavenging, punk ass bottom feeder. It's vicious, loud, looks intimidating, and ruthless; but a Hyena doesn't have a warriors' heart. It's a coward that makes a lot of noise and though it's lethal; it's a bitch! Unlike the Lion and wolf, the Hyena will go after prey that is weak, smaller, or sickly. A Hyena will never stand and battle with another predator. It will make a lot of noise and bare it's teeth, but it will never go toe-to-toe with Lion or Wolf. Hyena's run. My dad and I were sitting in his car by a basketball court. There were mad people out. Dudes were playing ball and a crowd was watching them. My pops had me look at all the black men & boys on and around the court as he dropped another gem on me.

Most of the dudes that I will encounter in my life will be Hyena's. Punk ass, bitch ass, soft ass motherfuckers that will roar like Lions and carry themselves like wolves. He advised me to closely watch and observe how dudes around me operated. How they carried themselves, spoke, behaved, the people they rolled with, and how to acted by themselves, versus when they had an audience. Pops told me to read people like a book, figure them out, and when I come across a Hyena type of motherfucker; Be a wolf. Not a Lion. When I asked pops what he meant by that, he stared at me for a moment, grinned, and replied, *"You'll know when the time is right, lil' man."* That time was now. My Hyena was a twelve-year old dude by the name of Keith Matthews. Apparently, Keith was something like ghetto royalty on our side of Newark. He came from a family of hustlers & thugs, his pops was an ex-local celebrity boxer, his moms thought she was a the Queen of the city, and Keith carried himself in the manner of spoiled and arrogant tough guy aristocrat. Son was a cocky, shit talking, light brown skinned pretty boy that thought he was untouchable.

The first time I ever saw Keith Matthews, I immediately detested his ass. It was at lunch on my first day at school. I was sitting at a table with my food, ignoring everything and everyone around me when Keith made his grand entrance. I was facing the cafeteria entrance, so when he strolled in, I had a clear view. He was with three other dudes. Just based on my first impression, I knew son was a dickhead from the jump. I don't know why, but I kept studying Keith as he and little crew got in line to get their lunch. He was the best dressed one amongst his squad. A crisp white Polo collared shirt with authentic Polo logo, a pair of dark blue denim jeans, and new looking low-cut white Nike Air Force's. His hair was freshly cut low, shape up sharp with a curving part and developing waves. Son had on a gold chain, and everything about his vibe irritated me. It wasn't his fresh haircut, name brand clothes, or that bling around his neck. It was him. The arrogant expression on his face, the way he smiled & laughed, and how he was speaking with his homies was in the manner of someone that clearly carried himself as better than any & everyone else.

As he was passing the table where I was sitting, we looked at each other. Keith stared at me for more than a few seconds, grinned like a snake, then sucked his teeth before saying something to his homie on his left. I didn't look back, but I heard them laughing at whatever was said. Though I had no visible reaction, I was on point. Keith Matthews was on my radar. Shit like that went on for the next two weeks. Whenever Keith and I saw one another at school, son always gave me this subtle dirty look before he smirked. Each time I passed him and his crew in the hallways, he kept probing me. Walking to close as we passed one another, made sure to shoot that look at me, flash that cocky grin at me, and he always mumbled something under his breath to his homies. Getting louder with each time in happened. The shit wasn't getting under my skin, but I felt the venom building in my veins getting more poisonous as time went by. After nearly a month of his hyena ass passively testing me, he finally worked up the heart to try his bully shit on me. Bad move on his part.

Part of me still wanted to become a professional boxer like I told my pops I wanted to be when I grew up. Just like we used to do together, I still ran to build my endurance. Because my aunt didn't really give a fuck what I did or where I went; it wasn't shit for me to just leave the house and not return for hours. It was a Saturday evening when I got tired of playing my video game. Aunt Vanessa was out doing her when I threw on my hoody, sweat pants, and Nike cross-trainers. I started running while shadow boxing. I ran the three and half miles to my school, then towards the park so I could run around the football field before heading back to the crib. When I got to the park, a bunch of people my age were chilling near the playground under a pavilion. Some were standings, others were sitting on the three picnic tables. I was jogging by when I heard a familiar voice call out,
"KEEP ON RUNNIN'!!!...BITCH ASS NIGGA!!"

I recognized Keith's voice immediately. I stopped, turned around, and pulled my hood down as I began making my way towards the pavilion. All of them were quiet as they watched me move closer. When I was few feet away, I made eye contact with Keith and inquired, *"What up, yo? You got a problem with me?"* Keith was all fresh and sharp in his crisp white T, gold chain, and black denim jean shorts. I ignored his clique of young niggas and chicks as I walked right through them. They were backing up as I approached him. I could see that he didn't expect me to step to him, but he had an image to uphold. He looked me and up down before going into his passive pre-hype mode. Keith's face changed into a look of pending aggression as he held eyes with me. I slowed my pace as he shot back, *"I don't who you are, but you better ask who I am, yo!...Who my people are?!...And yeah, I called you a bitch ass nigga!...What you gonna do about it?!! You don't wanna see me, yo!!"*

I didn't say another word as we tried to intimidate me with a bunch of empty threats. I may have been going on twelve, but I didn't give a fuck. About him, who he thought he was, his threats, or who his people were. I was a few feet away when he realized that I was stepping to him. Instead of him seeing that I was coming to bang, he made a move that put him in a fucked up position. Keith got hype, started to back up, his face twisted into an expression of fear driven aggression, and he explained how he was about to beat my ass as he began to remove his chain. Bad move homie. In a flash, I ran forward and caught him with a right hook. WHAP!!! I caught his ass flush on his cheek. From behind me, I heard several chicks go, *"Oooooohhhh!!!"* Keith grabbed his cheek and was stumbling as I unleashed the animal on him. His clique was hype and loud as they tried to motivate him to fight back. Son didn't take their advice. At all. He either covered up his head as I rained down punches on him, or he tried to grab & wrestle. After eating like twenty punches, he tried to out muscle me. By roaring like a lunatic as he attempted to put me in a head lock.

Keith received a body slam instead. I been working out & lifting weights since I was five. Both he and I were tall for our age, but he was mad skinny and weak as fuck. As he went to lock his arms around my head, I dipped on him. Grabbed his waist from the side, locked in my hold, and then lifted him off his feet. I slammed him on the concrete, making him holler like a punk. I dropped down and gave him the smoke he wanted. I held him down with one hand while punching him with the other. I busted Keith in the mouth, nose, jaw, and the side of his head. I

23

kept hitting him until he was curled up in a ball. Crying and begging me to stop. I did. When I stood up over top of his bitch ass, I looked at his homies and the young chicks that were kicking it with them. Not saying a word, I strolled away from the pavilion. Putting my hood back on. I didn't run though. I walked through and out of the park at a normal pace. I didn't have to run. I made my point. I wasn't the one they wanted to fuck with and the look I gave Keith's homies was an invitation. "WHO ELSE WANTED SOME WORK??" Not one stepped up to trade hands with me, so I bounced.

****

The drama with Keith wasn't over after I lit fire to his ass at the park. I guess he took his fucked up ass home and his people were none too pleased that he got his ass beat. On Monday, he wasn't at school, but I ran into him after though. He, his dad, and two of his brothers were waiting for me as I exited the school building. Keith's pop walked up to me and asked me to have a word with him. I walked with him and his sons until we were away from school and Marvin Matthews asked me a strange question. If his son wanted to rumble with me again, was I willing to? I looked that grown man in the eyes, glanced his battered and bruised son, then his two older, hustling looking sons before giving him both my attention and my answer. I walked to Keith's house with them, inside, and we went down to their basement. It was big as fuck and nice. Mr. Marvin explained to me that his son felt like I sucker punched him when he wanted to square up with me, so here, he and I were going to put the gloves on and handle our beef like men. Straight up and fair with no sucker shit. When he asked me was I good that, my response was simple. Where the gloves at?

Mr. Marvin laced up his sons gloves first, then he did mine. Just like his son, he was confident and sure of himself. As he tying my gloves on, he tried to get into my head. Telling me that he hoped I knew what to do with my hands, because he was once a professional middleweight contender and he trained all his boys *"How to throw them hands."* I didn't say a word. I glanced at Keith. Son was pacing back and forth, shadowboxing with a mean look on his busted-up face. He was down to his white tank top, I was in my jeans and white T, and when Mr. Marvin asked me did I want a mouthpiece and headgear, I shook my head no. Like in a real boxing match, Keith's dad brought us to the middle of our ring, and broke it down to us. The fight ended when one of us quit or got knocked out. As he stepped back, before the rumble commenced, it

24

dawned on me. This was a fight for their family pride. Keith's dad was making him fight me, because of their ego. They were assuming I was about to get my ass whipped in their domain. I recalled everything my own father taught me as I brought my gloves up, readied myself, and got to it.

I beat the dog shit out of Keith Matthews in his father's basement, in front of his father. Yeah, his pops taught him some boxing skills like mine did, but the difference was that I was born with the heart of warrior. Keith was born with the heart of pussy. He got some shots in, but he was not a natural born fighter. He was overly aggressively, his jab was weak, he was flat footed, and every time I landed a blow on him; he got mad. The more emotional he got, the wilder he fought, and the wilder he fought me; the more I lit his ass up. Keith and I rumbled for close to ten minutes before his pops ended the fight. I was giving his son the business, while ignoring my bloody nose and split lip. My nose was bleeding from a lucky punch, but my lip was busted from Keith's head butt of frustration while we were clinched; before his brother broke us apart to keep boxing. When Mr. Marvin had seen enough of his son getting his ass beat, he ended our battle. He stood us close together and informed us that our little beef was over. It was done and we weren't going to fight no more. There was no need to.

Mrs. Shanda Matthews, one of the prettiest light skinned chicks I've ever seen cleaned us up. I was given a fresh T-shirt and Mr. Marvin drove me home. Just the two of us. On the way there, he did something that I didn't expect. He complimented my boxing skills, my heart, and how I carried myself. Then, he invited me to come by the gym where he schooled some of the boys in the neighborhood. I agreed to drop by the gym, he shook my hand, and I climbed out of his car. My aunt wasn't home, so I made myself something to eat, took my food to my room, and did my homework while eating. Keith and I didn't speak at school, but the beef was over. That Friday, after school, I kept my word. I caught the city bus across town to the Newark City Boxing Club. Keith and his pops were there and my former enemies' dad looked excited to see me. He shook my hand before asking me was I ready to put in some work? I was given a locker, and when I came out in my basketball shorts and white T with my gloves and shit, we got to it.

I spent several hours in the gym working out with the Matthews. Keith's dad led me and his son in exercises to warm up, then we hit the heavy bag for a while. Keith went first, then I went, and his pops held the bag for us while giving us both advice, instructions, and encouragement. After the heavy bag, my new gym partner and I took turns hitting the mitts on his dad's hands. Mr. Marvin was strict as he schooled us, but not too hard or loud. We took a breather after the mitts, then moved on to the double end bag. Keith's dad pushed us to work hard and focus on his instructions. When we messed up, he corrected us. Harshly sometimes, but not with cruelty in his words. Somehow, Keith and I started becoming cool. We rapped a little as we worked out and it felt like our beef was really over. Mr. Marvin wrapped out the evening workout by putting headgear on us and having his son and I spar for a couple rounds. Neither Keith or I went all in on each other, but we got in four hard rounds of trading gloves. When his pops called TIME, we touched gloves before his dad told head on to the locker room to clean up.

I was ready to bounce and head home when I emerged with Keith from the locker room showered and dressed in clean clothes. Only Mr. Marvin had other plans. He invited me to dinner at his home with his family. About an hour later, I sat at the dinner table with them, getting down on a fire ass home cooked meal. Keith's mom could burn, yo! As we ate, Mr. Marvin and his wife made me feel like I was apart of their family. For some strange ass reason, I felt close to them and I opened up when they asked questions about me. Where I was from, about my people, and though I didn't want to talk about my parents, I did. It was quiet for a minute after I shared with them that my mother and father were murdered and that's why I was living in Delaware with my aunt. Keith's mom knew of my aunt, by reputation, but she didn't know her personally. When dinner was done, again, I was ready to bounce. That is until Keith asked me if I wanted to play the new madden on PlayStation? The 2002 edition had just dropped. I had it at home, but I accepted his invite anyway. To be honest, I felt compelled to stay and chill with him.

Keith and I had mad fun going at it on Madden. We played three games using our favorite teams. He was an Eagles fan, I rocked with my Giants, and we talked big shit as we played. I won the first game, he won the second match, and he almost beat me in the third game. I won by three points. He and I were smiling and still talking shit when Mr. Marvin came to his son's room to tell me that it was getting late and he was driving me home. My aunt was chillin' in the living room when I walked in. As soon as I opened the front door, I was hit with a haze of marijuana smoke. She was relaxed on the couch smoking a joint, sippin' on a drink, and watching a movie. We greeted one another and as I was heading up to my room, she informed me that there was some Chinese food for me in the fridge. I thanked her as I walked up the stairs. I knew that my aunt Vanessa cared about me, but she didn't stop living her life now that she had her nephew with her. She smoked weed in the house, she entertained men late at night, she went out a lot, and it was clear to me that she was in the game in some form. I suspected that she was a drug dealer or fucked with hustlers. Either way, she always looked good, always had money, and live life her way.

The Matthews were my new family in Delaware. Keith and I became tight in a short period of time. We kicked it at school and I became tight with his three life-long homies. Jerrell, Darryl, and Maurice. They went by Rell, D, and Mo. I finally came out of my shell now that I had niggas and Keith's parents welcomed me in like I was one of their own. When I wasn't in school, my time was spent with my homies and their people. My crew and I were always together. We worked out at the gym with Mr. Marvin, chilled on the weekends, and got into shit. We rumbled with young niggas in our hood, played football & basketball at the park, our hangout spot was the roof of an abandoned warehouse by the train tracks, and we had crazy fun. I didn't take long for me to catch on to what was up though. Mr. Marvin was trying to keep his son, me, and our friends out of the mix, but the signs were there.

Keith's pop was just like mine was. A gangster hiding in plain sight. Mr. Marvin, nor his wife worked regular jobs. Yet, their whole lifestyle was expensive. They lived in a nice ass house, drove luxury cars, and they had mad money. Keith had everything he could ever want. High priced clothes, sneakers, every video game known to man, but his two older brothers were different. Neither of them lived at home; yet, they also exhibited all the signs that they were paid out the ass. Na'jae was the oldest at 23 and Kareem was 20. Both of them looked ever the street niggas. They sported Rocawear, Sean John, Phat Farm, Enyce, Jordan's, and Timbs. Mostly I saw them in White T's, Dickies, and Polo shit. They always had fresh haircuts, chains, expensive looking watches, they drove fly ass cars, and they carried themselves like hustlin' niggas. When I was chilling with Keith and his brothers dropped by the house, it was like two living legends graced us with their presence.

To my homie, his brothers were his hero's. When they came around, Keith lit up and it was clear that he idolized Na'jae and Kareem. I watched them be all playful with their little brother, bless him with cash or a new pair of sneakers, joke with him, and it was evident to me as I studied them when they were together. Keith was not like them. His

27

older brothers were born with the thug gene in them. He wasn't. Na'jae and Kareem had that look in their eyes. The cold look of a killer. Niggas that were bred for the streets. Keith tried to be like them, but it just wasn't in him. He talked tough, fronted like he was hard, and though he had decent boxing skills; there was no lethality in his heart. Thus, why his father was grooming him to walk life on the straight path. Keith never noticed something about his pops and brothers. That was how they interacted with me. Mr. Marvin wasn't all preachy towards me as he was with his son. He wasn't all in my ear about becoming someone important when I grew up. He didn't talk about college with me. Advise me to start thinking about my future and shit. Nor was Mr. Marv and his older sons overly playful with me.

They shook my hand like a man. Na'jae and Kareem always dapped fists with me, we had serious conversations about life, and my friends' dad taught me something he didn't teach his youngest son. He introduced me to the steel. Mr. Marvin taught me how to hold, handle, load, and use a gun. The first firearm I ever touched was an all-black 9mm Beretta. I went with Keith's dad, just the two of us, to a shooting range. There, he taught me how to shoot. A few months later, my best friend's brothers started paying me to do favors for them. Take book bags to people in different spots all over Newark. I was firmly instructed to never open the bag and do exactly what I was told to do. Take the backpack to an address, deliver to whomever was waiting for it, and that's it. Don't shit else other than that. Na'jae or Kareem always paid me a hundred dollars to make the run for them. I didn't ask questions about what was in the book bags, but then again, I didn't have to. I already knew.

I was running drugs all over the city for them. At 12, I was in the game. This went on for two years. During that time, I was groomed by the Matthews differently from how Keith was. When I was with his dad or brothers, they schooled me on the streets. Unbeknownst to my best friend, I was receiving an education that he wasn't built for. Outside of school, boxing, and kicking it with Keith; I was with his father and brothers. Mr. Marvin molded me on how to conduct myself in the streets, how to think like a man, and about living by the code. Never snitch, never let a bitch make me lose my focus, live by my word, and back down to no man. Also, to be smart. Think before I act, keep my eyes open, and don't get caught slippin'. Na'jae and Kareem accentuated my thug academics by teaching me about narcotics. I learned mad shit about weed and cocaine. How to weigh it, bag it, the price scale, and how to pitch it on the streets. I was pushing 13 when I was officially put on.

2002 was coming to an end and drug dealers in the hood were getting younger and younger. I was thrown right into the mix.

They didn't start me off with coke though. Na'jae began my hustling path with trees. Smokers of marijuana in my age group were always on the prowl for bud, so I started selling it to them. Five and ten dollar bags of various strains. Jae' hit me off with three types of weed at $200 per flavor. Each one had a nickname. I was holdin' Reggie (Regular weed), Prince (Purple Haze), and Incredible Hulk (Hawaiian Green). My orders were to sell off my package and then bring back $600 to Jae' when it was time to get paid and re-up. Out of $600 my cut was $250. Keith knew that I was hustling for his family, but he was cool with it. He and I still rolled together at school and worked out at the gym with his dad; but when I got paged, I broke out to make my drop. Sometimes he went with me. He and I started smoking bud together with our crew. I was the only hustler in the squad. Though Keith, Rell, D, and Mo talked that thug life shit and carried themselves like they were gettin' it on the streets; we weren't the same.

They were straight laced young niggas from the hood. I wasn't. All of them participated in organized sports, they only kicked it on the corners, and they talked about going to college and shit after high school. Me on the other hand, I was a lil' thug in training. I didn't have a curfew. I could ditch school whenever I wanted to without consequences at home. They posted up on the corners as only spectators to the game; I was a developing player in it. They cell phones and pagers to talk to chicks; I had them to make money. Plus, I was only one among my crew that had a gun tucked in my waist band. Kareem hit me off with my first burner. A black Sig Sauer P250 9mm semi-auto. I never took my gat to school with me, but when I was on the streets; I was strapped. I also carried a blade. A spring loaded, black knife in my back pocket. Despite the fact that Keith and them were my niggas and it was clear that we were on separate paths in life; I still kicked it with them. We chilled at the park, on the corner, in the projects, and at each other's spot. The stark difference between them and me was how we behaved.

I was quiet, observant, chill, and reserved. Keith and them were loud, silly, cocky, and immature. They were also timid. When certain niggas hit the corner or projects courtyard where we were chillin'; they were quick to want to bounce. Sometimes I went with them, but most times I advised my dudes to go head and break out. I dapped them up and told them that I'll get at them later. Niggas in the game didn't mind me being around. I was far ahead of my age, they knew I worked for Mr. Marvin, and because I was Na'jae & Kareem's young nigga, no one ever came at me sideways. Though none of them fucked with Keith or our crew either, those older street niggas had my dudes shook. Niggas were packing heat, there were countless shootings where we kicked it, and the presence of wolves will always scare the sheep. I didn't judge my homies for bouncing when the thugs came out. This life wasn't for everyone and it was best to stay in your lane and be you. I stayed because I wasn't scared of nothing and I don't run from anyone. My place was in the streets. I felt like I was born and bred to be right where I was. Thug life was my life.

The streets was in my blood.

CHAPTER THREE

"I'm cut from a different cloth,
and they don't make that fabric anymore."

I had just turned fifteen, but I was far more man than boy. One, I was almost six feet tall and consistently working out, hittin' the weights, and spending hours in the boxing gym had my body ripped up. Also, I had more facial hair than the average teenager. A nigga wasn't even sixteen yet and I already had a man's mustache and beard growing. Keith was actually half an inch taller than me, but son was on the straight and narrow. He was still my dude, but on the real, we didn't kick as much as we did before. My nigga was focused on life after high school now. He rarely cut class, his grades were solid, and my boy was doing his thing on the football field. K was tearing it up as his school's star wide receiver. When we started the 7th grade, K decided that pursuing a boxing career wasn't for him. He had the skill, but not the heart for the blood & fire of combat in the ring. Mr. Marvin was cool with his son's decision to hang up his gloves and pick up a football. My nigga tried out for the 7th grade varsity team but didn't make it. They put him on the JV squad and my homie made the head coach of the varsity regret his decision.

Keith lit it up on the Junior Varsity squad as their one of their starting cornerbacks and primary kickoff / punt returner. My dude was fast as fuck and he had glue sticks for hands. He put himself on the map as a star and when our 8th grade year began, he didn't even have to try out. The coach put him on the team and by the time the season kicked off, he was their starting wide receiver and kick returner. I went the other direction. I wanted to get my diploma, but I wanted to get money more. I just stopped going to school and hustled full time. Still, I was at my homies football games every Saturday. Keith was the man, yo! There was no defender that could run with him, he burned niggas all day long, and he always scored multiple touchdowns in every single game. I showed my nigga love and I didn't dull the shine of his stardom. When he went to kick it with his teammates after a game, I didn't roll with him. Motherfuckers knew who I was and what I was about, so I didn't want my dude to fuck up his status by openly socializing with a drug dealer.

That was on a request from Keith's moms. She didn't have any less love for me or didn't want me around her son; she just asked me to fall back from him. Publicly. I felt where she was coming from and honored her wishes. When Keith wasn't at school, practice, or with his legit homies; we kicked it. Though we never spoke on it directly, K and I were like brothers. When we chilled together, son and I laughed, joked about shit, roasted one another, rapped about life, and I can't even front. I had mad love for my dude and vice versa. From time to time, Keith tried to lead me towards the road he was traveling on. Encouraging me to put my focus in the gym and make a run at making boxing my way out. He laughed as he claimed that I had it in me to dominate. That I could become a world champion one day. He was adamant about that shit. I always laughed it off and told him that I'd think on it. It was funny though. I believed that he was going to be something big in college football, but I didn't believe in what he saw for me. I never said it to him, but I wasn't going to leave the streets for the life of a professional fighter.

After my dude put up record numbers on the field as a freshman, college scouts and coaches from all over were on him. Keith received letters of interest from Penn State, Ohio State, the University of Georgia, Michigan, and Alabama. Even the big time Florida colleges were letting him know that he was on their radar. Son was big headed with his football fame, but it was all good. He earned that shit and he was that dope out there. Through all the recognition & hype about him becoming an NFL prospect; Keith and I still had a strong bond as homies. Whenever we could, we kicked it. One evening, I was in the projects chillin' on a bench near the playground. I was pitchin' product to the fiends when K rolled up. He sat on the bench with me and asked me did I wanna bounce with him and chill? He was heading over to his girl house and her cousin was in town. I grinned as I asked her what she look like? Keith laughed as he told me that she was bad. I eye checked a couple of dope heads lookin' shady as I told son let's roll out. I didn't mind kicking it with my nigga, but shorty cousin better be as bad as he claimed she was

****

On the way to Keith girls' spot, we picked up a couple of bottles. Some Henny for us, Alize for the females, and Dutch Master cigars. I had a couple of quarter bags of Purple on me. Keith's girl lived about twenty minutes from Newark in Wilmington. Shorty resided in the suburbs. The house was big and looked like those cribs only seen on TV. I followed K inside and we were met by not one, but two bad ass females. His girl, Kimberly, was sexy. Light skinned with long light brown hair, hazel eyes, and though she was tall and slim; ma was nicely built. She was definitely one of those redbone chicks that knew she was bad. Her cousin though! Shorty was even sexier. About 5'5, 150lbs, big chest, hips, ass, and thighs. Keith introduced us. A'Liyah and I shook hands and the smile on her face said it all. She was feeling me. Just like I was feeling her. I was diggin' everything about her. Especially her shoulder length jet black hair, panther slanted dark brown eyes, those plump lip gloss shining lips, and her best feature of all. Her smooth and healthy looking cocoa brown skin. She was ebony skinned like me and I was feelin' her chocolate ass.

Both shorties were dressed for a night of relaxation. Liyah, as she asked me to call her, had on a tight white tank top, black bra underneath, and a pair of high cut, dark blue denim jean shorts. We went out on the patio and popped the bottles. Keith poured everyone a drink while his girl began rolling the first blunt. Liyah was sitting close to me. As she and I got to know each other, I was checking her out. Like my pops had taught me. I was listening and responding to shorty, but I was assessing her at the same time. As she spoke, I focused on her teeth. They were even and pearly white. That meant she took care of her mouth. I was grinning as she smiled at something I said; but my eyes focused on her hand holding her glass of Alize Rose. Her fingers weren't gnarled or dirty. They were well taken care of. Manicured and pampered. I was diggin' her French tips style. The same went for her feet. They were pedicured and pretty. Her brown skin had a radiance to it, it looked soft as fuck, and I couldn't stop admiring her. I may have been only 16-years old and she was all of 17; but I knew that I was crushin' on a quality female.

We sipped and smoked as we chilled into the night. I had just started smoking cigarettes, as did Liyah. For a while, we had a four-way convo about various subjects. Laughing, exchanging opinions and talkin' shit as we passed the blunt around. Then, it turned into a two-way conversation. Between me and Liyah. Keith and Kim slid off into the house, leaving me and her cousin alone on the patio. That was cool with us. Sitting close to one another, Liyah and I shared another blunt as we talked. Only now, our conversation was casually flirtatious. Shorty rarely broke eye contact with me, I didn't break it with her, and we were on the same frequency. She wanted a nigga as much as I wanted her. I haven't been a virgin since I was fourteen, and though I've hit at least a dozen chicks since my first shot of pussy; I never wanted a shorty as hard as I wanted Liyah. We beat around the bush for a while though. She caressed my hand, kept giving me that dark & lustful stare, ma bit the corner of her lip a few times, and she did that rub her thighs together and sigh thing more than once. Then, she said fuck it. Guess a nigga wasn't catching the signs she was giving.

The truth though. I was catching the signs. Just wasn't gon' make the first move. My pops taught me that too. I watched for the signs that a chick wanted to fuck, then let her initiate contact. Pops said don't ever make the first move. Never ask to be let into the garden. Wait for the invite. The fruit will be riper by then. A'Liyah gently relieved me off the half smoked blunt, sat it in the ashtray, then stood up in front of me. I sat back as shorty straddled my lap and sat down. That was my invitation to the ebony garden of Eden. Ma moved my hands to her ass and then wrapped her arms around my neck. With her titties pressed against my chest, she kissed me. Damn, yo! Ma tasted like warm honey. Liyah softly moaned as we kissed. She was sucking on my bottom lip as I palmed her pound cake ass cheeks. When she started grindin' on me, I squeezed them tighter as our tongues fought each other. After letting my bottom lip slide out of hers, with our faces closes together, almost out of breath, she asked me one question. Did I have a condom?

In fact, I had four of them. Lifestyle XL's. Extra-sensitive. I always had rubbers on me. Liyah took me by the hand, led me into the house, and to the guest room where she was staying for the weekend. As soon as she shut the door, with the room dimly lit by a lamp, it was on. I was taking my 3X white T off as she removed her tank top. Ma was unsnapping her jeans as I pulled my 9mm from my waistband. Liyah didn't trip when I took my burner out. She was shimmying out of her jean shorts as I sat it on the dresser next to the bed. Ma stepped up to me and pressed her titties against me again, while staring up into my eyes as she undid my belt. Then my jeans. I used my feet to remove my J's and then she pushed my jeans and boxers down at the same time. I didn't even bother taking my socks off, because once Liyah had my dick and balls in her hands; I didn't even think about my socks. With one hand massaging my sack and the other slowly, softly stroking my pipe; she bit her lip as she let out an impressed *"mmmmmm!"*

At 16, I was packing a man's package. Never measured it, but I was certain that I had at least eight inches of grown man dick. Every chick that I smashed loved how big I was and my stroke game. A couple fronted like they weren't impressed, but they kept hittin' me up for the D. Liyah toyed and teased me for a minute, then she went down on her knees for a taste test. I groaned and locked my teeth together when she took my dick into my mouth. She did that shit like we were on our honeymoon. She first kissed the head, then she licked it. As if it was an ice cream cone and she was savoring the taste. She then softly licked and kissed down the side of my dick. She had me biting my lip as she slowly swiped her tongue up the underside back to the head, then she wrapped her lips around it as she took me into her mouth. Up to that night, I had my dick sucked more times than I could remember since I started fuckin', but no chick gave me head like Liyah did. For a long time, she made love to my dick with her mouth. Sucking it slow, hard, deep, and with patience. All the while she stroked in rhythm with her lips and tongue while massaging my balls at the same time.

Once she had me growling through clenched teeth and guiding her head as I stared down at the top of it; she took it to the next level. By taking my dick out of her mouth, but with the head resting on her warm ass lips, she whispered up at me,
"Sit down on the bed."

I did as she asked. I automatically opened my legs as she positioned herself in between on them on her knees. Shorty put her mouth on my dick again, but this time she wasn't all sweet and soft. With both hands cupping my balls and the base of my shaft at the same time, she kept moving her head down; taking more and more of my dick into her mouth. Shorty deep throated me, squeezed my sack, and then slid her head back up my dick. When she reached the head, she pulled back until her lips were on the tip of it, then she quickly deep throated me again. Ma had me on tilt with that velvety tongue and no gag reflex of hers. I had a fistful of her hair and was growling like a bear as went all the way in on me. Sucking my dick hard and fast. The feeling of her lips and tongue combined with the sloppy wet sound of her mouth had a nigga on cloud nine. I was starting to feel the tingle when she stopped, popped her lips off my dick, lifted it up and started licking and sucking on my sack.

I returned the favor not that long later. The first shorty I fucked taught nigga a thing or two about eatin' a chick out. I picked Liyah up off the floor, damn near tossed her onto the bed, and did my thing. I roughly opened her legs, pushed them up by the back of her thighs and put my face in her lightly hairy pussy. Ma was sopping wet as I began eating her out. She grabbed my head and moaned hard as I sucked her clit out of its hood. Then, I began rolling the tip of my tongue on it. I licked in a slow circle for a long time before I went faster. Harder. I sucked on her clit, pulled on it with my lips, and then finger fucked her with two fingers as she lost herself. She cursed, kept saying, *"Oh my God!"* and her ass was moving. A few times she tried to run on her back, but I held her in place. She even tried to close her legs, trapping my head between her thighs; but I held them open. I gave shorty the tongue until she came. Shaking, moaning, twisting her body, trembling, and trying to sit up. After the 5th time she told me to stop, I gave in and eased up on her.

Ma and I chilled for a minute before she told me to put on a condom. Once my sword was sheathed in latex, she moved into the doggy style position and I was on it. I slid into the pussy and gave myself a minute to marinate in how tight, wet, and warm she was. I held Liyah by her hips, watching her ass jiggle as I stroked. Not too hard or fast, but deep as fuck. I wasn't really all into that R&B nigga love making shit, so once I let her enjoy the long dick for a minute, I grabbed her by her hair and gave it to her. Shorty was loud as a motherfucker now. Moaning and looking back at me as she threw that ass back. I was loving everything. How her ass looked as it waved, the vice grip muscles of her pussy, that painfully pleasurable look on her face, and the wet sound of our bodies slapping together. We changed positions often. From doggy to missionary, from missionary to her riding me, back to missionary with her legs on my shoulders, and we finished on the dresser. Her legs around my waist, hands on my biceps and her face turned to the side with her titties bouncing as I roared like a lion. Bustin' a big nut in the condom.

A'Liyah and I used three of the four condoms before we were done. I was cool after two rounds, but shorty wanted go for a three-peat. Cool with me. A little head to roust the monster, wrapped it up, hit it from the back again, she came, I came, and we were out of gas now. It was damn near six in the morning. Though we were tired as fuck, when shorty invited me to join her in the shower, I obliged her. Liyah was looking at me, touching me, and bathing me like I was her dude. Ma scrubbed me down and spent extra time washing my package. I returned the favor, then we rinsed off and got out. Not too long later, we were hugged up on the bed. Shorty had on my white T and I was rockin' my boxers. As I stretched out on my back, baby girl was on my as if we were lovers. Head on my shoulder, her leg over my thigh, and arm across my chest. She gently ran her nails over my cheek as we lied there without speaking. Though I really wasn't the cuddle up-boo lovin' type of nigga; this shit felt good! Everything about A'liyah made a nigga feel right. I was mad chill with her and I was lovin' being close to her. Thug nigga or not, shorty made a nigga feel at ease.

****

Kim and A'liyah both hailed from Philadelphia. Only Keith's chick was a sort of rich girl. Her parents had several profitable business ventures in the city that afforded them the luxury to own a big house in the burbs and provide their daughter with a good life. Liyah was Kim's favorite cousin, but shorty still resided in the hood. Right in the middle of West Philly. Though Ma was street, she wasn't overly ratchet. Shorty was intelligent, wise beyond her years, and she had ambitions. After we hooked up that first night, we exchanged numbers and kept talking. Neither of us beat around the bush this time. She was feelin' me, I was feelin' her, we weren't that far from each another, and though she was still in high school; she made it clear that she had her eyes on the street nigga I was. Liyah and I talked all the time. At first, it was by landline at her crib. Then I got her a cell phone. Now, we could talk and text each other without limits. She was the first female I ever looked forward to speaking to on a daily basis.

About two weeks after the night we fucked, I made the forty-five-mile drive from Newark to Philly. In my new ride. A dark green GMC Envoy SUV. While niggas were coppin' Escalades and Navigators with spinners and tint work; I chose one that blended in with every other automobile on the road. An old school hustler in the projects dropped that jewel of wise knowledge on me. Until I had legit cover for my ill-gotten gains, never buy a LOCK ME UP mode of transportation. Niggas highlight themselves for the narcs and regular police patrols by rollin' around in BMW's and shit. Chromed out and tinted. By purchasing a normal ass vehicle, just as it was off the lot; I was mostly camouflaged from the law. The same ol'head impressed upon me some more real shit. The key to surviving and thriving in the drug game was to always limit my vulnerabilities. Low key exposure in the streets. No stuntin', flashin' cash, switch my routine often, don't talk about my business to motherfuckers I wasn't doing business with, and play smart. I was in the game to make money. Not popularity.

I picked up A'liyah and took her out for a night on the town. Shorty and I went to dinner at a steakhouse, then we rolled over to the movie theater. We did the hugged-up thing as we watched our flick. She had a bucket of popcorn and I held her Gummy bears for her. After the movies, we drove over the Benjamin Franklin Bridge and parked in the Wiggins Waterfront Park. We were on the Jersey side of the Schuylkill River in Camden. Liyah wanted to come here. On the way we fired up a blunt, so we were nice and lit as we walked along the lit path next to the water. Shorty was on some romantic shit with me. Holding onto my arm as we strolled and talked with the downtown Philly nighttime skyline in the background. We walked for a while and the vibe between us was strong. Ma was all smiles as she clutched my arm and I was calm in her presence. We stopped after a while and shorty moved into my embrace. Next to rail and with the river flowing beyond it; Liyah looked up into my eyes as she revealed to me what was on her mind.

I was the only dude she's met that has been real. She was loving my enite flow. How sexy I was, the way I was built, how my mind worked, my conversation, perspectives, my sex game was off the chain, and it didn't matter to her that I was thugged out type of nigga. She saw more than that in my existence, knew that I was deeper than what I did in the streets, and she was keepin' it real. She wanted me all to herself. I looked down at Ma, studying her pretty face, and looking deep into her eyes. I nodded my head with a cool smirk. That non-verbal answer was enough for her. Liyah eyes got a little brighter and she smiled while biting the corner of her lip. We held eyes for a minute until she pulled my head down to hers, closing her eyes as she kissed me. This was on some love story shit, but I was cool with it. Liyah was that type of chick. If flowing like this made her happy, who was I to stop it? My moms always told me that whatever I did to put a smile on a woman's face, if it didn't compromise who I was as a man; keep doin' it.

My time during the week was now split into two. Most of the week I was in Newark. Hustlin', dropping by the gym for a workout or to spar with a dude I was cool with, posting up on the corner or in the projects, and watching for the narcs. When I wasn't doing me, I was in Philly. I mostly made the drive on Friday afternoon to spend the weekend with A'liyah, but sometimes I showed up earlier in the week. Ma felt like she was getting the royal treatment when she walked out of school to see me waiting for her in my ride. I always took her to grab something to eat and to chill before dropping her off at her grandmothers' spot. Liyah's grandma raised her. After her parents died when she was four. That factor bonded us even closer when we revealed that we both lost our mother and father. At the same time. The only difference was how they died. Hers left this life in a tragic ass house fire. Mine were gunned down in a drug related ambush. Months went by and what we had only grew deeper. Despite being just as in love with A'liyah as she was with me, Ma was better at expressing it.

Bae' was open and had no qualms about not just telling me that she loved me, but exactly how much. Liyah had that sexy, no bullshit Angela Bassett look to her; but my boo was soft as a kitten. She was mad affectionate, she loved to be close to me, cuddle up, and she was always huggin' & kissin' me. When she stayed in Newark at my aunt's crib with me, behind the closed and locked door of my room; it was nothing but boo lovin'. Ma and I would lie on the bed snuggled up watching movies and shit, she loved to caress my beard as I fell asleep, and more than once I woke up to find her laying there staring at me with a warm smile on her face. There were nights that we smoked and chilled in my bedroom after fuckin'. She would lie on me, expressing to me how much I meant to her. How deep her love for me was in her heart. After six months together, Liyah told me that I was hers. I was her everything. Her world. I reciprocated, but not like how she did. I felt the same way about her, but didn't know how to verbally express it. Something in me was always in reserve. Still, I loved Liyah something fierce, and without smothering her; I was viciously protective of her.

****

Keith and A'liyah graduated the same week. Two days apart though. Son went with me to Philly for my girls' big day. Liyah walked up on the stage when her name was called to receive her diploma, looking good with her relaxed hair under her cap and high heels on her feet. Her grandma, Miss Carolyn, stood in between me and Keith. She clapped in between wiping tears of pride and joy for her granddaughter. Once the graduating class was done taking pictures and speaking to each other's people; we went back to Miss Carolyn's home to for Liyah's graduation party. Keith and I kinda played the background as my girl's fam and friends showed her love. Near the end of the day, Keith and I dapped, then hugged before he started back for Newark. Once Liyah's grandmother went to bed and her home girls bounced, so did we. My shorty and I had our own private celebrating to do.

I got us a room at the Four Seasons hotel and when A'Liyah walked into the room, her surprise was waiting for her. On the glass dining table were a dozen long step white roses in a crystal vase, a bottle of Dom

Perignon with a bottle of Patron silver, and shoebox size gift wrapped up like a Christmas present. My boo was eager to open her surprise. I watched her untie the bow, tear off the paper and then open the box. Her smile was ear to ear as she began taking out the contents of her gift. A diamond stud tennis necklace in a black velvet Zale's case, matching bracelet in the second one, two banded stacks of twenties in a total of $5,000, two packs of Apple flavored cigars and a two quarter bags of blueberry haze. There was one more gift, but I was holding that one back though. My shorty was smiling, but she had tears in her eyes as she hugged me extra tight and for a long time. Thanking me and telling me over and over that she loved me. When she kissed me, I can't even front. It was hot as a motherfucker, yo! Before we set the bed on fire, I popped the bottle of Dom, poured us both a glass, and then I touched my glass to hers. A toast for the high school graduate from the class of 2007.

A'liyah and I went at it hard and with fire multiple times. It was like we just got married and were on our honeymoon consummating our marriage. Ma attacked me like a Tiger in heat. We made love, fucked, sucked, licked, kissed, and pleased each other until we were damn near tapped out. Both of us were still naked as we threw back a couple of shots of Patron before I rolled a blunt and lit that shit up. We opened the windows to filter out the fog of haze. I sat on the bed and Liyah sat on my lap as we got blazed. She couldn't stop kissing my lips, cheek, or my neck. As normal, the weed, alcohol, and sex drained her gas tank down to E and it didn't take long for her to pass out. We went to sleep on our sides with her back to my chest and her juicy ass against my dick. It was just after two in the morning when we took it down, but we were up a little after ten. Liyah thought I was taking her back to her house after we stopped for breakfast. That was the plan, but I had to make a stop first. To give her a secret graduation gift.

Ma was over the top when I gave her the keys to her new car. A pre-owned but reconditioned to near perfect Infiniti G35 Sedan. I bought the joint three months before and had it refurbished. A nigga had to hustle a lot of product to customize it for my shorty. When I bought it, it was dark blue, but I had the paint stripped and redone in platinum with silver trim. The windows were changed to smoke and the interior remodeled with white leather and gray upholstery. Liyah was hype as fuck! She actually jumped on me, wrapped her arms around my neck, and repeatedly told me thank you in between kissing me as I held her up. I followed her whip in my SUV to her grandmothers. We went in, kicked it with her nana for a minute, and then went up to her bedroom to get dressed. My brother's graduation was starting in a few hours and he really wanted us there to see him get his diploma. Son put in the time, effort, hard work, and sacrifice for this day. My girl was heading off to Villanova after the summer, while my nigga was traveling down south to become a Bulldog when the college football season began. K was heading off to the University of Georgia on a full athletic scholarship.

There was no jealousy or envy on my part with my lady and homie going off to secure a positive future with a higher education. I wanted this reality for them and I supported their ambitions. Though I was deep in the streets and about the hustle game; being with Liyah and having Keith as a brother from another mother gave me something my parents death took with them. Hope. As I watched A'liyah graduate and dapped up my nigga in his cap and gown before he joined the graduating class; I felt that shit. A small sense of hope for myself. I started thinking that maybe I should take a run at boxing professionally. I was only 18-years old, Philly was a hard ass fighting city with plenty of top-notch trainers, and I was certain that I could step in the boxing world and bring the fire. With the right coach and my girl behind me, I could do it. I hadn't spoken my thoughts with anyone, but I was planning to. Right now, it was their time. Liyah and Keith were achieving what mad people from the hood never do. They were graduating high school and moving on to the next level in college. They were grinding for a better future and had me thinking that maybe I could to.

Live the African-American dream. That I could be something.

Something more than another thug nigga in the hood.

CHAPTER FOUR

"Rule number five: "Show no love. Love will get you killed."

-Majestic, Get Rich or Die Tryin'

My dude showed out when the principal of his high school called out his name to receive his diploma. Son got up from his seat with his gown on, but was rockin' a pair of gold framed Aviator shades and his cap tilted to the side. I smirked shaking my head while Liyah laughed. Keith's six-foot three silly ass was dancin' and boppin' all the way to the stage. He straightened his act up as he walked towards the principal. He was still smiling though as he removed his Aviators, shook her hand, and then accepted his rolled & tied diploma. K resumed his silly shit as he walked away from the podium. He put his shades back on and held up his diploma for the crowd with one hand, throwing up the duces sign with the other. That nigga was stupid, yo! Ever since he started playing football and focused on working towards this day; his whole style was different. Yeah, he still carried himself like he was chest deep in the streets, but my brother wasn't about that life. For him though, that was a good thing.

His pops and brothers were born with the cold center of a wolf in them. Keith wasn't. Son was strong, but he a good heart. K cared about people, he hated seeing those he loved hurt, he was a natural born athlete, and he was smarter than a motherfucker. My dude scored high as fuck on his SAT's and his college entrance / placement exam. He was consistently on the honor roll through high school, and though he was rumored to start as a freshman when he got to Georgia; son was planning for a future outside of football. K chose Business as his major, financial science as his minor. My homie was on the path to a lit future. I believed, just like the college football analysts and everyone else believed, that Keith was going to make it to the NFL. Son was a Five-Star recruit and the former pro's on ESPN were hype to see what he was going to do at the college level. Even so, if he didn't make it to the league, my dude was still on the road to glory. He told me that he was staying at Georgia all four years. To get his Bachelors and not have to rely on football to achieve fortune and success.

K, his teammates, and family balled out at his graduation party. It was held at his parent house and the shit was lit. The food & drink was catered, they hired a DJ, and everybody was having a good time. Me and Liyah hung back for the most part. We sat at a table sippin' drinks and watching everyone smile, laugh, and celebrate. Keith did come over to our table a few times. My nigga was so happy and animated that I couldn't help but smile. He knew that I wasn't into taking pictures, but I gave in to him and Liyah beggin' me to flick it up with them. He called Kim over and the cousins stood in between us and both K and I threw up the duces sign as his aunt snapped a few pics. I thought that was it, but he wanted one more. Keith put his arm around my neck, we put up our middle fingers, and both of us were rockin' our sunglasses as his aunt took one more picture of us. Son and I dapped it up and then he and his girl strolled off to keep partying.

Liyah and I bounced as it was getting dark. Before we left, I gave my brother his graduation gift. Even wrapped, he knew it what it was. A stack of clean banded cash in Georgia Bulldogs wrapping paper. I gave him the same amount I gave my chick. $5,000. They were going to college and even though they had scholarships, my gift to them was to get them started as they pursued their degrees. That was all I could give them. My girl was going to be closer, so I had her covered. Though Keith's parents had his expenses taken care of, he was my nigga. My homie. My dude. He smiled as he held the brick of gift-wrapped cash, then showed me love back. We locked hands and then bumped shoulders as we hugged. I told Keith to have fun with his people and hit me up the next day. We had a Madden beef to settle and I wanted my revenge. He laughed as he replied, *"No doubt, my nigga."* We touched fists again, then I climbed into my ride with Liyah and pulled off.

My shorty felt like having fun for just the two of us, so I drove to the place of her choosing. Dave & Buster's up in Philly. There were mostly white people there having a good time; but that didn't matter. Liyah liked it there, so that's where I took her. Bae' and I did the wings and beer thing, we talked about her future at Villanova, I got to enjoy watching her smile, and we played the games. I shot little basketballs into a moving hoop for D&B vouchers, she played whack-a-mole three times, we both played on the blackjack screen, and we went at it for six games of skeet ball. Ma was holding onto my arm and cracking jokes as we left. Knowing that she wanted to keep having fun with me, I didn't ask Liyah what she wanted to do. I just did it. I cruised around Philly with the Power-99 radio station on low and we conversed as we fired up a blunt. Anywhere else, I wasn't a conversational and comical type of nigga. With my lady though, I was. Not saying that I was an overly chatty and silly ass dude, but I catered to A'liyah's needs as a female.

The one thing I inherited from my father was his gentleman nature. He was raising me to be just like him when it came to women and I had his mindset. Naturally. I watch niggas treat females like shit, seemingly just to do so. They approach every chick like she a whore. Whether she is one or not. Most niggas I observe regard women in the same manner. With utter disrespect. Motherfuckers beat on women, cheat on them, lie to them, get them pregnant but then act like the life inside them is only the woman's concern, and they exploit women. For sex, money, an ego boost, their credit, a place to live, and for domination. Dudes be lying, abusive and disloyal ass pieces of shit, but insecure about who they girl talking to or possibly fuckin'. Niggas are possessive, controlling, and manipulative ass savages that will tear a good woman down to her core, turn her bad, then tell her she ain't shit but a broken, emotionally toxic bitch. When he was the very one that made her that fuckin' way.

I didn't roll like that. Whether a chick was a thot or a righteous female, I regarded both of with the same level of civility, decency, and respect. My pops taught me that when I was a youngin' and my moms reinforced his teachings. Thug or not, how I treat women is a matter of my character and caliber. It doesn't change because I do dirt in the streets, because I'm hard, or because I live that life. With A'liyah, I gave her what she required. I listened to her when she wanted to talk, when she desired intimacy I held her, every time she told me that she loved me I said it back, and when she wanted to silly, I catered to her goofy ass. Nah, I wasn't the most romantic and lovey-dovey type of nigga; but my girl was my beauty in the world. She was the peace and calm in my life. On the streets, I was always ready for whatever. My mind and heart were primed for violence as I made my money movin' work. I was always strapped, on the watch for niggas creepin' on me, and when I was on the block; I danced with the devil. Liyah was the angel that balanced out the demon of my existence. That's why I did whatever I had to do to keep her happy and safe.

After a long fuck session, more weed, a hot shower and some food; bae' and I took it down. I often slept on my stomach, and Liyah loved to sleep on me. As I drifted off, Ma was resting her head on my back, massaging my shoulder as she hummed a song. It took me a minute, but I finally caught on to the song that she was humming. Angel of Mine by Monica. That was her favorite song of all time. She played like damn near every day and it was the ringtone for my contact in her cellphone. I had my eyes closed, calmed by her presence and the sound of her humming. When she was done, she moved up to kiss my cheek, then whispered I love you in my ear. I mumbled, *"I love you too, boo."* She kissed me again then moved off of me to get comfortable beside me. Liyah truly loved a nigga and I genuinely appreciated having her in my world. Before her, there was only one female in my life that loved me with her entire heart. My mother. She loved me with everything she had and I felt the shit. The same as I felt it from my shorty. That love that can be seen in her eyes when she looked at me.

****

Back before I stopped going to school, I was a street nigga that actually paid attention in class. I didn't really have a lot of rap and it was known that I wasn't much of a talker. Yet, I did focus on what was being taught. In the 8th grade, I was in history class one day and the teacher was talking about Ancient wars & Societies. That week, the lesson was about the Rise and fall of the Roman Empire. Most of my class thought that shit was boring as fuck. I didn't. The shit had my intrigue. I listened to what the teacher was explaining about Roman society and being one the greatest & most powerful dynasties to ever exist. He talked about Emperors, their wars, how the Roman political structure was set up, and a bunch of other shit about their culture. What really caught my attention was how the Roman empire was destroyed. How it fell. It didn't come from rival Kings' army or another empire. Rome fell from within. It was crushed by people in power inside. Motherfuckers that the Emperor believed was loyal to the throne and Mother Rome.

There are two sayings in life that are true as fuck. Heavy is the head that wears the crown, and sometimes, the enemy that stabs you in the back, is the friend that your trusted to watch it. That was how the Roman empire fell, and how the Matthews family was destroyed. From within. A week after Keith's graduation party, I was with my girl in Philly. While Liyah was inside of a Korean nail shop getting a mani-pedi, I was outside waiting for her. I was leaning against my ride smoking a Newport and quietly watching people go by. As usual, I was in my typical attire. Tan short sleeved Dickies work shirt, heavy white T, matching Dickies pants, and my Timbs. I had gotten my hair cut the day before. My barber put a razor sharp touch up on my beard, and because the sun was out; I had on my Aviators. I felt my pistol on my hip, seated in its holster. I didn't use a holster before, but now I do. My joint bounced out of my waistband as I was moving down a flight of stairs, so I copped a holster to keep my shit secured from now on.

Liyah was just about done getting pampered when I received a text. It was coded. From Mr. Marvin. The code told me to call him ASAP, but not to use my cell. I spotted a pay phone a few stores down and went to use it. I called Mr. Marv and he answered on the second ring. The moment he spoke, I knew he was about to tell me something fucked up. It sounded like he was crying or about to as gave it to me straight. Keith was gone. He was dead. I felt my chest tightening up, I locked my jaw, I began breathing through my nose, and it was like I could feel the venom of toxic rage flowing through my veins. Mr. Marvin told me that he and his wife were at the hospital. Keith and his girl were in Atlantic City. Doing their Casino and beach thing. They were out partying the previous night, and on their way back to their hotel, they got lit up. Someone robbed them in their rental car, then shot them both. Mr. Marvin was crying as he told me that someone put two bullets in his youngest child's head and shot his fiancée in the chest. Kim was in critical condition and they weren't sure if she was going to recover.

Ice water replaced the blood flowing through my heart. Black smoke filled my mind, and through the volcano of anger I had become; all of it was concealed behind my calm exterior. I informed Mr. Marv that I was on my way to A.C. with Liyah and I'll call him when I was close. I hung up the pay phone, stared at it, felt my anger beginning to boil, and I bit my lip to keep myself in check. I was leaning against my SUV again when A'liyah exited the nail shop. I was smoking another cigarette as I watched her walking towards me through my shades. She was all smiles & beautiful energy as she walked up to show me her new nail style. Only my vibe and the look on my face when I took my Aviators off made her smile fade away. She looked at me with a concerned look as she asked what was wrong? Instead of answering her, I indicated with my head to get into the whip as I turned away from her to get in myself.

My shorty asked me again what was wrong with me as I drove. I could feel her staring at me. With my eyes on the road, I told her what was up. That Keith was dead and her cousin was in the ICU. As Liyah whispered, *"What?"* I went on to say that Mr. Marvin called me while she was in the shop to tell me that someone in AC got the drop on Keith and Kim. They robbed him, then lit them both up. Out of the corner of my eye, I could see Liyah sitting there covering her mouth with her hand with her eyes opened wide. I explained to her that K was killed on the spot, but Kimmy was alive. In critical condition. A'liyah sat there in the passenger seat, her eyes glued to the side of my face and when I stopped at a red light, I looked over at her. Tears were streaming down her cheeks as I reached out for her. She took my hand and when the light turned green, I held it as I pulled off. Heading out of Philadelphia.

****

Before I linked up with Mr. Marvin and my people, I took Liyah up to the ICU floor. The doctor filled us in on Kim's condition, then she left us with her. Closing the door to her room as she moved on to the next patient. Liyah was all the way fucked up. I stood next to her as she sat beside her cousin. Kim lied there with wires and tubes everywhere, the heart monitor attached to her was beeping slowly, an oxygen machine was damn near breathing for her, and it was fucked up to see her like this. Ma was like the sister I never had. Ever since she and Liyah came into my world, both of them showed me love. Liyah gave me her heart and Kim welcomed me into hers. She loved how I was with her cousin and how I treated her. In that, she and I developed a brother and sister like bond between us. I cared deeply about shorty and had love for her as if she was family.

A'liyah was hit so hard with grief that she unable to speak. She held Kim's limp hand against her cheek and cried while trying to will life back into her cuz. Though my eyes were dry, I felt what my girl felt. Pain. The difference was that Liyah's pain filled her with sadness. Mine filled me with venom. Potent, undiluted rage. It was a silent rage though. There was a fire rolling through me, but no one could see the flames. I left Liyah to sit with her cousin as I went down to meet with my fam. I found Mr. Marvin, his wife, and sons outside the hospital. They were the only ones in the smoking area. Keith's moms and pops were sitting together under the gazebo. Miss. Shanda was under her husband's arm, quietly crying into his shoulder. Na'jae and Kareem stood close to the parents. One with his hands clasped in front of him, the other with his arms crossed. I went to my surrogate mother, but no words were exchanged. I helped her stand and we hugged. Once she sat back down, her King stood up. We shook hands and then I embraced my older brothers.

I dapped and half hugged Keith's brothers before Mr. Marvin asked Kareem to stay with his mother while he spoke with Na'jae and me. We followed him out of the gazebo and began walking around the hospital. Mr. Marv led us to the boardwalk & beach. Which was only several blocks from AtlantiCare Regional Medical Center. We were indifferent to all the people out as we found an unpopulated spot on the boardwalk. Na'jae and I stood side by side. At the same time that I was lighting a Newport, Mr. Marv was firing up a Black & Mild cigar. His back was to us as he looked out at the Atlantic Ocean for a while. When he turned to face us, his focus was on his son first. Keith's pops ignored the tears rolling down his cheeks as he instructed his son to find out who killed K. Find out who shot his son in the fuckin' head. Twice. After taking a pull on his Black, then blowing the smoke through his nose like a dragon, Mr. Marvin fixed his pain & rage filled eyes on me. I held his cold gaze until he spoke. I was informed that he wanted me on standby, because as Keith's best friend and a member of his family; Vengeance was to be mine as well.

Without him saying it, I was going from hustler to soldier. Not once in the time that I've been sellin' dope for the Matthews' have I been tapped to put in any "wet work" for them. Not once have I been called upon to lay the murder game down. Mr. Marvin had goons for that. Niggas whose sole job for him was as trigger pullers. They were the soldiers that watched over our blocks, corners, and dope spots. Muscle that held shit down as niggas like me sold product and handled the cash. Though I was content with just trappin' and makin' money; I was always drawn to the goon side of the business. It was clear that Mr. Marvin was putting me on notice to be on some Grim Reaper shit for Keith. Before we left the boardwalk, he gave it to us raw. Once we found out who murdered K, we were going straight to the dark side of the Bible. An eye for an eye. There were niggas out there on borrowed time. The moment they put those bullets in my dude, they forfeited their lives. They were dead men walkin'.

I took Liyah home and stayed the night with her. Ma cried herself to sleep in my arms. Though we didn't speak much that night, my presence was enough of a comfort. Days went by slow as fuck for me. Keith's fam were making the funeral arrangements, his murder was all over the news, everybody was talkin' about it, and the fact that he was a high school All-American and top ranked college football recruit meant we had to fall back from the exposure. Up until the funeral, I still worked the block. Only at night now. During the daylight hours I was either asleep, with

Liyah, at the boxing gym, or putting int time at a shooting range. Mr. Marvin had one of the goons partner up with me to impart some soldier skills on me. Son's name was Isiah Bell, but he went by Prophet. Dude was 23 and originally from Camden, New Jersey. We were the same height, about the same complexion, and whereas I favored a low cut with waves and a fade; Prophet was old school with his hairstyle. Straight back, no frills cornrows with a sharp line up.

Proph was a non-talker like myself, so we got along perfectly. Every time I went to the range, he was with me. We spent hours emptying clips and he schooled me to enhance my marksmanship. Son even hit the gym with me and we sparred a couple of times. Dude was nice as fuck with his hands, but so was I. As much as possible, A'liyah wanted to be with her cousin in the hospital. I drove her to Atlantic City, but I didn't stay in the ICU with her though. Her and Kim's people were there all the time too, and despite them not saying a word to me, I caught their non-verbal vibe. They didn't want me there. At all. Most of them looked at me as if was responsible for what happened to Kim. It was one of my kind that tried to kill her, so they didn't want my particular breed of human being around them. I understood how Kim's people felt, but on the real, I didn't give a fuck what they thought of me. I wasn't there for their feelings and views. I was there for my friend & sister laid up in that hospital bed and my grief stricken girlfriend.

Yet, because I was a respectful ass nigga despite their judgments and opinions; I didn't stick around to make Liyah uncomfortable. I stayed close to the hospital so that when she was ready to go, I was able to scoop her up and take her home. Mad people came out to show the family love and to see Keith off on the day of his funeral. There were reporters and news camera, plus motherfuckers that showed up for a man's send off on some fashion show bullshit. I was looking at niggas real greasy during the whole funeral. Niggas arrived in pimp looking suits, chicks had on tight club dresses, short skirts, and exposed cleavage; dudes & females were dramatically performing for attention; and the media didn't make it any better. Cameras rolling LIVE and shit. Miss Shanda was a broken mess, Mr. Marvin was struggling to conceal his simmering rage, and I wanted my homie back. Related or not, losing Keith felt like I had lost a blood born brother. The shit hurt me something deep, but the smoke of rage in me over his murder was getting darker by the day.

I didn't say much at the repast for Keith. While everyone else was eating, drinking, and conversing; I was in Mr. Marvin's TV room with him, K's brothers, several uncles, and a couple of the top soldiers from the crew. Keith's pops made sure all of us had a glass of E&J and we threw down a shot for my nigga. The vibe in the room was painful, but also dark and violent. Before I left with Liyah, Mr. Marv pulled me aside. As he hugged me, he whispered in my ear. Be ready, Sha. Be ready. With that, I left with A'liyah and I drove her back to Philly. A week went by when the call came through. It was a little after ten pm and I was sitting on a bench near the run-down basketball court in the projects. Not five seconds after I lit up a Newport, my phone started vibrating. It was Prophet. Son hit me to inform me that it was time to get to work. Say no more, I replied. Ten minutes later, he pulled up in his Expedition and I climbed in. We touched fists as he pulled off and neither us spoke as he drove. The only sound was the music on the radio.

We rolled over to Prophets apartment to tool up. I followed son to his bedroom and he went straight to his walk-in closet. I watched as he carried out his arsenal of guns to lay out on his bed. When he was done, without looking at me, he told me to take whatever I wanted to use. As he began loading up a MAC-10 submachine gun, I picked up a sleek looking semi-auto. A charcoal gray & Black .45-caliber Ruger. I popped in a clip, racked the slide, then sat it aside. While Prophet got his firepower and shit ready, I took off my Black POLO T-shirt and put on one of the dark blue Kevlar vests. I strapped it tight, then my T back on. Prophet put the Mac-10 into a small gym bag along with a .40-caliber Glock and five loaded clips for each gun. He tossed me a black book bag and I put the .45 in it, four clips, a mini 12-gauge pump shotgun and a box of birdshot shells. Before we hit the road, Prophet made sure that we both had a ski mask and black leather gloves, then he put the rest of his arsenal away and we bounced.

****

The entire drive to Atlantic City, there was no conversation between me and Prophet. He had a D-Block mix CD playing at a moderate volume and there was no need for words. We weren't on a road trip to AC to gamble and fuck with the bitches. Son and I were on a murder mission. I smoked a couple of Newport's during the hour and a half drive. We left Newark a little after 11:30 pm. Prophet and I cruised around AC for about an hour before rolling into an apartment complex in the hood. I carried my book bag over one shoulder as I followed son into one of the buildings. We took the stairs up to the 3rd floor. Prophet walked up to the apartment marked 300-D and knocked on the door. Less than ten seconds later, a bad as fuck redbone chick with short hair in a tank top, tats everywhere, and a fat ass let us in. Shorty house smelled of weed and incense. Ma locked the door then returned to her couch and blunt.

Prophet had me follow him to the kitchen. Once in there, he ran down the game plan. We were going to lay low during the daylight but when come night, we gon' go out and do what we're here to do. From his bag, he pulled out two rolled up yellow legal envelopes. He took the rubber band off and handed me one of them. Son glanced in the living room, then looked back at me as he told me to wait until I was in the room I was staying in before I opened the envelope. Then study what was in it and get rid of all of it. Shorty directed me to the room I was crashing in as Prophet sat down on the couch with her. Once I was in the bedroom, I closed the door and opened my envelope. All that was in it was a sheet of paper with a name and a bunch of addresses on it, and a single, color photograph. I studied the motherfucker in the picture. I looked right into his eyes. This was one of the niggas that robbed and killed Keith.

Andre Lavelle Martin. I etched that niggas name into my mind along with his face. The picture was son's mugshot. He gave the camera the hard ice grill and son looked like one of those cold hearted, grimy ass dudes. The type of nigga that was down for whatever and didn't give a fuck about nothing and no one. I had a feeling that when it was time to move, me and Proph weren't going to hit these niggas together. I read and re-read the addresses on the paper until I memorized all of them, then I tore up the paper in the bathroom and flushed it. I did the same with Andre Martin's photo. The niggas face was burned into my brain. As I came out of the bathroom, I heard the sound of a female's mouth sucking and slurping, with the sound of Prophet groaning as shorty sucked his dick. I paid that shit no attention as I returned to my room and shut the light off.

In the darkness of the bedroom with the window open, I sat on the edge of the bed with a cigarette. Smoking as I stared off into the shadows of the night with several things on my mind. Memories of Keith, A'liyah, my mother & father, and my reality. Almost nineteen years old and I was here in Atlantic City to murder a motherfucker. Dude was one of two that killed my brother. They bodied my best friend and son wasn't even in the game. He was on his way to college, there was a chance that he was going to make it to the NFL, and my nigga wanted a different life than his pop and brothers. Keith wasn't built for the streets, but he was built for a life far away from it. He told me that was what he wanted. He wanted to make it so that he could live his own life and secure his own future. It dawned on him when I came into the picture. I was from the same breed as his dad and brothers. He realized that he wasn't, and put all of his focus on school and football. An education and athletic achievement were his way out.

Even I was feeling some hope through son. The game, and being in it, felt right to me. I had no second thoughts about hustlin', the streets, or thuggin' it out in the hood. I didn't question or regret what I did out there. I wasn't scared of shit, I was always ready to bang, and nothing rattled my cage. However, watching Keith ball out through high school, listen to him talk about going to college, and seeing positive hope for a better life and the fact that son frequently tried to get me to pursue a professional boxing career so that we could rise together; I actually considered it. I felt the urge to shed a tear for my nigga that was no longer here, but I didn't. My anger was greater than my pain. I didn't want grief. I didn't want sadness. It was blood I desired, yo. It was vengeance that I was hungry for.

And revenge is dish best served cold.

CHAPTER FIVE

"You're nobody till somebody kills you."

-Notorious BIG

Time moved slow as fuck as the day dragged on. I went to sleep that morning around 2:30. When I work up, it was 11:23 am. Prophet was still knocked in shorty bedroom and Ma was up. Daytime TV was on her flat screen and she was in the kitchen cooking. In a tight ass white T and gray stretch pants. She was cooking breakfast while smoking a blunt when I entered the kitchen. Before I could ask her what she had to drink, she told me what she had in the fridge. OJ, apple juice, spring water, milk, and Pepsi. As I was pouring myself a glass of orange juice, she finally told me her name. Patrice, but she goes by Peaches. I reciprocated by telling Ma to call me Sha. I almost didn't catch it, but shorty looked me up & down with a sly grin after we formally introduced ourselves. I acted like it didn't see her do it as I left the kitchen with my OJ and made my way for the living room. I ain't stupid or slow for a second. Ma was throwing signals my way, but I wasn't falling for it.

Whether or not Peaches was Prophets girl, there was no chance in Hell that I was falling for the Okie Doke. Ma was no doubt bad as Hell. About 5'8, 5'9; honey colored skin; gray eyes; pretty hair; nice sized titties, coke bottle figure, hips, and pounds of ass. Shorty was soft spoken, had a very beautiful smile, I was digging her tats, and from the sounds her mouth was making the previous night as she brained Prophet; she definitely knew what was doing on the sex level. I had no doubt in my mind that the pussy was fire as well. Nine out of ten niggas would dash to smash that without even thinking twice about it. I'm that tenth nigga that dudes would call stupid for not sliding dick up in her. They would be right about that too. They wouldn't see what I saw, or sense what I sensed about Peaches. Once again, I was thankful to my pops for teaching me what he taught me when I was younger.

A year before my parents were murdered, I was crushin' hard on this girl in my class. Her name was Heather and Ma was beautiful. I'm talking next level beauty. Even though we were only ten. Anyway.

Heather was mixed. Her mother was black and her dad was Rican. That combination was perfect in her. Shorty was real light skinned with both African and Hispanic features. Unlike the other dudes I went to school with, I wasn't scared to tell a chick I liked her. That's what I did with Heather. The shit worked too. It didn't take long for us to be on some boyfriend & girlfriend shit. Heather was my first kiss too. I was mad eager to tell my pops about her. When I did, he smiled and we went for one our drives. We talked about her, how I was feeling, and what I was thinking. Then, my pops shared his thoughts with me and took the opportunity to teach me a lesson about females and looking past a pretty face. He told me to do something with Heather to see if she was into me, as much as I was into her.

The entire following school week, I observed Heather how my pops told me to. She and I still sat together in class and at lunch and whatever; but I watched how she interacted with other boys at school. If she behaved with them how she was with me. She did. Heather was the same way with two other dudes how she acted with me. All smiley and playful, passing notes and carrying on like they were her boyfriends too. I told my father about it at the end of the week. Once again, he just smiled and broke it down to me. Girls like Heather were born pretty and they knew it. People catered to such a female because of their beauty. Once a girl realizes that being pretty got her attention, admiration, gifts, etc; they become consciously aware of it and use it to their advantage. Pops impressed upon me to be careful with beautiful women. See past their exterior and sweet smile, to sense out their true nature. At ten, it was a cute and innocent third grader that knew she was pretty and loved attention.

Now, at 19, I was posted up in the spot of a beautiful chick that was sweet looking poison. Back then, I curved Heather and acted like her ass didn't even exist. Almost ten years later, Peaches was giving me all the signs that I could fuck if I wanted to. I was chillin' on the couch when she brought me a plate of food. Breakfast shit. Waffles, cheese eggs, sausage, and hash browns. When Ma handed me my plate, she gave me that look again. That long and lustful stare with a thin smirk on her lips. I sat my plate on the coffee table as I watched her make her way back towards the kitchen. Ass shaking, bouncing, & jiggling the whole way. Peaches looked back at me over her shoulder as she disappeared into the dining room. She was a tease. Seductive. A game player. Definitely a freak. And there was no doubt that she was shady as a motherfucker. It was highly doubtful that she put something in the food, so as I dug in while watching the Price is Right; I figured out who and what was. A hustler, but she was also deadly temptation. A set up girl. A honey trap. One of those pretty AF chicks that easily lured niggas into an armed robbery. Or, a body bag.

I gave Peaches the cold shoulder as I ate and she sat on the sofa across from me. Sitting with her legs crossed, barefoot, alternating her eyes between her Pink BlackBerry phone and me. Though I wasn't looking at her as I focused on the Flat screen on the wall; I peeped her frequently glancing at me. Sometimes staring for a few seconds. I was hip to shorty game though. Ma was trying to tempt me. Hard. Reclining back on the arm of the sofa so that her titties were sticking out, crossing and uncrossing her legs, and even sitting with her legs open as she lied back. Angled so that I could see her pussy print through her tights. I saw all of that bullshit out my peripheral vision, but I didn't give shorty no indication that I even noticed that she was trying to seduce me. I didn't give a fuck about Ma being pretty with some nice sized titties and a juicy ass. One, I had a girl. Two, a chick being bad AF didn't move me. At all. Bad ass females were everywhere and a nigga like me wouldn't have a problem baggin' em.

Prophet finally woke up around two in the afternoon. By this point, I was chillin' in the room I crashed in. I was layin' on the bed thinkin about shit when son stuck his head in and told me that we were going for a ride. I put my vest on, checked my burner, slid it into the holster, then put my 4X black T-shirt on. Peaches was still watching TV when we left. She was smoking a blunt too. Prophet and I drove off and like him, as we cruised around AC, I gripped my pistol on my lap. Both of us were often checked the mirrors for cops on our tail. Son drove to a big ass garage not too far from the boardwalk and beach. He parked on the sixth level and we got out. He tossed me a set of keys, then pointed to an old ass dark gray Toyota Camry as he told me,
"That's you right there, fam…When we done, take that motherfucker somewhere isolated in the city, make sure there ain't no eyes on you, and then burn that bitch, feel me?"

I nodded my head as he went on to tell me the next move. That we were gonna separate for a minute. Go to a hardware store to buy two-five gallon gas containers, then fill them shits up and put them in the trunk. Once I was done with that, meet him back at Peaches crib. Prophet walked away, climbed into a forest green Nissan Maxima, climbed in, and was pulling off as I was opening the door to the Camry. Half hour later, I was at a Sunoco Gas Station filling up the gas containers with 93-Unleaded. I put them in the trunk when I was done and headed back for Peaches spot. When I arrived, I instinctively played it smart. I parked the Camry around the corner and two blocks down. Peaches left the door of her apartment unlocked for me. When I went inside, I didn't see her or Prophet. I didn't have to though. They were both inside the spot. In her bedroom. With music on, but not loud enough to drown out the sound of her moaning and the headboard of her bed hitting the wall. I wasn't in the mood to chill and watch TV while my partner got his dick wet, so I bounced for a minute.

I returned forty-minutes later. I copped some food for all of us. There was a KFC like six blocks away. When I returned, Peaches was rolling a blunt and Prophet was sitting on the edge of the couch next to her. Son was playing NBA LIVE 08 on the PS3. Ma finished rolling the Dutch, sat it down, and once more gave me that *"I wanna suck your dick"* stare as she retrieved the KFC bags from me. I sat down as she made her way to the kitchen. I watched Prophet ball out on the game until Peaches returned with two plates for us. Son switched from the game channel back to cable. The Wire running a marathon was on HBO. Peaches sparked up the L and after we smoked, the three of us got down on chicken & sides as we quietly watched season three of The Wire. Prophet commented that he was rockin' with Avon Barksdale, I shot back that I was riding with Marlo Stansfield, and we both fucked with Omar Little. Peaches didn't say a word. She sat next to Proph with her focus on her phone and cigarettes.

It was time to get to it. Just before nine pm, Peaches emerged from her bedroom dressed to kill. Her hair was done and she was barely wearing anything as she left for a night of bar and club hoppin'. I peeped when Prophet handed her a thick wad of cash before she went to her room to get ready. After she left, it was our turn to get dressed. I put my vest back on, checked my guns, made sure I had my gloves and ski mask, then Proph and I went over last-minute details. Right before we broke out, he called someone. From what I heard, he had eyes on his target and was confirming that the nigga was still out in the open. Once he ended the call, we left Peaches spot and walked off in different directions. It was on now and there was no turning back. I drove to the first address associated with Andre Martin. His baby mother's house. The first thing I did was drive past her apartment building, looking for Andre's ride. A black 2003 Lexus RX SUV. I didn't see it as I rolled by. After driving around the area for ten minutes, I returned to Andre's baby moms street and parked half a block down to wait.

I sat there in the dark interior of the Camry for just over an hour. Waiting for Andre to roll up. He didn't, so I sat still for another fifteen minutes then pulled off. The second address on the list in my head was my targets mother's spot. His moms lived in a nice townhouse in one of those upscale developments. I camouflaged myself by parking in a lot across from the house. Another hour and a half of waiting for the nigga show up. I was about to roll over to Andre's brothers house to see if he was there when a black Lexus RX cruised by where I was sitting in the parking lot. Music was bangin' loud from it as he parked in front of his mother's crib. The music stopped when the SUV shut off. I watched the nigga and a younger dude exit the Lexus and make their way for the house. Judging by how Andre and the young nigga were interacting, I'm guessing that little man was his younger brother. I watched them go inside. Now, I owned the motherfucker. Thirty-two minutes later, Andre came back out. Son was on the phone as he strolled with confidence towards his ride, climbed in, the engine-lights-and music started back up, and son pulled off. Unaware that I was on him.

✳✳✳✳✳✳✳✳✳✳✳✳

I followed Andre to his baby mom crib. He was only inside for twenty minutes before he exited the building and hopped back in his whip. He next led me to a dope house. The nigga didn't get out of his vehicle this time. He double parked in front of the house and a nigga strolled up to the drive side window. Something was passed to Andre, there was a quick conversation, and then the nigga was mobile again. I shadowed him to a bar and after waiting outside for close to half an hour, I went inside to see what the nigga was up to. I kept my distance, but I never lost sight of the nigga as he lived his best life. In between getting pressed up on by several females, I just sat in a booth. Sipping on a beer and watching the nigga across the bar. Ol' Andre was some kind of celebrity in this hood. He was in a booth with a couple of niggas and chicks. The nigga was rockin' white T under a black Dickie's work shirt, matching pants, fresh Timbs, and he was as shiny as the King of England.

Around the niggas neck was a Cuban link style gold chain with a large gold Lion head medallion with red ruby's for eyes. Lights sparkled off of the squared diamond studs in his ears and strapped to his wrist was a gold & silver Presidential band Rolex. Until the bar shut down, son was on his baller shit. Flashing cash, buying bottles, laughing and conversing with the dudes with him, and playing it smooth with the women. Especially the one sitting next to him. He and shorty were flirting hard and it was clear what was up with them when the bar cleared out. At 1:37 am, I was sitting in the Camry again. Gloves on and gun cocked. I finished off my Newport as I watched niggas and chicks exit the bar and drive off. It was a little after two when Andre left with shorty under his arm. From my vantage point, it was clear that son was drunk. Ma was damn near keeping him on his feet as he staggered and shit. I watched her help him into the passenger seat, walk around the front of the RX in her stilettos and tight ass jeans, climb in behind the wheel, start it up, and pull off.

As I followed the rear red lights of the Lexus, I was plotting on how to hit the nigga when my thoughts of murder were interrupted. By a moment of clarity. Something was off about the motherfucker that hit Keith. From what I was seeing with Andre Martin, shit wasn't adding up. The nigga was gettin' it in AC. He was hustlin' product on the streets on a level that it was clear that son was stackin' money. His baby mom and his own mother were living in nice spots, his BM drove a year model Acura TL, I was sure I witnessed a cash collection at his dope spot, and Andre himself pushed a fresh ass Lexus SUV. As I stared at the brake lights of his whip at a red light, I started looking at the situation from a different angle. Andre Martin was not the type of nigga that would risk his clearly profitable grind to ambush, rob, and kill a college bound football player from Delaware on Summer trip to Atlantic City with his girl. I felt my rage start to boil as the picture became clear. Keith wasn't hit on some random shit.

He and Andre Martin were on two different planes of existence. There was no way in Hell that this AC nigga would pull a lick on a random young nigga, rob him, then put two in his dome, and up the ante by shooting a female in the chest. Keith's murder and Kim laid up in the ICU was big in the media, yo. Yet, this nigga rollin' around his city like murdering a high school football star and attempting to murder his college bound girl wasn't shit to him. As if it never happened. I focused on the rear of the Lexus as it hit me. Keith's murder wasn't random. It was planned. My nigga didn't carry a lot of cash on him, and Andre Martin wouldn't randomly hit my homie even if he did. Niggas moving narcotics on Andre's level didn't commit armed robbery murders on some wild cowboy outlaw shit. My brother was set up. His murder was orchestrated. I was fuckin' sure of it now. Every instinct in me was certain that was the real deal. It was time to change up the game plan.

As Ma was pulling into a parking spot in front of an apartment building, I quickly parked on the opposite side of the street. Near the end of the block. I killed the lights, but left the engine running as I grabbed my ski mask from the passenger seat. Quietly as possible, I exited the Camry and cautiously moved across the street. I walked closed to the buildings to stay in the shadows as I watched shorty walk around the car at the same time Andre was climbing out. I kept moving like a panther in a dark jungle as I pulled the ski mask on over my head. I adjusted it so that I could see through the eye holes, then pulled my .45 from the holster and held it low next to my leg. Andre and the chick were heading for her building about twenty feet ahead of me. She was leading him by the hand as he staggered and laughed while admiring her ass. Telling her how he couldn't wait to eat her pussy from the back. Ma started laughing too, but stopped when she finally took notice of what was behind them.

Me. The very second shorty noticed me, it was too late. I was on their ass. She started to scream, but I didn't let it happen. I dashed forward and silenced her. With a quick and hard left straight to the temple. Baby girl was unconscious before she even hit the sidewalk. Andre was too drunk to react fast enough. Son looked at me into time to see my black gloved fist coming at his face. I hit the nigga between the eyes and followed it up with a pistol slap to the jaw. He stumbled back and hit someone's car. He was slumping down as I holstered my strap. I looked back and quickly checked shorty. She was lying on her side, breathing and weakly moaning, moving, but not trying to get up. Andre was taking a nap. Sitting against the side of the car, chin on his chest. I grabbed the motherfucker, put his arm around the back of my neck, and gripping the back of his pants and belt, I got him up to his feet and carried him towards the Camry.

Not too long later, I woke Andre Martin up. By kicking him back into consciousness. Two kicks to his ribs was all it took to wake him up. When the nigga opened his eyes, he was staring at the barrel of my .45. Before he could even think of making a move to try me, I gave him the right dose of encouragement to keep that ass still. I gripped his throat with one hand, at the same time I pressed the barrel into his right eye. We were in an abandoned apartment building in a very quiet area of the hood. There was enough light from the moon for us to see one another, and as he stared up at my ski masked face, I kept my voice low as I told him,

"If you don't want your moms, little brother, and baby mother to die tonight, when I ask you my questions, I better not think you're lying to me, aiight?" Son nodded the best he could with a gun pressing into his eye socket. I didn't waste a second. I pushed the gun in a little harder as I informed him that,

"Keith Matthews was my best friend, yo...My brother...We both know that you and your man murdered him and tried to murder his girl...Ya'll made that shit look like a robbery, but a nigga like you, with how smooth you hustlin' out here...ain't no reason for a nigga on your level to rob someone...especially someone like Keith....right?!"

Son didn't reply right away. He just stared at me with his left eye for a few seconds, then muttered, "Right". I bit my lip to control my anger, then asked my next question.

"Who put you on Keith? Who hired you to kill my dude, yo?"

When the nigga didn't answer me, I pushed the .45 into his eye even harder and moved my finger to the trigger. I half expected him to soldier up and say fuck it. Activate gangster mode in his mind and be like, *"it's whatever, dog. Do what you gotta do, because I ain't giving you shit. Pull the trigger, nigga."* Nope! He folded like a loser at the poker table and gave up a name. A name that sent my anger into fury level. I stood up over top of Andre. He lied there looking nervous as fuck as I stared down at him. The name he uttered fucked me all the way up. Part of me wished I had just put one in this niggas brain on the street after I knocked shorty out in front of her apartment. Had I done that, I wouldn't know what I now know. Thus, I would have returned to Newark unaware of the ultimate betrayal. A betrayal that killed something inside. I felt that shit die in me. That thing is called mercy. Keith was someone that I loved. Just like I loved my mother and father. I forgot how to cry from my eyes, but my heart was shedding tears of blood. I knew what I had to do now.

The nigga got out a few words of bitch ass pleading for his life as I aimed the .45 at him. His pleas fell on deaf ears as I pulled the trigger. POP! POP! Eye for an eye, motherfucker! I put two hollow points into Andre Martin's face. One shot to the cheek, the other in his forehead. I slid my piece into the holster as I left him on the dirty ass floor of the bedroom of the abandoned apartment. A short while later, with all of the gasoline dumped inside the Camry, with the license plate in my bookbag,

I tossed in a lit book matches through the open passenger window. I walked off as the car lit up. I stuck to the dark alleys for six blocks. I could hear the sirens in the distance behind me as I hailed down a yellow cab. When I climbed in, before the African dude driver could ask me where I wanted to go, I told him that I got $500 for him to take me to Philly and forget who his fare was. Homie from Nigeria was more than happy to drive me to Philadelphia, forgetting who it was that he drove there tonight.

Instead of going to A'liyah's, I rented a room at a motel. After locking the door, I turned my phone off and closed the blinds. With the TV off and my gun next to me on the bed, I went to sleep with my clothes on. Nine hours later, I opened my eyes. The first thing I did was take a piss. Once my hands were clean and dry, I lit up a Newport. Sitting on the edge of the bed, I turned my phone back on. Once that shit was connected, missed calls, voice mails, and text messages started coming through. Most were from Liyah, but the rest were from Keith's mom and my aunt. I called my aunt first. She answered on the first ring and before I could get a word in, she revealed to me what I had been suspecting and her veiled messages warned me about. Shit was off the chain down in Newark. There were nine murder's the previous night. Niggas from the Matthews crew were lit up and the police were all over the city. Seven of the niggas hit were either lieutenants that ran Mr. Marvin's dope spots or seasoned soldiers; while two were shot callers. Eddie White, Mr. Marv's right-hand man and the King himself.

I listened to my aunt tell me that my second father was bodied as I was bodying the motherfucker that murdered his son. My aunt told me that Mr. Marvin was meeting with his partner and lifelong friend Eddie when they were ambushed outside the bar they met up at. Niggas left them riddled with bullets in the parking lot. Without me saying a word, my aunt put Keith's mother on the phone. I could hear the pain and tears in her voice as she revealed the rest of the betrayal to me. Her own son's turned Judas on us. Na'jae and Kareem were the architects of plot. They had Keith killed in Atlantic City. He was used as a pawn to distract her husband. Prophet and I were sent to kill Andre Martin and his dude to clip the loose end while they initiated their takeover of the empire that their father built. Miss. Shanda paused to compose herself, then finished telling me what I needed to know. She was kicking it with a friend over in Wilmington when it all went down. One of her husband's soldiers hit her phone and let her know what was going on, then told her that she had two choices.

61

One was to stay where she was. Two, was to go somewhere safe with someone that she trusted. Miss. Shanda went with option two. She and my aunt Vanessa became cool over the time Keith and I were friends. After getting word that her own children were taking over the Kingdom and that her man was gone, she called my aunt. Who picked her up and the two of them put some distance between themselves and Newark. When she told me that they were actually close to Philly, staying in a Motel 6 in Upper Darby; I informed them that I was on my way. Twenty minutes later, as the hack cab driver focused on the road, I called Liyah. It took me a little over ten minutes to calm her down. She hadn't heard from me in days and she knew what was going on in Newark. Ma was all emotional. Crying, angry, scared, and demanding that I come to her. Once I assured my chick that I'll be with her once I met up with my aunt and Miss. Shanda; Liyah cooled down and we ended the call.

When I arrived at the motel in Upper Darby, after we did the hug thing, I sat down with my aunt and surrogate mother. Half an hour into talking about the situation, I had to face the obvious. The life we knew was over. Miss. Shanda couldn't go home. Her sons unleashed the demon in them and there was no doubt they would murder her too. They killed their own brother and father. My aunt and I were on the same page. She was at risk as well, because of me. I suspected that Prophet was involved with the plot, so it was logical that them niggas would come at me as well. I knew too much and would be seen as a loose end to be cut. Being that I clipped Andre Martin. Plus, the Matthews brothers knew how deep I was with their brother and there was no doubt that they would see me as a threat to them. That meant they would go at my aunt to get to me. Unlike Miss. Shanda, my auntie wasn't all emotional. She was calm and collected as she informed me that she had access to her money and could take care of herself. I looked at Keith's mom, made eye contact with my aunt, and with no hesitation, she nodded her head.

Miss. Shanda was leaving with my aunt Vanessa when she departed to rebuild somewhere. I left them at the motel to discuss the details of their travel arrangements and new life together. I took my aunts car and made the drive back to Philly. Before I met up with my girl, I cleaned up. My .45 went to a watery grave in the Schuylkill River, while the license plate from the Camry went over the rear fence of a metal scrap yard. Back at my motel room, I trash bagged everything I wore in Atlantic City before I jumped in the shower. I re-dressed in the shit I picked up at Sneaker Villa on the way to the motel. I drove off again, making a quick stop in an alley. To drop the trash bag under a pile of them in a dumpster. Listening to older niggas on the block talk about dudes that got locked up for murder paid off. I got rid of everything that connected me to Andre Martin's murder. Even my cell phone. I grabbed a new prep-paid from a corner store before I picked up A'liyah. She was waiting for me on her grandmother's porch when I pulled up.

My shorty was fucked up. Not two seconds after she climbed into the car, she was on me. Hugging me, squeezing me, crying, and she couldn't stop kissing me. Ma was mad, upset, but relieved that I was ok. I didn't say much as Liyah smothered me with her love and worry. When she calmed down, I told her that we needed to talk. For over an hour, as we drove around Philly, I told her what was goin' down in Newark. About Mr. Marvin, his sons, Miss. Shanda, and my aunt. Bae' was quiet as I broke it down to her. The empire was gone, my people were gone, Keith's mother was leaving with my aunt Vanessa, and I was going to have to get low myself. For some reason, my chick just sat there next to me. Quiet. She stared at me for a while, then she turned her head and looked out the window for a while. I gave Ma her space and focused on the road as I smoked a port. When Liyah finally spoke, she told me that she was hungry and wanted to stop somewhere to eat.

We ate, mostly in silence at a Cheesesteak spot. It was clear as day that my girl was deep in thought. She sat across from me in the restaurant, not saying much as she ate. A few times, she stared off in the distance towards the door. She didn't know that I caught it, but more than once I saw her wipe away tears before they could fall down her cheeks. After we left the restaurant, a few minutes after we pulled off, Liyah quietly made a request. Without looking over at her, I replied, *"Aiight."* Our first stop was a liquor store and then we met her cousin on a Diamond Street corner. For some weed. About thirty-minutes later, we were in a hotel room close to Center City. As Liyah stood at the window with a cup of Henny and crushed ice, I rolled up a Dutch. We sipped and smoked in silence. I was sitting at the table finishing off a Newport when Ma walked around the table and began to straddle my lap. I crushed out my cigarette as she cupped my cheeks, made me look at her, stared into my eyes for a long time, and then kissed me. Softly. Tenderly. With a gentle fire burning on her lips.

We went at it for hours. It was still light out when we started fuckin'. By the time both of had nothing left, it was dark outside. We were tired and sore as we lied on the bed. Naked and half covered by a sheet. I was on my back and Liyah was on me. Head on my shoulder, arm across my body, and her leg over mine. I stared at the window while running my fingers through her hair. Liyah lied there on me, caressing my chest, trying to not cry as we embraced in silence. Every so often she sniffled, or sighed. She also trembled a little. She fell asleep on me without saying a word, but there was nothing to say. I knew what was up. Though I didn't tell her directly that I killed one of the dudes that murdered Keith; I didn't have to. She knew. She sensed it. Reality finally caught up to us. My girl was a high school graduate going to college in the fall. She was smart, with a good heart, ambitious, positive, and she had dreams. Reality showed her who it was that she was in love with. Life showed her the truth.

The truth that she was an angel in love with a demon. Ma always told me that she saw something better in me. She accepted that I was a thug, but she had more hope in me than I had in myself. Liyah thought if she loved me hard enough, that I would change. That I would turn my back on the streets, stop sellin' dope, and toss my gun for a better life on the right side of the tracks. Periodically, I gave her hopes for me some thought. We talked about me living right and pursuing something righteous. Then, Na'jae and Kareem murdered their own father and brother. Awakening the beast in me. I looked down at A'liyah's beautiful sleeping face on my chest. She saw the real Sharif and it compromised her love for me. Bae' was torn into two. One side was holding on to me, the other half was pulling away. She was struggling to make a choice, but I saw her decision in her eyes. Staying with me was a risk to her safety, life, and future. Thus, this was our last night together. Liyah was moving on the path of life without me. It hurt to know that was coming, but it is what it is. It's her life, her choice on how to live it. There was no use in asking her to stay.

It was better that she wasn't with me for what was coming next.

There was still a few more niggas that had to die.

CHAPTER SIX

"The wrong people will always teach you the right lessons."

I was on my own now. The next morning in the hotel room, Liyah did what I had anticipated. She broke up with me. Ma did a lot of crying as she explained why she couldn't be with me no more. I was who I was and she couldn't be with a nigga like me. My life, and what I did with it was a threat to her. I was a thug and there was nothing she could do to change that. We sat on the end of the bed and she held my hand in both of hers as we stared at one another while she kept it real with me. She loved me with all of her heart, but there was no room for a drug dealing criminal in her life anymore, She could see the truth now. I wasn't going to give up the street life. Not even for her. Behind my calm exterior, part of my heart felt like it was on fire. I didn't show it, but it hurt like a motherfucker that shorty and I were no more. I loved Liyah and I wanted forever with her, but as my pops used to tell me; God and Life don't give a damn about what you want or your plans. A'liyah and I were over, she was leaving me, and even if I was the begging type, it was pointless.

Liyah and I shared one last long hug and kiss before she exited my aunt's whip. I dropped her back off at her grandmothers' spot. She and her people were going back to Atlantic City. Kimmy was conscious again and she wanted to be there to take care of her cousin. I watched her walk towards her grandma's house and go inside without looking back at me. I nodded my head, bit my lip for a second, acknowledged the fact that I lost the one chick that truly loved me, and then in an instant, I buried that shit as I pulled off. I spent the rest of the day with my aunt and Miss. Shanda at the motel. I chilled on the recliner chair watching TV, smoking cigarettes, and sleeping. There wasn't much convo between the three of us as the day turned to night. We had Chinese takeout for dinner and then watched the Sunday Night football game. The Eagles played the Cowboys in Dallas. The Birds won 41-13. Two hours after the game, my aunt Vanessa and I left Miss. Shanda at the motel as we climbed into the car and rolled out.

Like me, my aunt was armed. When we arrived in Newark, I drove to our neighborhood, but parked a few blocks away from the house. Down the street from a Seven-Eleven gas station. My aunt stayed in the car while I went inside the store. I returned to the whip a few minutes later with a cheap pre-paid phone. Auntie set it up and then we left the car together. Sticking to the alley's, we cautiously made our way to the back of the house and waited. Checking to see if niggas were watching the house. With her Glock 9mm in hand, I left my aunt concealed in the darkness beside a neighbors' garage while I scoped the street in front of the house. I spotted them near the end of the block. Niggas in an SUV parked on the opposite side of the street in front of my aunt's house. I watched them for a few minutes, then crept back to the alley. We moved like ghosts to our back porch, then I told my aunt to do her thing. With the phone I bought at the gas station, she dialed 911.

Using a fake name and real address on the block, she told the dispatch operator that suspicious looking men in a dark colored SUV were sitting on her street and she thinks they were waiting to break into someone's home. Once the operator informed her that the police were on their way and the call ended, the phone was powered down. After nearly ten minutes, we heard the sound that we had been waiting for. The whoop-whoop of a police cruiser in front of the house. Aunt Vanessa quickly used her key to unlock the back door and we went inside. Both us made our way to the living room window and looked out. Two Newark police cars had the SUV blocked off and the patrol officers had their guns out, ordering them motherfuckers in the Tahoe to exit the vehicle. There were three of them. All dressed in dark clothing and they were fucked, yo! The cops found guns on them after the pat down. We watched them niggas get cuffed and placed into a paddy wagon that was called to transport them.

After the police bounced, we turned the lights on and got busy. I went to my room and quickly packed what I needed. In my Nike gym bag, I first put my cash in. I kept my bread under the floor board in my closet. Along with my guns. Two nines, a .40 caliber, and a .44 Magnum. I put my straps in the bag along with the ammo for each gun and the clips. In my book bag, I tossed in eight and half ounces of weed in zip-lock sandwich bags, four ounces of coke I hadn't rocked up to sell yet, and the pictures of my parents in an envelope. My aunt was just like me. She was traveling light. A large Gucci shoulder bag and a matching backpack. I could tell by the look of her pack, her money was in it. We were leaving everything else because we had what was important. The lights were left on as we exited out the kitchen door again and made it back to the car four blocks away as fast as we could.

Back at the motel in Upper Darby, we settled in for the night and got some sleep. In the morning, I went to IHOP with my aunt and Miss Shanda for breakfast. After we were done eating, auntie gave me some advice. She and Keith's mom were out, so she dropped some jewels on me before their departure. She told me to take care of myself, watch my back, be smart, and do what I needed to do. Miss. Shanda held my hand as she thanked me for being a real brother to her son and that she was going to miss me. I walked them out to the car, hugged and kissed them both, then watched them drive away. Heading for a new state to start over. Because of Keith, my aunt and Miss. Shanda became tight as Hell. Aunt Vanessa was a true hustler, Keith's mother was a gangsters' wife, and I knew they were going to be cool together. Now that they were in the wind, it was time for me to get to it.

****

The first thing I did was get my hands on a vehicle. Instead of going to a pre-owned dealership, I bought a whip from private seller. I found a Navy blue, 2003 Jeep Grand Cherokee in the paper. The older brother in Southwest only wanted $6500 for it. I paid the man, we did the transfer shit at Penn-DOT, and that was that. Now that I had wheels, I needed a residence. Once again, I went to the newspaper to find a crib. I found just what I needed. A one bedroom, second floor apartment in a reasonably quiet area of West Philly. I set up my spot quickly, found a boxing gym close to where I lived, and then started checking out the west side drug trade. It took me a week to get a lay of the land. I had some product to sell and though I peeped that there were fiends all over the place; moving my work in Philly was not as simple as it might seem. Philly niggas were viciously territorial and were not shy about puttin' bullet holes in unknown niggas that try to fuck up their money by sellin' dope in their hood. It wasn't about being shook to sell on these niggas block. My plan was to avoid unnecessary and stupid ass confrontations.

I thought about several possible moves, then came up with an idea. It was bold as fuck, and dangerous, but I was like fuck it! I drove across the bridge to Camden and spent a few days scoping out the hustling action on several blocks. I watched how niggas moved, what they drove, and like a wolf, when I spotted the perfect prey; I began stalking my next meal. A pretty boy looking corner hustler was making steady money selling dope. When I saw that son was the flashy type that liked to ball out in the bars and loved to flash cash and look good; I marked that

67

nigga for a lick. I never pulled a robbery before, but I was confident that I could get it done. So, I watched homie like a stalker for almost three weeks. I studied his every move, followed him without being discovered, and I learned son's entire routine. He was hustlin' coke, and like clockwork, he re-upped on the same day, at the same time every week. Saturday night. For two weeks straight, I followed him to a row house. He was inside for half an hour, then exited with a bright orange and white Nike box under his arm and brand-new sneakers on his feet. That was smart as fuck. Anyone watching would assume that the chick that lived there was his girl and she bought her man a new pair of sneakers.

Only I saw through the subterfuge. Dude and his connect, the shorty that lived in that house with her man, the supplier; were creatures of habit. My target arrived both times between 12:00 and 1:00 am. Yeah, he came out with new Nikes on his feet, but the sneaks he had on when he went into the house weren't in that box. His product was. After the second time he re-upped, I didn't follow him back to his baby moms' crib. I stayed right where I was. The second-floor window of the abandoned row house across the street. I sat in the shadows on an old chair in the bedroom of that vacant watching the supply house until dawn. I had to confirm that was indeed the re-up spot. My target arrived at 12:35. The next hustler showed up at 2:10. Number three at 3:08. And the last exited the house at 4:42. Now that I knew son's resupply schedule to a certainty, I didn't have to follow him anymore. Unless he got murdered, arrested, or decided to leave the game; I knew exactly where he'll be next Saturday night.

A week later, I was chilling on the couch watching TV. A shorty by the name of Myiesha sat on the opposite end. She smoked a cigarette as she stared at the large flat screen. We were watching the UPN show called Girlfriends. It was a marathon and shorty was watching it when I knocked on her door. Just because I had come over, there was no reason she couldn't keep enjoying her show. It was just the two of us anyway. Her five-year old daughter was spending the night at her grandma's house. It was a little after one am when I heard a key slide into the lock in front door. That was my cue. Less than a minute later, Brandon Myles strolled into the living room. He was just greeting his girl and daughters' mother when he froze where he stood. He averted his eyes from his lady to me. Then, at the .40 caliber Sig Sauer in my hand. Aimed at the side of his girl's head. Son was a deer in headlights as I calmly instructed him to come on in and have a seat.

I stood up when Brandon sat down. Deer in the headlights was the only way I could describe how homie looked. Son sat there in the recliner chair, looking up at me with fear burning in his eyes. I had him put the Nike box on his lap, warned his chick to sit there and be quiet, then I sat down on the arm of the couch close to the recliner. I raised my gun and pressed the barrel between his eyes as I broke it down to him.

"You just gon' have to eat this one, champ...You got caught slippin' and it is what it is...In a minute, you gon' take me to where you stash your paper at, then I'm a bounce with your product and cash...but check it out though, son....there's a silver lining here for you, my dude." I pressed the barrel in a little harder as I told him that,

"You get to keep your life, fam....your girl too...I just want the work and money, feel me?...But yo...It would be wise for you to take this hit on the chin....because if you come looking for me, you better get to me before I get to your people, na'mean?...Me and ya girl had a nice little chat before you came home...I know who it is you love and care about...So, if you come after me lookin' for payback or go to law...son...I don't think you got the financial expenses to cover that many funeral costs, feel me?"

Brandon swallowed, I saw the bitch in his eyes, and then he nodded that he understood as I removed the .40 caliber. I made him and his girl get up and walk ahead of me. As we left the living room, I asked him where was his stash. Safe in the bedroom he replied. Once in there, I gave son a roll of duct tape and had him wrap up his girls' wrists and ankles, then put a strip over her mouth. He did what I told him to do and then I ordered him to lay her on the bed. I then told Ma to just lie there and chill. Brandon went into the closet with me on his heels. He uncovered his safe and as he punched in the code to open it up, I placed the cannon to the back of his head. Just to keep him docile and in case he had a gun in the safe.

Son opened the safe and I tossed him a black trash bag I pulled from my back pocket. I stepped to the side with the gun still on him as he placed rubbed band held wads of cash into the bag. I had to admire homie. He was for sure a money stackin' hustler. He had to put at least 30, 40 grand into the trash bag. When he was done, he handed the bag back to me and I told him to stand up.

I walked dude to the opposite of the bed from his girl and made him sit on it. He was looking up at me when I put him out. With lightning speed, I grabbed him by shirt collar and hit the nigga with the flat side of the

Sig across his temple. The first hit rocked him, I kept him up by his shirt, hit a second, then a third time. Son was out cold as I let him drop onto the bed. I went around to Myiesha. Shorty was crying with her eyes squeezed shut. I knelt down and told her to remember what we talked about. Forget that this night ever happened. Or, her daughter gon' be raised by grandma. With that, I left their bedroom with the trash bag of cash, picked up the Nike box in the living room, and quietly departed their apartment. I took the rear stairs out of the building and walked to my ride around the corner. I stashed my score in the trunk and casually drove away. I made a quick stop at McDonald's when I was back in Philly and then took it on home.

I came up big with Brandon. $38,575 in cash along with twelve and a half grams of vanilla colored cocaine. I smiled as I looked at the fruits of my first lick on my dining room table. I then stashed everything, ate my quarter pounder meal while watching ESPN, hopped in the shower, and then crashed on the couch. The first phase of my plan was in the bag. On to phase two. Build a foundation of my own crew. It was time to recruit a couple of hungry young Philly soldiers and put them on. My 19th birthday came and went as the weeks went by and I didn't even notice. My mind was preoccupied as I searched the City of Brotherly Love for my team.

For weeks, I just rolled around the various hoods of Philly to watch certain spots. I clocked the hustlers and other corner boy looking niggas as they did their thing. Posted up around corner stores and in front of row house stoops on their thug shit. Hustlin' dope, fightin', talkin' shit, and runnin' from the cops. I was looking for a particular breed of goon, so I watched niggas closely. When I spotted a potential recruit, I snapped a picture with a digital zoom camera.

Philly was a vicious ass city with vicious ass niggas on its streets. As I said before, Philly dudes were fiercely territorial. Motherfuckers just can't stroll up on a block or corner without provoking a violent altercation. Especially in North Philly. I did however spot three young niggas that piqued my interest. One from the North side, one from Southwest, and one from South Philly. Though I wasn't scared of anything or anyone, nor was I shook to put bullets in a body; the focus was my goal. To recruit. Not provoke a shootout. I had to get at these niggas through the backdoor. Thus, I used the best asset to get a niggas attention. Women. On each side of the city that I marked a recruit, I started hittin' up the bars. The females noticed me right away. I walked up in the joint as the new nigga that caught their eye. One, I knew how to dress. Two, I was over six feet tall. And three, I was a hustling lookin' nigga with cash. I flirted with various chicks, bought drinks, and I went home with more than a few.

I finessed information out of three chicks after I buttered them up. Good dick, great tongue, I had fire weed, and I didn't mind spending money. Hotel rooms, bottles, dinners, and I paid for trips to the hair & nail salons. Though it was a costly investment, I got my return in spades. Three of the chicks I bagged, once I got them comfortable with me, I made a deal with them. I showed them the picture of the nigga from their side of the city that I wanted to recruit and presented shorty with $1000 to approach son with an offer. An offer to potentially make serious money on the streets, and all they had to do was call a number. Shorty left with half the money to do what I asked and a white business card with my pre-paid cell number on it. All three chicks were motivated to get the other half of that grand. They went out and found the niggas in the pictures, presented my offer, and within a few days my phone would ring. As anticipated, the young niggas were on guard. Suspicious of who the fuck I was, but drawn in by the potential of making money like a moth to the flame.

To ensure these dudes that I wasn't a cop, nor was I setting them up, I had them meet me individually in a public place. The first prospect met me at 30th street station. I told son what I'd have on. When he walked in and saw me sitting by myself in the food court by Burger King, wearing fitted Yankee cap and jersey, I nodded to him. I was rising from my seat with a large fountain soda as he nodded back. I indicated with my head for him to follow me and we exited the station. We started walking across the Market Street bridge and I gave Ramiq a moment to light his cigarette before we discussed what I wanted from him. Son was 18 and the same height as me. 6'1. He wasn't as stocky as I was though. He was brown skin and athletically slim, but like a lot of dudes in Philly; he rocked a thickening Muslim beard. He kept his neatly trimmed and well groomed. As was his hair. Cut short, his shape up was razor sharp, and his waves were three sixty. I instinctively liked Ramiq. His facial expression was hard, but it wasn't forced. I knew he was cut from a thugs' cloth for sure!

We walked through downtown and I kept it 100 with him. I told Meek, as he preferred to be called, that I scoped him out in his hood. That I was scouting for niggas to build a team with. Meek nodded his head as he walked with his hands in his pockets. Without looking at me, he calmly inquired,

"*So why me, fam?...Out of all the niggas you saw on my block, why you pick me?*" My eyes momentarily followed a cop car as I rolled by, then I replied with,

"*Because you stood out, yo...You wasn't on no bullshit and games, feel me?...From my vantage point, son...You was the only one I saw out there on some soldier shit...not talkin' a lot, being loud, jokin' around, or really trying to be noticed...With what I'm building, yo...I ain't got time for dogs that bark and make a lot of fuckin' noise....I'm lookin' for wolves, my dude....silent but deadly, na'mean?*"

Meek glanced at me as we strolled and nodded his head. With a devilish grin flashing through his beard. He replied that he liked the sound of what I was offering, but there was a question on his mind. Why should he run with me? What was I offering? I was waiting for him to ask that question. Still walking, I told him that I had $3,000 for him. 1500 just for coming to this meet, another 1500 to show up to the next one, and if he decided to run with the wolves, he was going to make more money than he ever has on the corner. I guarantee that! Meek was quiet for two blocks, then he looked me dead in the eyes, weighing his options, and then dapped fists with me as he told me to hit him up when I was ready for the second meet.

****

Four days later, Meek arrived at Midnight Tavern on Jefferson Street in West Philly. It was ten minutes after twelve in the afternoon. In between scouting and recruiting, I built up a bond with the O.G. that owned the bar. Leon Miller was definitely a gangster from back in the day. At least two nights a week, I stopped by the tavern. To drink, flirt with the women, and kick it with the ol'head. It didn't take long for Leon and I to become tight. I sat with him in his personal both and we knocked back shots, rapped about the sports, converse about females, and he schooled me on handling business in the streets. As O.G. and I became closer, I started dropping hints about some of the plans I had in the works. Leon was interested, so I let him in on what I had brewing. He was as an avid weed smoker and he like younger women. Chicks in their early twenties and pretty. I catered to the old head by hittin' him off with high grade smoke and I surprised him with a 22-year old, bad as fuck, ebony toned stripper I hired to rock his boat in a hotel room.

72

Leon was now apart of my plan, so I had full use of his establishment. He closed the bar for a few hours so that I could have a private meeting location for my recruits. Meek was the first one to arrive. Twenty minutes later, my second prospect knocked on the door. I let son in and dapped him up. Xavier, aka Zay and I walked over to the table where Meek was sitting. I introduced them and then we sat down and went back to smoking and sippin' on Henny. Almost a half hour later, the third and final recruit showed up at the bar. That would be Ahmir. Known as Cannon on the street. Now that all three of the goons that I reached out to had arrived, once Cannon had a glass of cognac in front of him, we got to it. The first thing I did was keep my word. I handed a rubber band held wad of cash to all three of them. The second $1500 I promised them for showing up. Now that I had paid out almost ten grand, they valued my money and my time. I sat at the head of the table and gave it to them straight and raw.

I told the three of them that I was recruiting them to run with me as a squad to get what all street niggas want. Money, Power, and Respect. Looking at Meek, I spoked to all of them as I explained that the $3000 that they have is only a taste of what I had cooking. I then reached down under the table and reached into my book bag on the floor. Onto the table, I lied a gallon sized zip-lock bag on table. Two-quarters filled with Brandon vanilla toned cocaine. With the bag sitting in front of me, I explained that if they're in, the first thing we going do is sell off this coke. Once it was gone and we all got some cash to sit on, we gon' step it up. I anticipated they were thinking about a connect, but I had something else in mind. I told my prospects that we ain't working for nobody. Fuck a connect. Fuck a consignment deal. We ain't moving nobody's package. Once this coke was gone, it was time for that outlaw shit. We ain't puttin' up no buy money for product from some middle man intermidiary. We gonna take what others got. We gon' get money with other niggas product.

It took Meek, Zay, and Cannon about two whole seconds to make their decision. It was unanimous. They were in. Now that they were on board, I laid out the continuity of leadership. I was in charge. Though I was only 19 and Zay was the youngest at 17, I made it clear that this was my show and I was the leading star of it. In no uncertain terms, I told them that this was my team and my team was a Republic. Not a democracy. It was going to be about respect amongst us, but when I make a decision on what we do, or how we made a move, it wasn't up for debate unless it was mutual fuckin' discussion. Once I had their understanding, I impressed upon them the code. One: Do not talk to anyone outside of this table about our business. Two: Do not make a move on your own that will put the whole team at risk of getting locked the fuck up. Three: Fuck everyone except for those in this room. Four: Think before you fuckin' act! Five: Live quietly to stay rich and out of jail. And rule number four. Death Before Dishonor. I looked all three of them in the eyes as I broke down the 4th code.

If any of them broke the 4th code, dishonor equals death. I wasn't fuckin' playing about that shit. I pulled out my .40 caliber and lied it on the table next to the bag of coke. I stared across the table at Meek for a few seconds, then I focused on Zay as I revealed my thoughts. If anyone, including myself, breaks the 4th code; automatic death sentence. If anyone snitch, backstab the crew by running with other niggas against us, turn sucker for some pussy and get us in deep with the law, and especially if any one of us double cross any one at this table; then you better hope God grants you refuge. Because the Devil will be coming for your soul. As raw as I could say it, I told all three of my goons that if they break the 4th code, they better murder me in the process. Because I will be coming for their life and one of us will end up in a body bag. I paused after I spoke those words, studied each of them for a second, and offered them an out. Now. By saying that if these rules and codes of conduct was too much for them, there was the door. Leave now. No one stood up and I was satisfied with what I saw. Calm faces and hard eyes. The wolf pack was born.

We set up shop in Southwest Philly. Using a hood rats row house as our lab, we got busy processing our coke for distribution. Just like I was taught by the Matthews, we turned the powder cocaine into crystalized rock. Old school style. A pot of boiling water, a glass jaw, swirling cocaine in water with a cut of B12, and ice cubes to harden the mix. Once the large rocks of crack dried, using latex gloves and razor blades, we cut up the chucks into pieces. Zay and Cannon did the chopping at one end of the table, while shorty and her sister used gloves and tiny spoons to scoop powder coke into glass vials normally used for cologne oil. The rocks went into small baggies of various colors. For the soft coke, we used two different sized glass. Five and ten dollar vials. With the crack pieces, it ranged. We had two, five, ten, and twenty-dollar bags. My people spent hours in the lab. By the time they were done, we had the full package to put out on the street.

One-hundred and sixty five and ten-dollar vials to go with seventy-five crack bags of all four colors. Red, blue, green, and yellow. That was only half of the twelve and a half ounces of coke that I relieved Brandon of. Though I only put a quarter ounce cut of B12 for every one ounce of cocaine for every cook; that shit really inflated the actual product. Though it meant dropping the purity level of the coke a bit, it didn't matter. Fiends were still going to smoke and snort that shit. While my two goons and the chicks were baggin' up, Meek and I were out and about. He knew someone that had access to firepower, so he called his people and we met with the nigga that had the guns. I dipped into my stash of dough again and bought us a load of hardware. Some pistols, a couple of shotguns, three automatic submachine guns, ammo, and a vest for everyone. Meek arranged for a chick he knew to rent a storage unit for us just outside the city and I gave Ma the money to lease that bitch for six months up front. We stashed the arsenal inside the unit and drove back to the lab. Zay and Cannon had the work ready to go, we paid the shorties for their work, then we bounced.

While my crew went off to do whatever they felt like doing, I left the product with Meek before I hit the highway. There was something about Ramiq that I really liked. Son just had this feel to him and though it was clear that I ran shit with my new team; dude was definitely going to be second in command. It was just his overall vibe that I knew I was able to trust him. I drove down to Newark and spent the evening cruising around the city. I was hidden by my tints and I didn't plan on interacting with anyone. I drove past my aunts' old house, by Keith's, I stopped at the high school to look at the field where my dude used to scorch niggas up and down the grass, then I rolled by the corner and projects where I used to do my thing. Where I posted up, hustled, and got into fights at. Eventually, I drove past spots that were hot with niggas moving product. Even from Philly, I knew all about the Matthews brothers. I kept my ear to the streets and they were talking about Na'jae and Kareem.

Keith's snake ass brothers had it on lock in Newark and other places. Like Wilmington. Word was they had a strong connect and were majorly stacking money. When niggas were really getting money like that in the hood, motherfuckers talk. I picked up on that chatter in Philly. People in the city had family and shit in Delaware. When it came to money and the niggas making it, word travels all over the place. Niggas and females talk about shit and eventually, someone like me will hear about it. Chicks I rapped with in the bars or was fucking told me about this or that what they heard about Na'jae and Kareem from their cousin or whatever in Newark. I soaked up all that was shared with me, storing that shit in my memory banks. I had another plan brewing in my mind, but for the t being, I was keeping that one to myself. I stopped at a gas station tc up before heading back to Philly. I pulled up to Pump #4. In front o1 at #2 was a snow-white colored BMW S-series with smoke tints chrome trim work. That shit was nice. I exited my SUV and made way for the store.

I normally paid with my debit card, but I had to piss and I want Pepsi and a fresh pack of Newports. As I reached the doors, a wo. was coming out. Being the gentleman my pops raised me to be, I ope the door for her. Ma slowed her pace as she exited, looked me in face, and in an instant, she had my attention. We did the same thin the same time as she passed me by. We sized one another up. I feeling what I was seeing, and judging by the look in her brown eyes was she. She turned her head straight and kept walking, but I was looking at her. Nah, I wasn't all love struck or no bullshit like that. Y was intrigued. Ma had to be in her thirties, but she looked younger t what I was guessing. She was about 5'8, thick but in shape, cocoa br skinned, with long jet-black hair. It was silky and it shined. I was dig her face and body, but I was really feeling her sexy but casual d style. She was just reaching her ride, the BMW, when I went into store.

When I came back outside, I expected the BMW to be gone and like fuck it. A missed opportunity. However, it was still sitting at pt #2 when I exited the store to fill my gas tank. I paid for $25 dollar gas inside, selected 93 unleaded at the pump, put the nozzle in, and s to fill the gas tank on its own and I made my way to driver side of BMW. Ma rolled her window down when I stepped up. I leaned d and introduced myself and she told me her name as we shook ha Nina. Nina Stevens. We began talking and neither of us beat around bush. I told ma that I was 19, she revealed that she was 38, I asked if had a dude, she relied no, asked if I was single, I said yeah, and a biting her lip a little, with a sly grin, she held eyes with me and aske I'd like to join her for dinner? Staring in her eyes, with my own smirk, I asked her what was she in the mood for? And its on me, if don't mind.

Minutes later, I followed Nina's car as she led me towards restaurant of her preference. An Italian spot called La Casa. Dinner just the appetizer. I peeped out her vibe and knew what was going down later on.

Looks like I was staying the night in Newark.

CHAPTER SEVEN

"Where I'm from, you carry the load, you ain't supposed to bitch / That's why I watch who I'm around when I pose for flicks / And I don't talk none of my business around these nosey chicks / I control the strip, potent shit, my solider's pitch / I got what you need / whether you pop, shoot, smoke or sniff

-Paul Cain, Bars R Us

Nina was one of those women that had a lust for younger thug type of niggas. Ma was bad as fuck. Sexy was too light to describe her really. She was beautiful in the face, her hair-makeup-& nails were on point, she looked good as a motherfucker in that black pants suit and white silk blouse, and the cut of her suit showed me everything without revealing anything. Her body was riper than every fruit in any garden. It was clear from our conversation as we dined that she was not a window dressing sort of female. Her self-esteem and self-assurance were real. She carried herself with poise, and when she spoke, her vocabulary was intelligent and her words were delivered with confidence. There was no doubt that she wanted the dick, but she made one obvious miscalculation with me that she quickly picked up on. I wasn't the typical street wise, but brain dead-incompetent-or illiterate ass nigga from the hood.

Shorty was a sexy cat that liked to toy with her playmate before she sank her claws into him. Over Italian food and wine, with a lit candle between us and all that bullshit, she attempted to establish intellectual dominance over me. After a bit of feeling each other out topics, she engaged me in a deep, real talk conversation about life. She held eye contact with me as she shared her views and philosophies about the black community, issues, and the state of black people in America. I gave her my full attention as I absorbed her intricate use of wording, her super confident tone, and her dissecting eyes as she flexed her intellectual muscles. Aiight. I dig it. Ma one of those HBCU, higher learning females. Cool. When she finished and asked for my thoughts on the subject, I responded. With the very own style of highly knowledgeable, deeply philosophical, and wise beyond my years dialogue, I replied with full detailed opinions on every subject she spoke about. Without parroting back anything she had said to me.

When I finished speaking, Ma was taken aback, but she did a smooth move in covering it up. She smiled at me with a raised eye brow as she picked up her wine glass and took a sip. I grinned a little too as I thought to myself. That pussy just got wetter now that she knows she fuckin' with a street nigga with a high IQ. I may have dropped out of high school, but I still fed my brain. Whenever I could, I read deep books. I also watched the news and black documentaries. I kicked it with older brothers at the park where they taught me how to play chess and always dropped wisdom & knowledge on me. Before my father was killed, he had schooled me to always feed my brain. Useful and important shit. It was a habit I've had since I was a little nigga. Dudes always wondered why I didn't have a lot of rap when I was on the corners and in the projects with them. Even as a young buck, I didn't have any interest or tolerance for mindless, ignorant ass conversation. About dumb shit, pointless shit, or bullshit.

Instead of going back to her place, we went to a hotel. Once we were in the room and the door was shut, it was on. Nina pounced on a nigga like Jaguar. As soon and I closed the door, she was on me. Backed me against the wall and pulled my head down to hers to kiss me. We kissed hard and aggressively. I was feeling that about her. She wanted grown ass sex. None of that R&B love making shit. As she was opening my belt and jeans, I unbuttoning her suit jacket. She moaned as she kissed me, sliding her tongue deep into my mouth. I got her jacket off as she opened my jeans and stuck her hands inside my boxers. With my lips between hers, she let out a sultry, *'Mmmmmmm!'* as she took hold of my dick. Yeah, a nigga was packing a titan down there. Long and thick. Nina pulled my dick out and stroked it as I led her backwards into the room. When we reached the queen-sized bed, Ma stopped kissing me. She started unbuttoning her silk blouse as I pulled off my T-shirt and kicked off my Jordan's.

Nina's titties looked delicious in her white lace bra. They were big as fuck. She had on matching seamless panties and her hips looked just as good as her breasts. Ma was just pure chocolate thickness. Her eyes were locked with mine as she reached back to unhook her bra as I removed my boxers. I knew what she wanted without saying a word. Less than a minute later, I had Nina on her back in the middle of the bed, pleasing her titties. I held them together and sucked-licked on her nipples. She caressed my head and moaned. I tried to suck the life out of her through her breasts. I went back to kissing her before I moved down her body. She lifted her hips as I pulled her panties off and tossed them over my shoulder. Without wasting time, I moved her into position. Nina sat up on her elbows, watching me as I put my face into her pussy and started eating her out. I swirled the tip of my tongue on her clit as I gripped the back of her thighs. Pushing her legs up higher and wider open.

I sucked on her clit and fingered her dripping wet, cleanly shaven pussy until she came. Moaning hard and loud as fuck, grabbing my head, and rotating her hips. Nina told me that she wanted to suck my dick, that she wanted to feel it in her mouth; but I ignored her. I was busy. Busy still eating her pussy. I kept licking, sucking, and fingering her until I got what I wanted. Her begging my ass to stop. I didn't until she came again. Ma dropped back on the bed and I moved up towards her. I took a fistful of her hair, picked her head up, turned it towards me, and she opened her mouth as I slid my dick into it. Propping herself up on one elbow, she stroked my dick as she sucked it. I bit my lip and groaned as I watched her top me off. She looked up at me, licking the head and sides of my dick, deep throated it, and had it wet and dripping with spit. Her head game was top notch. I was loving how skilled she was with her lips and tongue, she stroked it right, her mouth got wet as fuck, and Ma had almost no gag reflex as she deep throated me.

Though she made me bust and stared into my eyes as she licked and swallowed every drop, we weren't even close to done. I retrieved a gold package Magnum from my jeans pocket, put it in on, and Nina was already in position. Doggy style. I fucked her like that for a long time. Pulling her head back by her hair, gripping her waist, and slapping her ass as it jiggled and shook with each stroke. Nina was vocal as Hell as I dicked her down. Constantly calling out "OMG!" and "FUCK!", or telling me to go deeper and harder. I catered to her requests and each time she said something, I gave it to her raw. Stroked extra deep, or harder, or I gripped her hips even tighter. I wasn't really vocal while fuckin', but when the pussy was this good, it had a nigga making noise. Groaning and growling, biting my lip and locking my jaw. After doggy, I got my back and she straddled me. I held on to and played with them heavy titties as she rode me. Properly. Other females I fucked did all that horseback riding, bouncing shit. Not Miss Nina Stevens.

She kept her hands on my chest or shoulders, eyes locked with mine as she snake-rolled her pelvis. Keeping my dick deep inside of her, sliding her pussy up & down it. Feeling every inch and making sure her G-spot was stimulated with each and every roll of her hips. She didn't go too fast or hard. Marinating this dick on some fiery seduction shit. When she was about to nut again, she picked up the pace and I clutched her ass cheeks as she came. Once again, loud and hard. Not long after her orgasm, I had her in the missionary position. On the edge of the bed, legs opened wide, and she held herself up as I gripped the back of her neck. Our heads were close together as both of us looked down. Her titties were bouncing as we watched my latex and milky female secretion covered dick rapidly slide back and forth in her pussy. When Nina started begging me to cum in between trying to breathe right and moan, I started banging away. Going deep and hard, ignoring the sweat on my face and her nails in my arms. I cobra clutched the back of her neck and growled like a full-grown Grizzly as I busted a nut in the rubber.

We stayed where we were for a minute. Both of us breathing hard as fuck, covered in sweat, and with her eyes closed, trembling with her chest heaving, she kept whispering, "Damn." I slowly pulled out and stood up as she lied back on the bed. Arms over head, which was turned to the side and her eyes still closed. I deposited the condom in the toilet before taking a piss. I then got my Newports and lighter out of my pants before making my way towards the round table near the window. I opened it before I sat down and fired one up. Nina finally found the energy to get off the bed and use the bathroom herself. When she was done, she did what a few chicks have done with me before. She came to me and sat on my lap butt ass naked as I smoked. Ma studied my face as she got all touchy-feely and kissy with me. I didn't say nothing. I just let her do what she feel. I messed her up, her eyes were tired, and I could feel her still trembling a little. Yet, she couldn't keep her hands off me or stop kissing on me. In my mind, I grinned to myself. Job done.

I wasn't looking for any kind of relationship, but this was a high-quality woman that I wouldn't mind fucking with for a while. Nina was not only beautiful in the face with a sexy ass body; she was top shelf. A successful college educated interior decorator and realtor, single, no kids, had her own money-car-and home. Her head skills were elite, the pussy was fire, and I knew by her interactions with me before-during-and after we fucked; I was in with her. Nah, I wasn't looking for a wifey; but I'd settle for a temporary Queen. She told me that she lived just outside of Newark. In New Castle. She was born and raised in Wilmington, attended & graduated from Cheyney University, and had family all over Delaware. That's why she was in Newark. Her sister hosted a female only get together at her home. I met Nina when she was on her way to hers in New Castle. Ma and I took shower, housekeeping was called to change the linens and shit, and with that sweet lady look in her eyes, she asked me to spend the night with her. I did, but she best not get used to this. I wasn't her dude, she wasn't my woman, and what we had between us wasn't a relationship. She was just the current bad ass chick that I was fuckin' with for the moment.

****

We set up shop in two areas of Southwest Philly. Both spots were prime locations to get money. The first area was in the cluster of a row house heavy neighborhood. Zay knew this part of the city, so he was our hand to hand dealer in that area. Meek was his muscle. His protection. A hood rat let us use her crib to sell from. Her row house became Meek and Zay's lay up and fall back spot. With the rise of snitches and city cameras all over the place, we went lo-tech with how to move our product. Zay worked the streets and gave out the number to his pre-paid phone. When the fiends wanted to cop, they hit his cell and met him in various alley's or vacant buildings around the hood. Never at shorty crib, out in the open on the street, or on any corner. Meek was always with Zay when he made his drops. If they were posted on a corner and got a call from a buyer, the transactions were never spoken about in detail over the phone. Everything was vague and in code.

When a customer was looking to buy something when they called, all they said was the street they were on. But add in how much they were spending by sliding it in as the street number. That was the code, in which Zay or Meek would tell them where to meet them at. For a little over three weeks that was cool. Me and Cannon did the same thing in our spot. Son and I were set up in a chicks crib in this projects like apartment complex. One of those developments where most of the occupants were either 9-to-5 working types, motherfuckers on social security, or single mothers on welfare who got a reasonably nice apartment through section eight housing. Ma that let us use her spot, Cannon set that up. Met her at a bar and finessed her with drinks, weed, flashin' his cash, and then dicked her down at a motel. She had a kid to some nigga in prison upstate for twenty-years and her week was spent working eight hours a day at a call center as a representative to collect student loans. We hit Ma off with a couple hundred dollars a week to work from her spot and Cannon hit her with the dick to keep her happy.

Almost a month in, I switched up the format. We were selling off our product, but I wasn't feeling how we were operating. All that in and out, phone tag, meeting buyers all over the place shit was putting us in the

82

light of exposure too often. It felt like we were had established a predictable and vulnerable pattern. I called a meet with my crew at shorty apartment while she was at work and her daughter was at daycare. I told my niggas that we changing up how to we did business. It had taken me a week, but I set up two new spots for us to hustle from. The first was an apartment building on Warrington Avenue, between 56th and 57th street. I had scoped the area with Cannon and arranged a deal with a sexy ass stripper that lived in the rear apartment on the ground floor. I did the same thing on Elmwood Avenue, right before 71st street. Only with this spot, it wasn't a chicks home we were working out of. Through a cutie with a fat booty, I was put on to an ol'head that owned and ran a pool hall / takeout spot.

Back in the day, Shaun Holmes was a major player in the Philly drug game. From the mid-eighties to the early-nineties, he was that nigga when it came to selling dope. Word from shorty was that Shaun was apart of a mafia style crew that had several sections of the city on lock. Then, the Italians and the law banged on them niggas until the kingdom folded. A lot of dudes got murdered, fled the city, or got indicted. Shaun got hit with a ten-year sentence by the feds in October 1994. He came home January of 2005. Ma used to be married to and had a nine-year old son to one of Shaun's nephews, so she knew the whole story. When homie got out, his brother kept him straight by signing over his pool hall to him so that he could make his money the legit way. It was a front though. Shaun's older brother was kind of a made nigga in the city, so they ran drugs and other illegal shit through the spot. That is until 2006, when big brother Holmes was murdered and his drug business died with him. Since then, Shaun has been doing whatever he could to keep the pool hall's doors open without the backing of drug money.

The 42-year old former hustler was quick to strike a deal with me when I presented my offer to him. To let us use his business to move our product. Cannon and I set up our shop in back room of the pool hall. The rear door to the alley was in the room and we stayed out of sight when we were on the clock. Cannon put on a shorty from his hood to act as our relay. While he and I were in the backroom with a two TV's *(one for regular watching and the other for the security cameras),* a video game, and the cocaine ready for distribution; baby girl pretended to be one of Shaun's workers up front with him. It took a minute to establish a flow, but once we did, our exposure was basically zero. Cannon and I rarely left that backroom. We watched movies and shit, played Madden-NBA2K-Mortal Kombat, the bathroom was right across from the backroom, and we put two couches in there. When we got hungry, we hit shorty phone up front and she brought us some grub from the kitchen. Business was really poppin' at night, so we were in the shop from around eight to like four in the morning.

Twelve and a half ounces of cocaine is a lot of dope to some niggas, but to me, it was just a starter package. The silver lining was that Brandon's coke was good shit. The fiends that smoked rock was coming back to cop multiple times a day and those who snorted powder were too. We would have sold off the entire package much faster, but due to the Philly PD and City Hall initiating a Zero Tolerance crackdown on narcotics trafficking; we had to take a pause now and again to avoid the narc boys discovering our operation. While on hiatus from the paper chase, my time was spent doing shit that I normally did. Hittin' the boxing gym, swinging by the shooting range, reading, and down at Nina's spot. Frequently getting my dick sucked and sliding up in that fire pussy. Though Ma was showing all the signs that she was fallin' in love and wanted a boyfriend, I didn't trip. I was planning my exit from her life, but stuck around to continue enjoying the fruits of her body.

I still kept my eye on Na'jae and Kareem. The pause in the flow of what I had going on in Philly gave me time for three things. Planning moves to level up my gangster, stalk the Matthews brothers, and continuing to build my team into something vicious. Meek, Zay, and Cannon truly looked up to me. None of them bucked the system I set up, they did as I asked, and I never had a problem with them doing dumb shit. I had got into their heads and they believed what I believed. That we were going to get paid out the ass and establish ourselves as a power crew in the game. I played shit close to the chest though. I didn't tell them all the plans I had brewing in my head, but at the same time, I was preparing them for the next phase. When the police eased up on the hood's we were selling our product in, it was back to business. However, I had my team on a schedule and disciplined program. Meek and Zay hit a gym like me and Cannon did. All of us worked out, lifted weights, and sharpened out fight skills by sparring and running through various boxing exercises. That was the physical part.

At the shooting range, we shot up targets like we were Marines getting ready for a war. I even took my goons out deep in the woods far away from Philly, towards central Pennsylvania to work on our marksmanship. I met a white dude at the range that was cool as fuck and liked to smoke weed. He also had a thing for prostitutes. I set up a little tryst for him with two nasty ass chicks from the website backpage.com. Homie had the freak night of his life in the motel room I paid for. Dude had a bottle of liquor, some fire bud, and two nympho chicks all to himself for a night. I hook, line, and sinkered my man. All to get access to what I needed. My new homie Kyle was a gun loving white boy ex-soldier that owned acres of property in the middle of nowhere Pennsylvania. He came to Philly every year for this big gun show and had stopped at the range to break in his new rifles and shit before heading home.

Kyle lived alone in the boondocks and gave us hustlers from the streets of Philly full run of his custom made shooting area. Because he had all the right licenses, permits and shit; it wasn't unusual for him to shoot on his land. Me and my crew spent hours capping off hundreds of rounds. We shot semi-automatics, revolvers, assault rifles, shotguns, and Kyle even helped us fine tune our shooting skills. Payment for him was a package of weed and a freaky bitch from backpage to that made the trip with us to suck & fuck him while we focused on the guns & ammo. When the coke we had was down to an ounce and a half, I put my crew on notice. Re-up time was coming. We sold off the rest of our product, my goons had a little savings built up, and now it was time to resupply. Though we could have pooled buy money together to re-up from a local source in the city, or possibly in New York or Baltimore; that wasn't in the plan. I gathered my team at Midnight Tavern and gave them their mission orders.

Meek was traveling to Pittsburgh, Zay was heading for a city in PA called Johnstown, and I was sending Cannon out of state. He was going to Cleveland, Ohio. They weren't being sent to those cities to search for a connect to purchase dope from. They were being sent to be conduct what the military calls reconnaissance and intelligence gathering. My goons were going on a scouting mission. Their job was to travel to those cities, find a female to finesse to set up a spot for themselves, and then scour the city until they find what I was sending them to locate. A target. A nigga getting money on a high level. A motherfucker out there selling weight, stacking money high. Once they found a player like that, report back to me. The goon of mine that finds the biggest prey, that's where we hunt. I could easily link up with someone in the city or close to Philly and buy product from them to put on the streets, but fuck that! My mindset wasn't on negotiating to get what I wanted in this world. It was going to take what I wanted, from whoever I wanted to take it from, however I had to take it.

****

My wolves had been in the wind for almost a week. As I waited for them to send what back on potential targets, I had my own mission to carry out. Originally, I was just going to fall back and wait for my goons to report in. I was going to chill, get my dick wet, and vent on niggas in the ring. Dudes that thought they were the next boxing superstar challenged me to trade hands with them. After brutalizing a handful of motherfuckers during sparring sessions, I had a rep at the boxing gym. Niggas started calling me Sha The Menace. Dudes thought they were tough and nice with their hands foolishly invited me to spar with them and got their ass lit the fuck up. One, I'm lethal as a cobra with them gloves on; and two, I didn't believe in mercy during a fight. My style is viciously brutal and I ain't gotta fight dirty to rip a nigga the fuck up once that bell rings. On the outside, I come off as a cool-laid back-quiet type of nigga. On the inside though, I was filled with venom.

Anger, frustration, turmoil, and hate. I felt that shit all the time. The pain over my parents, Keith, losing A'liyah, and the betrayal that cost me Mr. Marvin and Miss. Shanda had consumed me with a constantly burning ball of rage. Fury. I was content to exorcise that shit on the weights and heavy bag, but so many niggas that thought they were cut from a killer's cloth wanted to try me. At the gym, dudes would arrogantly invite me to lace up the gloves and headgear to jump in the ring and spar. Thinking I was an easy win for their egos and shit. They saw it as a means to gain a popularity boost. I saw it as an opportunity. To vent, and to prove a point. Be careful who you cross in this world. Wolves love to hide in sheep's clothing. I beat blood out of niggas, made some quit, beat a few senseless, and knocked three dudes straight the fuck out. I made my point. I was not the one they wanted to fuck with! Yet, no matter how many motherfuckers I beat the breaks off of, it did nothing to lessen my anger. Five days after my goons hit the road, I decided to direct my focus at the niggas I had a vendetta with.

After buying an old Dodge Stratus from a car lot, I started spending a lot of time in Newark. I worked the fiends at night to learn which one of Na'jae and Kareem's dealers was a good target. By good, I mean which one of their dealers was making a lot of money for them. I was pointed in the direction of a nigga by the name Jermaine. I found him in less than a day. Imagine my surprise when I found out that it was Jermaine Harris Jr. A nigga Keith and I went to school with. Son was a basketball star that was recruited by Duke and had graduated when Keith did. He never balled for the Blue Devils because he ruined his hoop dreams when he put hands on a chick at a party a few weeks after graduation. He was drunk, shorty said something foul to him, he punched her, got arrested, and Duke pulled their scholarship offer. Jay only got probation for hittin' shorty, but no school would touch him. That's bad news for homie.

Because I was about to.

CHAPTER EIGHT

"Keep your friends close and your enemies closer."

-Sun Tzu, The Art of War

Ⅰt only took one full day of stalking Jermaine before he presented me with a window of opportunity to make my move on him. I was in son's shadow for almost 18-hours and he never made me. Starting in the A.M., I followed him from the moment he exited he and his girl's apartment. They lived in a nice ass spot. Rent had to be at least $1200 a month. I watched J stroll to a dark blue Yukon, climb in, and drive off. His first stop was IHOP for breakfast. From there, he rolled past his moms' house. His mother still lived in the same crib. He was inside for about two hours and then he drove to his shop. A small block near the projects I used to post up in. I parked a block away, facing the corner where he had young niggas out hustling for him. 16, 17-year old's from the looks of them. I watched Jermaine hold court on the corner. Getting report from a tall youngin' with the beginnings of dread-locks and a white T. One of the other young dudes handed him what looked like a potato chips bag, but by the way he was holding it, I knew what was up. That was the money from the night shift's product sells.

After following Jermaine to a row house on the other side of Newark, an hour later, he came back out and drove off again. I assumed that residence was the money drop. Good. Na'jae and Kareem were still operating from the same playbook their pops had designed. I stored that knowledge away and continued following Jay. He returned to his block and posted up on a row house porch. Across the street and three houses down from his corner. From where I was parked, I could see the porch he was sitting on and his youngin's across the street in front of the store. It was a good thing the Stratus I bought had smoke tinted windows. I reclined my seat back a little with my gun on my lap as I settled in to study & observe. For hours on end, I sat there behind the tints as Jermaine watched over his area. The young niggas served the fiends using the pick & roll method. The crack head would approach the youngin' by the pay phone, tell said young dude how much he wanted, a hand signal was given to the runner, and the runner disappeared around the corner.

The fiend walked off in the opposite direction, going around the corner as well. Once in the alley behind the houses, the exchange was made. The junkie motherfucker passed off the money, the young nigga handed over the crack, probably still in caps, and they two went on about their business. A few minutes later, the young buck that made the delivery smoothly passed the cash off to the tall kid in the white T-shirt. Everything was how it was before and during the transaction. Jermaine was on the porch talking to some thick chick with big ass titties, while the young niggas on the corner were standing around talking shit and chillin'. After six transactions over the course of two hours, the youngin's cleared the corner. I watched Jermaine stroll into the house, and like that, the block was dead. When I checked my watch, I knew why they shut down the corner. From behind me, I watched a Newark PD patrol car come cruising down the street. The cruiser rolled past my car, slowly, then parked in front of the store. Where it sat for the next twenty-five minutes.

Jermaine's crew knew the patrol schedule and the police knew this was a drug dealing block. The war on drugs was a joke. The cops knew they could indict this corner and pop the niggas working it. They probably knew who they all were. Yet, unless there was a reason to lock shit down and make a bust; it was business as usual. The police make their presence known, the crew running this spot scattered, business slowed up for a hot second, and right on time; Mr. Patrol Officer put his cruiser in drive and bounced. Within twenty-minutes, J was back on the porch and his crew returned to resume business. Only now, they were posted up in the middle of the block, about thirty feet away from where I was parked. They took over a stoop in front of someone's house. I sat there for another two hours, and then Jermaine closed up shop for the day time shift. The youngin's dispersed again, he went inside the row house with young buck in the white T-shirt, and ten minutes later, he was in his Yukon and mobile again. I followed him to a hair salon, where I watched a chick in tight jeans and an equally tight shirt climb in and he pulled off.

They went to eat first and then to, I'm guessing her spot. A high-rise apartment building close to downtown. That made sense. Ma looked like she was one of those chicks that was catered to by hustling niggas such as Jermaine. One, she was sexy as Hell. Two, her body was right. Three, by her manner of dress and the way she carried herself, she was definitely sucking money out of Jay through his dick. At a minimum her apartment cost her seven to nine-hundred dollars a month. An hour and a half later, J came swaggin' out of the front doors of the apartment building on his phone as he exited. He was smiling and shit. He walked right past my ride and I could tell by the look on his face that he was speaking to a female. Son was still a playboy I see. He had the chicks on his dick when he was ballin' for the high school and homie loved that shit. Mad females were on him and he was a notorious cheater. Had bitches fighting over him all the time. Not really a surprise though. It's like that when you're a six-three senior, handsome, rumored to eat pussy with supreme skill, and a college bound superstar with NBA level potential. I see shit didn't change even though he a drug dealer now. Sex was still this niggas addiction.

Jermaine and I made the drive from Newark to Chester, Pa. I shadowed his ride staying three cars back the whole time. When son parked in front of a nice ass house in a quiet neighborhood, I pulled over half a block behind him. I killed my engine as his rear lights went out. I watched him climb out of his Yukon, walk up to the house, and he didn't knock or ring the doorbell. Son went straight in and closed the door. Two hours later, twenty-minutes after the living room lights went off and a light in the master bedroom turned on, my pre-paid phone vibrated. It was a text from Cannon. There was no message. Just a dollar sign with three exclamation points. I sent him a cryptic message in response. "Eyes on." My nigga spotted a possible target for us to hit, so I told him to keep his "eyes" "on" the nigga. Zay and Meek haven't hit me yet, and as much as I wanted to wait for the find a potential mark; I made an executive decision.

I hit their phones with new orders. Head for Cleveland and link up with Cannon. Keep a low profile and wait for me to join them out there. I put my phone away and returned my attention to the job at hand. The light had changed in the bedroom window. It was now dimly lit by candles. J was up there with another female. Ten minutes later, I pulled off and found a McDonald's about six blocks away. I ordered a #3 value meal in the drive thru and sat in the parking lot to eat. When I was done, I made a stop across the street from McD's to pick up a few things from a few things from a Lowe's hardware store. A flat head screw driver, black latex gloves, a box cutter, a three pack roll of duct tape, and a painter's shoe covers. I had some time to kill, so I cruised around Chester for a minute until I saw niggas ballin' on a lit-up basketball court. I sat on the hood of my ride, smoking Newports as I watched them ball. Calmly waiting for the night to get late.

Jermaine's Yukon was still parked out front as I quietly broke into the house. It was 1:45 am and all the lights in the crib were out. When I had returned at 10:34, the candles were still burning in the bedroom window. J was still getting his dick wet or boo lovin'. Instead of sittin' in my whip on the street, like a rookie nigga dying to get caught; I parked a few blocks away and found a dark spot to watch the house from the cut. A house across the street was for sale and it was easy getting into the crib through one of the basement windows. I sat in the master bedroom on the window sill and just waited until son and his chick went to sleep. The candles went out at 11:28pm. Nothing happened for two hours. A few cars cruised by, but other than that, it was a dead quiet night. Which was perfect for me. I got ready, waited for a little while longer, and then moved away from the window.

With my ski mask and latex gloves on, I gripped my .40 caliber Sig as I moved through the house like a ghost. I kept my footsteps slow and silent as I cleared the living room. Then the dining room. After moving through the living room, I paused at the bottom of the stairs. Listening for the sound of movement above me before I continued on. I waited for thirty seconds and then started going up. Fortunate for me, the stairs were carpeted. Still, I moved slow and silently. When I reached the top, I began for the front bedroom like a phantom with my burner aimed at the door. For some reason, my heart was beating like a motherfucker. I could hear it in my ears along with the rhythm of my breathing. I stopped at the cracked open bedroom door and peeked in. The moonlight from outside was enough for me to see Jermaine and shorty sleeping. On their sides, all intertwined and hugged up. The smell from the room was a mixture of scented candles, weed, and sex. With my free latex gloved hand, I softly pushed the door open and breezed in.

Not that long later, Jermaine timidly taped his chick up as I aimed the .40 caliber at him. When I woke them up, I first turned the bedside lamp on and tapped son on the forehead with the pistol. The moment he opened his eyes and saw my ski masked face and the barrel an inch from his nose; his expression morphed into instant fear. I had him wake his sexy as all Hell, dark chocolate, all ass and titties girl up. Ma was shook as fuck too. I told her to keep her fuckin' mouth shut and she'll be fine. I had Jay close the blinds before I tossed him a roll of duct tape. At gunpoint, he taped up his chicks wrists and ankles, then I told him to put a strip over her mouth. I told Ma to sit still as I took her man by the back of his neck. In his boxers, I walked him out of the bedroom. We returned a few minutes later. I made Jermaine get on his knees next to the bed as I showed shorty what I took from her purse. Her driver's license and her cell phone. As held the gun to Jay's head and looked into her tear shedding eyes, I told her why she was going to keep her mouth shut about what happened this night.

I knew everything I needed to know to not only end her life, but the lives of everyone she loved. I went into her contacts and recited off a few people she wouldn't want to see dead. Her mother under the contact "Mommy". Her "Sissy", "Auntie Mel", "Big Bro", and "Bestie". The look in her eyes told me that she wasn't going to say shit. I pocketed her ID and phone before making Jay stand up. I had him put his clothes back on. Except for his socks and shoes. I gripped him by the back of his neck again, reminded shorty one more time to come down with amnesia, then we departed. As Jermaine unlocked and opened the front door, I removed my ski mask. When we reached his Yukon, I made him get in behind the wheel as I slid in behind him. A minute later, he pulled off and I directed him to where my ride was parked. In an alley. We got out, I walked him to back of my whip, opened the trunk and made him climb in. I shut the trunk, climbed in, and casually drove away.

****

I drove Jermaine back to Newark and we parked in a rundown lot close to his corner. When I opened the trunk and he saw that it was me, the look on his face was priceless. He recognized me immediately. I backed up and told son to get out and shut the trunk. Once he did, I stepped up to him, gun in hand, and broke it down to him. First, he was going to call the nigga that was running his corner for the night shift and have him shut it down. Tell him that the narcs were conducting block sweeps. Second, he was going to have the all the product and cash delivered to him. Right here. And third, once the drop was made, we were going to swing by his spot and I was taking his money. Once I got what I wanted, and if he didn't try any slick shit, I was going to bounce. I gave Jay his phone back, and with me staring at him, he called the dude running the night shift on his corner and relayed what I had told him to say.

Twenty-three minutes later, a Nissan Altima pulled into the lot. It rolled up to my ride and stopped. I moved out of the shadows of a vacant house close to the parking lot and quietly crept up on the Altima' blind side. Jay's nigga climbed out of the car and was approaching his boss as he sat behind the wheel of my vehicle without the keys in it. Youngin' had a bookbag by the strap as he approached my ride. Son did as I told him to do. He stepped out of my vehicle and kept his nigga distracted as I approached him from behind. My sneakers made noise on the asphalt, causing son to begin to turn around. He was half way when I took his ass out. His side profile was perfect for a straight right. I socked homie in the jaw hard as fuck and I heard it crack. Dude dropped to the ground; asleep. I told Jay to pick up the bag and hand it to me. I returned him to the trunk and we rolled out. Leaving his lieutenant stretched out in the lot with a broken jaw, but alive. Son was just a pawn. Not a name on my kill list.

Jermaine wasn't so fortunate. Once he handed over his cash, a little over $55,000; I clipped him. Quiet and painlessly. My former classmate liked to get his drink on. He had mad bottles of liquor in the kitchen of his apartment. I popped the top on a bottle of E&J and made him start guzzlin'. I sat across from him in the living room and watched him drink himself stupid. When he was finally unable to lift the bottle to his mouth, he blacked out on the sofa. He was miles past fucked up and numb. I moved son to the floor, grabbed a pillow from his bedroom, placed it over his face, and the pressed the barrel of the Sig into it. When I pulled the trigger, there was a hard, but muffled POP! I left the pillow over J's dead face and searched for the shell casing. I found it on the couch, grabbed the bag of cash, and quietly left the apartment.

I began heading back to Philly to get ready for my road trip to Ohio with a nice little score from Newark. I had close to $75,000 in cash, a little under ten ounces of cocaine, and a pound & a half of weed. Jermaine's spot was a shop that sold both. I was going to bless my crew with a little bonus from my lick on Jay, the coke was going on ice until we came back to PA, and the weed was going to be enjoyed. The monetary and narcotics rewards were cool, but I got a taste of what I really wanted. Revenge. My move on Jermaine wasn't personal with him. Son ain't never do me dirty and we were kinda cool. The only reason he was now meeting his maker was because of the Matthews brothers. Taking their dope from him and murdering him was a shot at them. That was the first act of the war they started when they betrayed Keith and their parents. Jermaine was a sacrificial lamb. I had a thirst for blood and war. For the time being, it was quenched and now it was time to fall back. I wasn't done with those two back stabbing snake motherfuckers by a long shot though.

I stashed my ride in the storage unit and caught a cab back to my spot. After getting some sleep, I was on the move. The first thing I did was contact a chick that I fucked from time to time and made a her a deal. For $2500, she agreed to drive me to Cleveland. I packed what I needed and shorty picked me up in her silver 2009 Acura RL. Ma and I stopped for something to eat and to top off the gas tank before we hit the road. Almost seven hours later, we pulled into Burger King in West Cleveland. I didn't want Ma too see too much, so I told her to go into the restaurant to use the bathroom and get something to eat. She caught the message and I hit her with an extra $500. Once she was out of sight, I climbed out of her car and grabbed my bags. Meek was waiting for me three vehicles away. I tossed my shit into the back of his Durango, hopped into passenger seat, and son pulled off.

Fifteen minutes later, we were linked up with Meek and Zay where we were going to be staying for the time being. Cannon set us up with a local chick that had a big crib with space for all of us. Ma's name was Kyana, she was 29, no kids, and all about gettin' money. Shorty was average in the face, but she had dick suckin' lips and about 40lbs of ass. I was diggin' shorty. She was definitely hood, had that ride or die feel to her, and within an hour of chillin' and blowin' some weed with her and my goons; I saw the writing on the wall. She was fuckin' both Cannon and Meek. Ma was flashin' eyes at me, but I wasn't going there. If my soldiers wanted to pass her around, that was their business. Their thing. Zay didn't seem interested and I was definitely wasn't either. I wasn't into the sharing pussy thing. That night though, I did hollah at Meek and Cannon when shorty went to bed. I told them don't let no pussy fuck with their flow. Period! Smash all they wanted to, but I expected them to stay on point. At all times.

We didn't talk business that first night after I arrived. The rest of the evening was spent chilling in Kyana's crib. We blew down a couple of blunts, ordered Chinese, watched the Lakers dust off the Pistons and then OKC blowout the Spurs. NBA on TNT was lit that night. Cannon went up to dick down Kyana, Zay was smoked out and asleep in one of the rooms, while Meek and I got busy on the Xbox 360. We boxed it out on Fight Night, then we got in a game of Madden and split screen on Call of Duty. I was ready to call it a night, when my nigga hit me off with a gift. Meek hadn't been in Ohio for a week, but had already made playboy moves. He sent a text and then had me roll out with him. We drove across the city to an apartment complex. We went into one of the buildings where we were met at the door of the apartment marked #12D by a redbone cutie in a tank top and booty shorts. She let us in and there was another chick chillin' in the living room. This one was my flavor. Chocolate. The light skinned chick took Meek by the hand and led him towards her bedroom. Leaving me and her friend alone to get to know each other. Ma fixed me a drink, I had three Magnums on me, and shorty looked like she was ready.

****

The next day, while Kyana was out and about, me and my crew got down to business. Since Cannon found our target, I let him handle the run down. He introduced us to East Cleveland dope dealer Gerald Foster. He went by Geeno on the street and Cannon chose this nigga after hearing his name ringing out all over the place. Apparently, Mr. Geeno was that nigga in the hood out here. The talk on the street that Cannon picked up was that son was a triple threat in the game. He was moving coke, dope, and weed. We passed a blunt around as Cannon explained that Geeno was definitely a major player in the game. The nigga was rolling around the city in a customized Navigator, he was always dressed fresh, his closest dudes were just as sharp, bitches were always talking about him, and his name carried weight on the streets. In Cannon's opinion, Geeno was a high-risk, high-reward target to hit.

I agreed with him at face value, but I wanted to see the motherfucker up close and in person. Cannon and I bought a dark gray, late 90's model Ford Focus that afternoon then waited until it was dark to find a path to Geeno. Kyana called a home girl of hers and we took Ma with us as we hit the streets. Shorty played tour guide as she led us from one trafficking spot to another in our targets' territory. Keeping a low profile, the three of us watched the corners, projects courtyards, and dope houses from a distance. We clocked the niggas hustling, the fiends coming to cop, and how shit was set up. The game was different out here. One Geeno's corners and his spots in the housing projects; transactions were made out in the open. Fiends showed up to buy, nigga passed off the product, received the cash, and off the junkie went. The exchange was subtle, but it was still right there for all to see. Only at the dope houses did the customers go inside and buy their drug of choice in the residence and then bounce out the back. None of the fiends were seen coming back out once they went in.

Geeno's weed was sold almost exclusively by females. Kyana's home girl, Ta'lahni, she copped her bud from one of the chicks that worked for our target. Sis was a dealer hiding in plain sight. Her legit cover was a hair dresser at a hot spot salon called Queen Diva's. We set up on the salon and when Ma showed up, Ta'lahni pointed her out. Miss Dionne was a tall and sexy piece of work. Butter scotch colored skin, short hairstyle, slim but nicely shaped body, and was dressed in the finest high-end name brand designer wear. Ta'lahni sat behind us and gave us our direct link to Geeno. Dionne was his cousin. The other chicks that sold weed for him reported to her. She also handled the re-ups and the female dealers dropped off her big cousin's money to her when they checked in to restock. I looked at Cannon in the driver seat and we both smirked. I sensed that son had the same thought that I had. Stalk Miss Dionne until we put eyes on Geeno. If Ma was that high in her cousin's food chain, there was no doubt that it was only a matter of time before she met with the nigga face-to face.

****

Though I was only twenty-years old, my age had no bearing on my skill sets in the streets. My pops taught me as a youngin' to use my brain, I was bred to think like a warrior, I inherited my father's viciousness, and I was fortunate to be schooled by old school gangster's. OG's like Keith's father. Mr. Marvin and others took me under their wing and filled my mind with street knowledge. However, it was on me to take those lessons and apply them appropriately. One of those teachings I took to heart was given to me by an ol' head in Newark. That lesson was no matter what I did in the street, any move I make is to be made with intelligence. Think before I act, thoroughly plan shit out, and always, ALWAYS have a backup plan. Most niggas in the hood just do shit. Whether it's selling dope, robbery, even committing murder. Half of the time, it's all for the popularity. Dudes want their names to be spoken in the streets with infamy and reverence. These type of nigga's are ego driven, attention & admiration seekers.

The other type are those brain dead, retarded motherfuckers. Stupid, low IQ ass criminals that fuck the game up. Niggas that sell dope out in the open, making it publicly clear that they're drug dealers. By rockin' shiny ass jewelry while being obvious with their drug trafficking, loud, and they tend to be very dumb with their decisions. Decisions such as beatin' up their baby mama's, brag about their illegal activities, show off by driving vehicles that the police always identify as a dope boy ride, and when it comes to guns; they might as well advertise the murder in the newspaper before they shoot. Nigga spray bullets in neighborhoods in broad daylight; or, they brag & talk about committing a homicide to gain thug celebrity points. Then they ass get identified, arrested, and have the audacity to be like, *"Who snitchin'?!!"* when those Homicide Detectives come through with that first-degree murder warrant.

That's what separates me from them. I ain't in the game for the notoriety of my name. I ain't trying to be some kind of legend in the hood. My goals are simple. Money and revenge. The money is my avenue to do whatever I feel like doing and getting revenge was my motivation. The way I was raised, how I was bred, and the bloodline that I come from was built for this shit. I think, I strategize, I plan, and I play the game in the streets like a chess player. Three moves ahead at all times. No glam, no stuntin', and no time for bullshit. Traveling to Ohio and targeting this nigga Geeno wasn't just about hittin' a major score. To my crew, it was a come up for dope and cash. To me, it was a piece being moved on the chessboard. Now that Geeno's cousin was our way to the motherfucker himself, I kept my eyes on her. I had my team watching her big cousin's dope spots and corners while I stalked miss Dionne.

In doing so, I saw a window of opportunity to close the kill window on a rising Cleveland drug lord.

I decided to go In Too Deep with this shit.

CHAPTER NINE

"Conceal your Intentions and Master the Art of Timing."

-Robert Greene, 48 Laws of Power

Once I learned Dionne's habits and patterns, mappin' out her day-to-day schedule became easy. It took me more than a week of stalking and watching her like a hawk to learn her routine. After clocking Dionne's every move for five days straight, she presented me with an opportunity. To infiltrate Geeno's domain. It was a risk, but I was like fuck it! Risk it is. Because hittin' a major dope dealer like Geeno was tough, we needed time to formulate a solid plan. After a few weeks in Cleveland, I started to notice something about my goons. They were getting restless. All we did was watch, study, learn, surveil, chill in Kyana's crib, eat, smoke, sleep, and occasionally get our dicks wet. I mean, we were on some real vampire shit most of them time. More than half of the daylight hours, we were indoors. Watching TV, movies, playing Xbox, catching a basketball or football game, or blowing down weed. Throughout the evening, I had my crew out gathering information, but I was the only one that spent most of the day away from the house.

I assigned Dionne to myself because she was an important target. My goons were vicious, but not very high up there when it came to handling business like a professional. Meek, Cannon, and Zay were foot soldiers. We were all wolves, but I was the alpha. The brains of the pack. Still, I had to keep my team hungry and busy. I was planning to make my next move, but I gave them something to do. Me and Kyana went for a drive to talk. When we returned to the house, I told my crew to get ready for a road trip. We drove two hours away and set up in Pittsburgh. Kyana had a cousin that lived there and her cuz was willing to help us take off a weed dealing nigga. Homie was selling high-grade bud. Thus, he was sitting on serious cash. It took us two days to figure the nigga out and I let my team do the dirty work. Like the pure goons they are, Meek led Zay and Cannon on a late-night home invasion, beatdown-armed robbery. They did the black hoody and ski mask thing. After they dumped all evidence, we drove straight the fuck out of Pittsburgh right after they hit the niggas' residence.

My team was happier than a motherfucker with their lick. They got son for sixteen pounds of weed and a little over $50,000 in cash. When we got back to Cleveland, they put fifteen pounds of the bud on ice, left one pound out to smoke, and tried to split their score of the cash with me. I sat at the dining room table with them and pretended to accept the $10,000 they slid my way. Later on, around six in the morning, while my team was smoked and knocked out, I split the ten-grand. Giving Kyana and her cousin five a piece. Me and the ladies were the lookouts and get away drivers. Because none of my squad knocked off Kyana's cousin Lana, and being that she was exactly my type; ma and I left the house to get us a room before she headed back to Pittsburgh. With my team satisfied with some action and a nice score; it was back to business for me.

I decided to keep my crew in the dark about this move I was making. If I pulled it off, then I'll let them know. It came to me quick that Dionne was single. Through binoculars, I could see that she didn't have a ring on her finger. She lived in a luxury studio apartment and she drove a black Mercedes Benz SLK350. Which I never followed to a boyfriends' crib or a hotel for a sexual rendezvous. Dionne spent most of her time at her salon, and though she seemed like one of those females that liked to socialize with her girlfriends and shit; it was clear that she wasn't. When she was away from her business, baby girl was truly a lone wolf. She went out to eat by herself, worked out at the gym without a partner, shopped solo, and went out on runs without company. Shorty liked her wine, Chinese food, she was a fairly decent boxer from what I observed of her hitting the heavy bag at the gym, and she was an avid weed smoker. I knew that because I was standing behind her in line when she bought four packs of sour apple flavored wraps at a gas station.

The gym was the best place for us to "meet". Due to knowing her entire schedule, I showed up at the gym half an hour before she arrived. I paid the guest fee for the day and got to work. I was hittin' the free weights when she showed up in her Royal Blue on White Nike warmup sweat suit and matching gym bag over her shoulder. Her long brown hair was back in a gym-day pony tail and she carried a clear cup of healthy fruit juice with crushed ice. I kept doing what I was doing as she disappeared into the female locker room and returned less than ten minutes later. In a tight White sports top, Black spandex pants, and White on Black Nike cross-trainers. I watched Dionne go through her routine. Stretches in the open area, about twenty-minutes of that aerobics-yoga shit, then after a break, she hit the weights. Put in some work on her upper body, then her legs. I was doing some shoulder work on the cables as she listened to music on her IPOD while doing hanging knee lifts to sculpt her abs.

I tracked Dionne's workout progression as I did my own thing. She saved hitting the bag for last, so I made my way to boxing area as Ma was doing crunches. I wrapped my hands, put on my leather bag gloves, and started hitting one of the heavy bags from an angle to see her coming. When she came over to wrap up her workout, she looked around the heavy bag area. There was a white dude three bags down from me. My man was not a legit fighter, but was going extra hard on the bag to show that he was. If son was a really a boxer, he was going to get his ass trucked in the ring. Two bags down from him was a blonde haired, blue eyed white chick. Shorty wasn't a boxer, but it was clear that she realized the fitness benefits of boxing. I was focused on the bag as I hit it with crisp jabs, hard straights, body shots, and hook combinations. Alternating my stance and ignoring the sweat trickling down my face. All the while I was watching Dionne watch me out of the corner of my eye. I put on a good show for her, then stopped to catch my breath.

Ma walked over and made first contact. By saying hello. I gave her my attention, and though I have looked at her many times over the week I had been stalking her; she looked prettier standing this close to me. She had a bright smile and though she had those light brown, relaxed, sexy bedroom eyes; they were friendly. Inviting. Almost innocent. I flashed a grin at her as I replied hello in return. She first moved loose strands of hair away from her face. Still smiling at me, she looked almost shy as she asked me,
"If you don't mind, will you help me put my gloves on?" I held eyes with her and my smirk remained as I replied,
"Yeah, no doubt"

I took my gloves off, sat them down, and with her eyes still locked with mine, she handed me her gloves. White & Pink 12-ounce Everlast gloves. I saw that she had wrapped her hands right as I put the first gloves over her hand, strapped it tight, and then did the second one. Dionne thanked me, I told her your welcome, and following the game plan I had in my head; I began to return to my workout. Before I made it one step, luck was on my side. Her sexy as fuck voice called out to me. Asking me was I professional fighter? I smiled in my mind. I was in. I lied and told Dionne that I was about to go pro. I still had a few more amateur fights before I competed in a make believe boxing tournament in New York City. Even if I didn't win the Amateur title belt, I was still turning pro. Dionne seemed to be impressed. She looked me up & down, and when she did that subtle bite the corner of her lip thing; I knew that I had her interest. We conversed for a moment, then she asked me if I was willing to show her a few things?

A few things turned into a several lessons and us working out on the bag together. I showed Ma how to throw her jabs with more technique and precision, how to roll a hook off the jab, tuck her chin, and land crisp and powerful combinations. I played it cool though. Keeping my distance at first, but gradually progressing towards physical contact. Positioning her by her hips, touching her shoulders, and standing very close to her from behind as I schooled her. She was self-conscious when it began, but it didn't take long for her to like it. Dionne and I spent over an hour together when I hit with the bait & snare tactic. I checked the time, then told her that I had to go. Just as I was hoping for, a subtle look of sadness flashed across her pretty face, but it quickly disappeared. I caught it, knowing what it meant. She was having a good time with me. She liked me and didn't want me to leave just yet. Now that I had Ma in the snare, I pulled that shit a little tighter.

Dionne and I exchanged numbers, I promised to hit her up soon, and we shared a hug before I left the gym. Hook, line, and motherfuckin' sinker! I drove back to Kyana's crib, hopped in the shower, blew down some haze with Meek, and got down on KFC with the team and shorty when she, Zay, and Cannon returned from getting food. I didn't say anything to them about Dionne, but around 8:30 that night as we were chillin' and watching Nas & DMX in Belly on DVD; Ma texted me with the classic. *"Wyd?"* We did the text thing for about an hour, then I went out on the back porch with my Newport's and we took our conversation to the phone. Dionne and I talked for close to two and a half hours. She was definitely feeling a nigga. Even when our age difference was revealed. She told me that she was 29, about to hit 30, while believing that I was 23. When she asked about my accent, I told her the truth. I was from New York. Ma went on for a bit about how she loved my accent, asked questions about NYC, and we had a casual convo about boxing.

The call came to an end with her telling me to text her the next day when I wasn't busy. After we hung up, I stared at my phone for a minute. Smiling at it. Dionne was a beautiful, financially secured lonely chick. Ma was the type that falls in love deep and loves hard. She didn't say it during our conversation, but I picked up on it. She's been hurt. A lot. Niggas did her wrong. Probably beat on her. Definitely cheated on her. That's typical with females with her kind of beauty, at her financial level, and with her personality. Motherfuckers dog women like her out. Being treated and hurt that way makes a woman shy away from relationships, prefer to be alone, become suspicious of men, and put up a wall around their heart. It also makes them lonely, crave affection, jones for sex, and vulnerable as time goes by. I met Dionne at the perfect moment. All of that loneliness was getting to her and she wanted to feel again. It was in her eyes when she looked at me, the way she smiled at me, and how she spoke to me. That wall around her heart was still up, but time has made it weak.

****

In just three weeks shit going smoothly in Ohio. On one side, I had my team preoccupied. To keep them busy, I let Meek oversee a little side action with Zay, Cannon, and Kyana. On the low, they bagged up and sold the weed that they took from that Pittsburgh nigga. Kyana knew people and acted as their go-between to conduct business. I also let my dogs off the leash a bit. By letting them live. When not hustling weed, my crew got to turn up. I had shorty chaperone them outside of Cleveland to party and bullshit. Still, I had to remind them of one thing. No noise. No gunplay unless it was absolutely motherfuckin' necessary. I told them to get their drink on, fuck with the bitches, do the strip club thing, and chill; but to avoid confrontation with niggas. Hold their tongue, keep their guns on safe, and maintain discipline.

On the flipside, I had Dionne in the viper's nest. We did the casual, get to know each other thing for a week. Texted, talked on the phone, we went out to dinner and shit, and then she invited me over to her spot to hang out. It was a Chinese and wine type of date that included some blunt smoking, soft music, and one kiss lit the fire. Several hours, four condoms, and multiple orgasms later; Dionne and I were naked and asleep on her bed. Her head on my chest, arm across my body, softly snoring into my neck. Ma was sleeping good. I kissed, licked, sucked, and fucked her for hours. I had her to the point where she was unable to keep her hands off of me. Where she was unable to stop kissing me. I melted that ass like butter. From that first night, until three weeks later, I was at Dionne's apartment two, three times a week. She texted and called me all day long. All we did was chill, drink, smoke, and fuck. She couldn't get enough, always wanted me around, and played right into my hands.

After a week and a half of fuckin' her brains out and making her feel like a natural woman again; I had Dionne exactly where I needed her to be. Comfortable. Over the course of three nights, as she was asleep or in the shower, I went through her phone. Copying numbers, going through her Facebook page, and sending pics to my phone then deleting the trail in hers. I had what I needed, but kept playing the role of the man in her life to keep the deception going. As Dionne was expressing her love for me and believing that she and I were heading towards being official; I was moving the pieces in place. My crew was stalking their targets, we were planning our moves, and everything was falling into place. All of the time and work we put in finally paid off when I locked eyes on Geeno himself.

Dionne was at the salon when her big cousin made an appearance. I was watching her from my ride when his custom Navigator pulled up to the shop and parked. I watched him stroll inside to receive Kingpin love from all the stylist and shit before he and Dionne disappeared into her office to have a private discussion. They were inside for twenty-minutes, then the nigga bounced. With me on his tail. I followed the nigga all over the city for hours. He met with a couple more business owners, dropped by a lawyers' office, and then he met with his lieutenants. On a few corners, the courtyard of a housing projects, two bars, and then a ghetto ass strip club. I knew exactly what the nigga was doing. Showing his face to the people that ran his domain right before the new package was delivered. It was re-up time in the empire. I picked up on that from his coded messages to his cousin. It was time to make our move.

It was just after two am. I sat on the reclining chair in Dionne's living room watching her sleep on the couch. All she had on was a tank top and panties while I was fully dressed again. Just a few hours before, we had returned to her spot from date night. We went to dinner, then a movie, and before we fell back to her place, we had some fun. At an arcade. We played a bunch of games, laughed and fooled around like a couple deeply in love, and did a whole lot of boo-lovin' and kissing. Once we were at her spot, she gave me head as I smoked a blunt, I ate her pussy as she toked it, and then we fucked like two horny ass Lions right there in the living room. We then showered together and chilled on the couch. Ma had herself a glass of white wine as we snuggled and watched TV. After Dionne fell asleep, I got up, put my clothes back on, and sat next to the couch. Staring at the TV as I waited. At 2:32 am, my phone screen lit up and vibrated. Three minutes later, it did it again. Six minutes after that, once more.

That was my crew. Meek, Zay, and Cannon handled their end. Now, it was time for me to handle mine. I took a moment to light a Newport and smoke it while watching Dionne comfortably sleep on her side. Ma was actually in love with me. I saw the fire of it in her eyes. She thought she had a good nigga. One that she was more than willing to give her heart to. She was always hugging me, kissing me, touching me, telling me how she felt, and wanted me near her. Though I was playing a role, how she was with me fucked with my character at times. Dionne's affections often reminded me of A'liyah. My first was the same way. Gentle, intimate, and pure. There were times that I started to get too comfortable with the chick that I was deceiving. Dionne made me smile for real. I liked lying in bed with her, I enjoyed the sex just as much as she did, and a few times when I told her that I loved her too; I felt like I did. As I watched her lie on her side with strands of her hair crossing her face, it wasn't doubt that I felt. It was a fading sense of regret. Dionne was damn near the perfect woman and she had to meet a nigga like me.

I woke Dionne up. Once she was conscious, I told her that I needed her to do something for me. Call her cousin Geeno. She looked confused as fuck as she just stared at me. I picked up my phone from the arm of the recliner and open Meek's message. Then showed it to her. Dionne's eyes opened wide as she looked at a photo of her aunt. Geeno's mother. With her wrists tied together and a strip of duct tape over her mouth. Tears from her terrified eyes, running down her cheeks over the tape. Dionne looked up at me with tears forming as I opened Zay's photo message. Ma covered her mouth as she looked a picture of her cousin. Tabitha. Geeno's beloved younger sister. D looked at me in utter denial and disbelieve with tear shedding eyes as I showed her the third picture. Her best friend and the mother of her cousins' twin daughters. Sharon. The same as her aunt, both women had their wrists tied with rope and duct tape over their mouth. I watched the light fade from Dionne's eyes as I calmly instructed her to call Geeno. I told her what to say as I passed her own cell phone to her.

With the phone on speaker, she told her cousin what was going on and what I wanted. I stayed quiet as the nigga started ranting that gangster shit. How we didn't know who we were fuckin' with, what he was going to do to us, we must not know who the fuck he is; and yada, yada, yada!

Mid-rant, I reached over and hit the end button. As I was attaching the photos to the message with his number on my phone, Dionne's started ringing. I ignored it until it stopped, then I hit send. Exactly one minute later, I called the nigga from her phone again and son was quiet now. Staring at his cousin, I reminded the nigga of my demands, that the lives of those he loved were on him, and exactly what he was going to do. Before we ended the call, I informed him that he had three hours to get it done and be at the spot. Then I hung up on him. Dionne looked at me with broken and red eyes as I told her to get dressed. We had work to do.

****

I took Dionne to her salon and she cleared out her safe for me. I now had a gym bag full of cash that she was holding for her cousin. Next, we went to where she kept the weed at. I bagged that too and put it in the trunk next to bag of money. I then drove us to a quiet spot where we sat in the car to wait. Dionne sat beside me looking out the window into the night, silently crying and not saying a word. No begging, pleading, or trying to reason with me. I just smoked and let her be with her silence. When it was close to go time, I offered her a cigarette. She didn't smoke, but a menthol seemed like a good idea at the moment. With a look of growing revulsion and deep pain in her eyes, she stared at me with utter hatred as she accepted the Newport and I struck my lighter for her to fire it up. I stared out of my window as she smoked. A few minutes later when I looked over at her, it was done. The poison I laced the with the tobacco before I refilled the cigarette tube did what it was supposed to do. Knocked her out and her heart was slowly slowing down. I reached over and removed the mostly smoked Newport from between Dionne's still fingers.

After moving her body to the backseat, I drove to the meeting spot. A rundown industrial area in what was essentially a dead zone in Cleveland. As I waited for Geeno to show up, I got ready. Fifteen minutes later, I was smoking a cigarette as I watched son's SUV with the lights out round the corner of a building and slowly make its way towards where I was parked. I pulled my ski mask down before I opened the door and climbed out. Leaving the driver side door open and concealing my .45 behind my leg. Geeno stopped about ten feet away from me, killed the engine, and I began approaching as he was exiting his ride. I took aim on the nigga and he put his hands out. I walked up on him, turned him around by his shoulder, and put the barrel of the Colt to the back of his head. I walked him towards the rear of his Navigator and had him open up the rear hatch. There was our score. His coke and dope packed into two black suit cases and hundreds of thousands of his money stuffed into a duffle bag.

I told Geeno that his cousin was in the car and to go on and get her out. As soon as I let him go and he began to walk away from me, I canceled him. He was only a foot away when I raised the .45 and put one in the back of his head. Son dropped to the ground face first and I began my exit. I carried the suit cases and duffle bag to my ride, pulled Dionne out of the backseat, carried her to the Navi, put in, left her cousin lying where he was, and then got the fuck out of there. As I drove away, I texted my crew. Telling them to bounce. Now. Hit the motherfuckin' road. We were all set to leave Cleveland as soon as we had the score. All three of my goons had their exit strategy in place. Meek was heading for his cousin's down in Virginia, Zay had family in Chicago, and Cannon was off to lay low with his sister in Atlanta. Once I was done with the cleanup, I was in the wind too. I linked up with Kyana at a motel. She let me into her room with the bags and we got busy.

As I took a hot shower, scrubbing down every part of my body, Kyana took the trash bag with everything I had worn in it to the dumpster. Once I was dressed again, Ma and I repacked all the product into clean luggage and then I blessed her with her cut. $50,000 in cash and five-pounds of high-grade weed. Key earned herself a big come up with us. I made sure to keep money in her pocket while we camped out at her house, my niggas threw cash her way too, and now she had 50K and enough marijuana to build something for herself when she got to Kansas City. Kyana was a rider and because I trusted her code of silence, I made sure that she was good before we parted ways forever. We left the hotel room together and she climbed into the vehicle I arrived in, as I put the suitcases into the trunk of the legally established vehicle I set up weeks before. A gray 2006 Hyundai Sonata. My subterfuge was in place as I began leaving Ohio. All of my luggage and what I was wearing was from the University of Ohio State.

At twenty-one years old, 6'1, with an athletic build and how I had my hair cut and beard groomed; my outfit and props made me look like a college boy. Not a thug nigga. Kyana got everything I asked for. In the trunk with my suitcases of dope and money was a mix of sports equipment, a football, workout clothes, and a couple pairs of sneakers. In the back seat was my bookbag of text books, a laptop, a bunch of papers and shit from Ohio State University, and Kyana, true criminal she is, got me some real camo. On the car was a parking decal from the college and she got me a student ID badge with a lanyard to hang from my rearview mirror. As the sun was lighting up the sky, I was heading east towards Pennsylvania. By ten am, I was tired as fuck and was halfway back to Philly when I decided to check into a Travel Lodge motel and get some sleep. Five hours later, I was back on the road. Immediately upon arriving in Philadelphia, I drove straight to the storage unit and stashed the dope. I left the car in the unit, took a gym bag with me, and caught a cab to 30th street station. Where I bought myself a one-way Amtrak ticket.

To Memphis, Tennessee.

CHAPTER TEN

"Be careful who you call your friends.
I'd rather have four quarters, than one hundred pennies."

-Al Capone

I'm almost certain that my father had the same ability that I have. Intuition. Foresight. Peter Parker, aka Spiderman, called it a spider sense. The keen ability to feel shit before it happens. My spider sense didn't start tingling in Memphis for a couple of months. When I first arrived, for the first week; I didn't do much. I set up in a motel, kept my head down by day, and did a little roaming at night. I was close to the hood, so that's where I went. I found a low-key bar, a barbershop run by a nigga that was originally from Baltimore, a bunch of restaurants were in that area, and I spotted a strip club that I made a mental note to check out. My goons checked in to let me know that they were good and I kept my eye on the news in Ohio. Due to Geeno being a major trafficker of narcotics, his name and murder ran for two days and then wasn't mentioned again. The same for Dionne. For a week, I hit up a local Memphis library every evening before it closed to use one of their computers.

To check the open source law enforcement websites. None of our names were attached to warrant postings. Neither in Cleveland or Pittsburgh. I checked everywhere. Looking for my goons and myself on a wanted site or in the Cleveland or Pittsburgh newspaper. Day after day, nothing. None of our names popped up. Though we were clean, I was playing it safe. One at a time, I had my wolves link up with me in Memphis. Meek caught the Amtrak, Zay flew in from Chicago, and Cannon drove in from Georgia. They met with me on different days, in different locations. To simply pick up their cut from the Geeno score. Then bounce. Head back to where they were, keep their heads down, and wait for my call. Once my crew was paid and in the wind, I started doing my own thing in Memphis. The barbershop on the South side of the city became my new chill spot.

Maurice, the former Baltimore dude that own and ran Prime Cutz was an ex-dope dealing nigga that found success in the south. As son and I got to know each other the more I kicked it in his shop, he shared with me how became a permanent resident of Memphis. Originally, he came down to get money. He had family in the city and he traveled from B-More with a couple of niggas to hustle. Shit got hot after eight months. They felt that the police, and or feds were closing in on them; so the Baltimore niggas packed up camp and went home. Except for Maurice. He liked it down in Memphis. A bad ass local chick was pregnant with his seed, he loved the food, he was feeling the southern vibe, and there was nothing for him back in Baltimore. No family, real friends, roots, or a life off the streets. Thus, son made the decision to stay in Memphis and build something for himself.

That was twelve years ago. Since then, Maurice married his shorty, they have three kids, his wife family made him blood, and he built one of the hottest barbershops in the city. In private, son told me that he laid bricks of his shops' foundation with his dope money. Once he was making serious legit income, he was out of the game. It made sense. Prime Cutz was a cash cow with both the loyal local customers and the VIPs. All over the walls were framed photos of rappers, a couple black movie stars, and professional athletes. Shit really got poppin' when Maurice formed a deal with a chick that ran her own salon. They bought the store front next to the barbershop and opened the Prime Stylez Hair Salon. I was on vacation, so I definitely enjoyed myself. I got my hair cut once a week, but I was always at the shop. Chillin', blowin' down fire ass weed with Memphis niggas behind the building, watching the young bucks run around, and conversing with Maurice and the other niggas that chilled in the shop.

We rapped about women, sports, politics, cars, whatever. To be honest, I kinda lost myself for a minute. I stood in front of the barbershop and watched dirty south niggas spit in freestyle cypher's, ran basketball with dudes at a nearby park, was a spectator at a parking lot custom hood car show, and I dined with Maurice and his family at his home. I even did a little socializing with the niggas I kicked with. I hit the bar with them, I was invited to cookouts and a one of their kids' birthday parties, and one night, Reece's brother in law and two of his homies took me to that strip club I wanted to check out. It was called Chocolate Paradise and the spot was off the hook. It was a motherfucking freak show! I strolled up in the with a fresh cut, waves flowing, dressed in black Dickie's, new Timbs, and a pocket full of money into a stable of pure thoroughbreds. There were no white bitches there. Every stripper was a different shade of brown, young or youngish, and bad as fuck!

I wasn't a nigga that was tender in the dick region, but I liked wh.
saw at Chocolate Paradise. Pretty faces, full glossed lips, big titties, th
hips, stallion thighs, and monster asses. Niggas were wildin' up in the
Making it rain cash on chicks, getting lap dances, turning up in
private rooms, and dropping money on dancer's at the bar. I was in
booth with the niggas I arrived with. Once we had our drinks, they
the night started by calling over a couple dancers to get to it. A bad
red bone shorty did her thing on me, so I slipped her a couple of twent
and that was that. It didn't take long for the niggas I arrived with
venture off to do what they do, leaving me in the booth by mys.
Which was fine by me. There was someone that caught my eye anywa.

Out of all the sexy ass dancers all over the place, one of the bar tend
had my attention. I sat there sippin' a henny on ice as I sized Ma up. S
was mocha brown, about 5'9 or 5'10, she had to be about 160lbs, a
everything else about her was right. From her long silky black h
sleepy brown eyes, plump full lips, her obvious big chest under her bl
silk blouse, and I could tell from her shape and form, that she was
thickness below the waist. Being that I wasn't a hesitating or nervous
nigga, just as I was just about to go over to the bar, shorty gave me
green light. She looked in my direction, focused on me for a minute,
held eyes, and then she flashed a smile at me. Then gave the nigga at
bar his beer. That was my cue. I made my way over and sat on a stool
wait for her to come to me.

Me and Danisha, Nisha for short, rapped for over an hour as
served drinks. Ma did far more talking to me than she did serving nigg
their preferred poison. The other chicks bartending took over for h
being that I had her attention. Ma sipped her own drink as we talked a
the flow of our convo was smooth. She was definitely into me and I w
feelin' her, but on some real shit, it felt like she was trying to put a sp
on me or something. The brown bedroom eyes of hers were a li
hypnotic. Sexy as all fuck, but she was on some cobra shit. I   lik
it though. It was close to three in the morning when the niggas I roll
with were ready to bounce. Danisha dipped off to get ready to cl
down when I rolled out. I had my own ride, so when Reece brother
law and his homies bounced, I pulled off in the opposite direction a
decided to cruise around for a minute. Taking the time to smoke a
listen to some music. It was ten minutes after four when I rolled ba
into the strip clubs parking lot. To find Nisha standing next to her c

She had texted me twenty minutes before to tell me that they were almost done closing the club down for the night.

I followed Nisha across Memphis to a dark and quiet neighborhood. After I parked behind her dark purple Charger in the driveway, I quickly checked my .40 caliber and tucked it into my holster. With a round in the chamber and the safety off. I climbed out and followed Ma towards her house. As she unlocked the front door, all I could hear were those loud ass down south crickets. I trailed her inside and she turned on the living room light as I entered. Aiight, cool. No niggas waiting inside to ambush me. Thus far, it wasn't a set up. Nisha told me to come on in as I closed the door. As I locked it, she asked me if I'd like a drink? Yeah, I replied. I looked around as she went into her dining room towards the kitchen and I sat on the couch.

Nisha's crib was nice! From the furniture, to the carpeting, electronics, and her spot was clean as fuck. She had pictures of her people all over the walls and it wasn't hard to tell that she came from a big family. When she came back out, instead of the drinks being already poured, she brought out two glasses with ice in them and a bottle of Patron. Ma handed me a glass as she sat down next to me. As she opened the Patron, I smoothly looked into my glass. To make sure nothing was in it. Other than the ice. Nisha half-filled my glass, then her own. We got comfortable, started sippin', and resumed our conversation from the strip club. Over Patron and a blunt, I got to know shorty some more. She was 27, obviously single with no kids, she was the oldest of five, and outside of bartending and doing hair on the side, she was about to start her second year at Southwest Tennessee Community College. I asked her what was she studying and she replied that she was in two course programs. Business and finance. She went on to tell me that her plans for success in the future, and I genuinely listened to her.

I was no different from most dudes in society. I loved pussy just as much as any other man. The difference between me and most niggas, I wasn't about no desperate-thirsty ass shit. I didn't jones for pussy like most dudes. Nisha and I talked for a long time and though that sexual vibe was there between us, I wasn't pressed to get my dick wet. I was present for the entire conversation and Ma saw that I was. As the sun was coming up, things got physical between us. It started with us kissing on the couch. Once that fire started to cool down, we took it to the bed. She led me to her bedroom by the hand and closed the door. We weren't on no real romance shit either. She undressed me, I undressed her, my gun was placed on her dresser, and onto the bed we went. Shorty firmly pushed me onto my back and I put my hands behind my head as she moved in between my legs.

I kept my eyes closed and my lip clenched between my teeth, groaning as Ma sucked my dick something special. Nisha softly moaned as she gripped my shaft and balls, making love to my dick with her warm mouth. She had me growling and gripping her hair as she sucked, slurped, and licked. My dick and my sack. She alternated between doing it slow & gentle, to hard & fast. I was trying not to nut before we fucked; but she made me bust off. Loudly. Ma swallowed, kept sucking and licking for a while, and then it was my turn to return the favor. Not too long later, Nisha was on her back with her legs hooked over my shoulders, sitting up on her elbows, moaning and rotating her hips as she pulled my face deeper into her pussy by the back of my head. I sucked on her clit as she drenched my fingers inside of her. Her pussy got wet as fuck and I was enjoying all of it. Not only did she have a fat, shaved pussy with a big clit; she was clean.

After making Nisha cum all over my face, I sheathed my dick with a Magnum and Ma climbed on it. With her hands on my chest, mine on her hips, and our eyes locked, she rode me. Slow, deep, and with the sexy as Hell snake roll motion. No bouncing or quick movements. My dick was not only thick, it was long. Nisha showed her appreciation and skill by keeping me deep inside her, put a vice grip lock on my dick, and making love to every inch with long wet strokes. I had a death grip on her waist and she was biting her lip and moaning with her eyes closed as she kept riding me. She picked up the pace and her moans grew louder by the time she came. Not long after she stopped shaking on top of me, it was my turn. I read the vibe of her body and the look on her face. Ergo, I gave her what she wanted. From the back, I gripped her waist and watched her ass cheeks ripple and wave as I pounded her pussy. Making her moan and scream as she looked back at me. Until I took a handful of her hair and pulled her back. Still beatin' the pussy up as she threw it back at me.

****

Bomb sex, some cold water, a Newport, a hot shower, and seven hours of sleep later. I woke lying on my side. With a headache and a full bladder. I could feel Nisha asleep behind me. Her soft breath on my neck, titties pressed against my back, and her arm around me. I only kept

112

my eyes open for a second, before I closed them and lied there for a minute. Enjoying the moment. I can't even front. It felt good being there with Nisha. The sex was fire, but lying with her like this; her presence; felt good as fuck. I was relaxed. At ease. Comfortable. With the plan I had in my mind for the future, feeling like this felt off. Wrong. But, as I lied there with this bad ass southern chick behind me, I just embraced it. I put my plan in the back of my mind and lived in the moment.

About half an hour later, Nisha found me on her front porch. Siting on one of her big ass white porch chairs, smoking a Newport and chillin' in the early morning quietness. Ma had her hair back in a pony tail and was dressed in her chill at home gear. A white tank top and white stretch pants with no panties on. In that cute, but thick ass southern accent of hers, she asked me if I was hungry? Because she was "fixin" to cook something for breakfast. I nodded yeah and she went back into the house to get to it. Less than an hour later, Nisha and I were having breakfast together. Scrambled cheese eggs, pork sausage links, and buttermilk pancakes with OJ. We ate in the living room with the TV on, watching re-runs of House of Payne on BET. This was definitely going to be a chill day. As Ma was cooking, we shared a blunt, breakfast hit the spot, neither of us had plans for the day, and without saying it directly, Nisha asked me to spend time with her.

I picked up on it earlier that morning. Danisha wasn't lonely. She was just alone. Ma had goals and ambitions. She was on a grind and focused on her success. That's why she worked, had a side hustle, lived alone, and was in college. She was making up for lost time from a past mistake. She shared with me that her heart got her in trouble. She followed her first love and his drug dealing ways to a three-year prison sentence. At 21, she found herself in state prison, doing time on a conspiracy charge. When she came home at 24, her aunt looked out for her. By setting her up in the house she now lives in, hooked her up with a bartending job, and gave her a little money to get on her feet. Her auntie also got in her head about making a way for herself and achieving something positive. Nisha put almost all of her focus on her goals and hasn't really allowed a man into her domain. That worked for a while, until a certain type of nigga came into her world.

That's me. It was how she looked at me. The way she spoke to me. And how she was with me. Open, comfortable, and vulnerable. I don't know why I have this effect on women, but certain ones are powerfully drawn to me. Never realizing what I truly am or even seem to sense it. Nisha, just like Dionne, looked at me as if I was something special. The kind of nigga they wanted to spend the rest of their life with. To love. I don't know what it was about me, but none of them see what, or who I truly am.

Danisha and I did the ghetto love thing for three months. When she was busy, working, or in class; I did me. Kicked it at the barbershop, ran ball, I found a shooting range outside of Memphis, or I chilled at Nisha's crib. I checked in with my goons too. Unbeknownst to them, I checked up on them in person. Just to see in real time if they were keeping it all the way 100 with me. Being that Cannon was the closest to me, I drove to Atlanta to see what he was up to. Son was keeping a low profile. He was shacked up with a chick and making zero noise. He time was spent playing video games, gettin' his dick wet, and smoking haze. Good. I shot up north to Virginia and checked on Meek in Richmond. He too was playing it low key. Staying with his cousin, he was fuckin' with a sexy ass projects chick, and was causing no ripples. After dropping off the rental car at Enterprise, I caught a cab to the airport and boarded a one-way flight to Chicago.

For some odd reason, the entire time flying to Illinois, this feeling kept creeping into my mind. About Zay. That something was off about him. Not once since I met and ran with the nigga did I feel that he was foul in any kind of way. Son was just as solid and vicious as Meek & Cannon. He carried his weight in the crew, there was no bitch in him, and he handled business without hesitation. However, the entire flight from Virginia, I couldn't shake this fuckin' feeling that something was off with my goon. My spider sense was tingling like a motherfucker. Following my instincts, I decided to see for myself what was up. No sooner than I rented another car, I hit Zay's phone. Telling him that I was in town and where to meet me at. We linked up at a McDonald's parking lot, rapped for a hot minute, dapped, half-hugged, and then he rolled out. Without knowing that I was following him.

Zay drove to the southside, parked in front of an apartment building, and went inside. An hour later, he and a super bad light skin chick came out and climbed into a tinted-out Denali SUV. With her behind the wheel and him riding shotgun. I followed the GMC all over the hood as Zay met with niggas on a couple of obvious drug trafficking corners, a row house, when he and his chick stopped to eat at a Chinese buffet, and then over to the mall to do a little shopping. Zay spent well over a thousand dollars on his shorty. I trailed them back to their apartment, waited again, and when they came back out; both of them were dressed for a night on the town. This time, I followed my goon and his chick to a high-end looking bar. I slipped in twenty minutes behind them. I saw Zay, his lady, and what looked to be a crew of niggas and bitches in some kind of VIP area. Ballin' out. Everybody was fly, jeweled up, they were poppin' bottles, and living their best life. Zay was doing big things in Chi-Town, and that presented a serious problem for me.

Several hours later, I stood in front of my vehicle and looked out at the Chicago skyline across the lake. It was nice and dark where I stood. I heard tires slowly approaching behind me, but I didn't turn around. I knew it was Zay. When son reached me, we dapped fists and I handed him the blunt I was toking on. After taking a hit, he asked why a second meet? He thought I was on my way back to Tennessee? I accepted the blunt from his hand, took a hit, and after exhaling, I looked son dead in the eyes and brushed his questions off by telling him that I knew that he was running his own little operation up here. That he lied to me about laying low and staying off the radar. Zay didn't respond. He just looked at me with insolence in his eyes and cold indifference on his face. After a few seconds of silence, he replied that he was his own man. Free to do whatever he wants. He saw an opportunity to make big money in Chicago, so he took it. I nodded my head, held his stare, and responded to him with the facts.

He was selling dope in a city he's not from, with niggas he don't know. That he was styling & profiling, riding dirty, and flashing cash like he was in a motherfuckin' hip-hop video! And let's not mention the high-priced girlfriend he had. Zay kept that *"I don't give a fuck"* look on his face as he replied, *"And?!"* I looked son dead in his eyes as I gave it to him raw. I explained to the motherfucker that he was making himself a prime target to get popped by the narcs or Feds, while knowing too much. About Philly, Cleveland, and Pittsburgh. That he knew about the drugs we sold, niggas we robbed, the money, our names, and the fuckin' bodies we dropped! My voice was gettin' louder as I informed this nigga that with what he was doing in Chicago, if he was to get knocked, he had the golden ticket of information on us to make a deal. And it wasn't going down like that.

I had the niggas attention on my eyes and voice that he never noticed my hand. Which hand slipped into my jeans pocket. In the blink of an eye, I removed the 9mm semi-auto I bought from a Chicago nigga that a dope fiend led me to. It was already cocked with the safety off. Zay barely had time to react before I took a step back and lit him up. POP!!

Right in the face. Under his left eye. No sooner than his body hit the ground, I walked up and gave him two more to the head. POP!! POP!! Though we were pretty much in the middle of nowhere across Lake Michigan from metro Chicago, I still moved quickly. Took me a few minutes to find the shell casings, remove Zay's cell phones and ID from his pockets, pick up the mostly smoked blunt and then bounce. I drove off in the old Nissan I paid another smoker to use. Once back in the city, I dropped the 9mm Taurus and shells in a sewer on a back street, then got rid of Zay's phones and ID by wiping them off and tossing them into a dumpster.

Once the crack smoking chick had her car back and another $200, I began my departure from Chicago, Illinois. Instead of catching a flight back to Memphis, I bought an Amtrak ticket and waited for the train to arrive. I had two hours to kill, so I sat on a bench outside of Union Station. It was almost five am as I sat staring at nothing in particular. Smoking a port. Feeling no regret for bodying Zay. The nigga went from friend to enemy, homie to a dead memory in matter of seconds. That motherfucker let money and the grimy crime life inflate his ego. Put a battery in his back and led him to just start his own operation while runnin' & gunnin' on my shit. I told the nigga when I recruited him that my word was law and don't go against the grain. By trying to build his own little empire in Chi-Town and playing the game his way, it was only a matter of time before the law got their hands on him. I wasn't leaving it to chance that his ass would turn state's evidence and burn all of us to escape a conviction. The law would have rolled out the red carpet for him if he had the chance to drop the dime on us and tell them all the shit we've done. Fuck that! Son got what his hand called for and I had no regrets that I smoked him.

****

Danisha was just like Dionne. A sista with a deep heart who made the mistake of being willing to give it to a nigga like me. A thug that didn't want it. Or deserve it. Almost two weeks went by after I returned from Chicago. Nisha was settled into being my lady. Ma was really happy to have me in her life. Always smiling when I was around, boo lovin' on me, suckin' & fuckin' me like crazy, and catering to me as if I was a King. She fed me, cleaned my clothes, we did the chill & smoke thing, and she hit me with the *"I love you."* Not with her words though. With her eyes. With how she kissed me. Her actions. Ma was waiting for me to say it first. I never did. I cared about her, I liked being around her, and

I enjoyed the vibe & fire between us; but I had to keep it 100. I didn't love her. Even when I thought I did. Fuck, I even tried to. It wasn't there. I came to a realization as she slept with her head on my chest one night. I wasn't built for love. I wasn't made to be the man in a woman's life. Love, intimately romantic love, wasn't meant for me to have. Or to give.

Ma was still asleep when I left. Her home and her life. I did leave a gift for her though. $20,000 on her dresser. I was walking out of Danisha's world and I left the money because I wanted her to achieve her goals. Unlike Dionne, Nisha couldn't identify me to the law. She didn't know anything about me that was true. Where I was really from or what I was into. She didn't even know my real name. She believed that my name was Lamont Greene. From Newark, New Jersey. Everyone I knew in Memphis believed that's who I was and where I was from. I got my Sonata out of storage and hit the road. Meek and Cannon were mobile as well. We were heading back to Philly. It was time to get to it. It was time to go to war

Time doesn't heal all wounds and vengeance doesn't have an expiration date. By now, the Matthews brothers probably done forgot all about me, but I ain't forget about them. Not for a fuckin' second. Everything I had done and every move I made was in preparation for my vendetta against Na'jae and Kareem. I kept my eye on the crime report back home. Week in and week out, waiting to see their names. I even scoped out dudes and chicks Facebook pages to siphon second hand info. Females talk about shit all the time, so it wasn't hard to figure which niggas were hustling for the brothers. Thus, by default, I locked on to the same niggas to figure out which ones to target. By selecting dumb motherfuckers braggin', posting their brand-new Jordan's-money-guns-and everything fuckin' thing else these social media superstars love to advertise. Once more, I was thankful that I was raised and schooled by old school gangster niggas with old school gangster philosophy.

Always keep your business out of the public eye.

You never know who's watching you.

CHAPTER ELEVEN

"Never interrupt your enemy when he is making a mistake."

-Sun Tzu, The Art of War

Meek and Cannon didn't shed a tear for Zay. I told them why son had to get bodied and they accepted it for what it was. He went against the grain and didn't give a fuck about the risk to us. Thus, they didn't give a fuck about him being dearly departed. It is what it is. Now that we were a triple threat instead of four horsemen, nothing changes. At my spot, I revealed to them the plan I had formed in my head that they had no idea they were unknowingly apart of and had been preparing for. Though we had quite a bit of product and money to build something of an empire in Philly, my plan was bolder than that. Meek and Cannon listened as I broke it down to them. About Mr. Marvin, Keith, Na'Jae, Kareem, and their operation over in Delaware. Then, I shared the vision of my plan with them. When I was done, I didn't even have to ask them were they down to ride. It was in their eyes and overall aura.

We got to work immediately. It was late October and starting to get colder outside, so that meant a lot of niggas weren't going to be on the streets much. The true dope boys were, but in the growing time of bitch made niggas, we were going to have to go Hi-Tech on em'. I had Meek and Cannon start making *"friends"* with chicks in Newark. Cash was the best tactic to ensure their way in, so they each bagged a couple of ghetto dimes and buttered their sexy asses up. Shopping trips, weed, bottles, some cash in their hands, and some dick work just for good measure. Once my soldiers had three or four chicks on the hook and willing to do *"favors"* to make some money, the next phase of the plan was initiated. The street level dealers were young niggas that were all over social media that I had previously targeted, started getting mad attention from Meek & Cannon's honey traps. One by one, the ladies lured these niggas in. It didn't take long for these dudes to start taking the bait on a hook. The girls were more than happy to suck & fuck these niggas after they received a nice wad of Ben Franklins.

I gave it a little more than a week before me and my goons began getting our hands dirty. Meek and Cannon were receiving information about the Matthew's brother's street level action, but a few of the dumb ass young niggas had direct lines to the next tier above them. The older niggas they worked for who reported to Na'jae and Kareem. I needed to know who their lieutenants and shit were. Two of the young niggas were marked for direct contact. Meek and Cannon had one, I took the other dude. We used the bitches to draw both of them into an ambush. My goons caught the first one arriving at shorty house. They snatched the nigga up, tossed him into the SUV they were rolling in, and off they went. I met with them when they done. Meek told me that son gave up what he knew as soon as they put the gun to his head. We now knew the name and other details of the nigga his corner crew reported to. I didn't have to ask about the nigga they snatched up. Cannon informed me that they dumped the body in the bushes behind an abandoned building.

Young nigga number two arrived at a motel thinking he was about to get some head and pussy from his little side piece. *A couple of hours after posting on FB that his girl was pregnant.* Son arrived in a cab, knocked on the door, baby girl let him in, and by the hand, she led him to the bed. Ma told him to get naked. Once dude was nude, on the bed, and ready to get his dick sucked; I strolled out of the bathroom in black hockey mask with a .45 in my gloved hand. I thought the nigga was about to have a heart attack on me as I told shorty that she could leave now. After she was gone, by the throat, butt ass naked, I escorted son into the bathroom. And shut the door. We had a calm chat about a few things as he lied in the bathtub and then I made an executive decision. I decided not to body him. Instead, I made him an offer that he definitely didn't refuse. I was taught that fear does two things to a nigga. It makes him too scared to fight, or willing to do anything to live. Dude was the latter. I could see it in his eyes. In that moment, he became much more useful to me alive.

Meek and Cannon handled the first lieutenant without a problem. They stalked homie for a few days and then caught the motherfucker slippin'. My man was just leaving his baby mama's crib in Wilmington when my goons let him have it. Both of them in all black and ski masks lit son up with .40 caliber's right there on the steps of his BM's row house. They ghosted the area, got rid of everything, and then made their way back to Philly. I got the text from Meek as I sat on a chicks couch watching Pay-Per-View boxing. I smoked a Newport as Shanice rolled another blunt beside me. Me and Neecy went back to when I first moved to Delaware. We went to school together and was always cool. Not only was Ma cute as fuck with a nice body, she was crazy smart and about her money. Neece was bi-sexual, didn't do relationships, was a true lone wolf, and I knew without a doubt that I could trust her.

I wanted Shanice to be a part of what I intended to build and she didn't hesitate to want in once I explained it to her. For now though, we were just chillin'. Smoked an L, crushed an order of pizza & wings, and decided to order the fight on Pay-Per-View. Floyd Mayweather and Juan Marquez were in the 9th round when I got Meek's text. Good. One of the Matthew's brother's lieutenants was in the bag and it wasn't going to take long for word to get back to Newark. Enough time for me and Neecy to finish the blunt she was sparking and the fight. Floyd was dominating Marquez and this was shaping up to be a good ass night for us. Money Mayweather won by a unanimous decision and it was time for me to handle my end. Shanice and I climbed into her dark blue Chrysler 300 and off we went. I sent a text to my inside man and told him that it was time to move. Neecy and I were sitting in the dark on a side street when son hit my phone. An hour had gone by. As soon as I saw the words, "GAME TIME" in the text, along with the location, I told Shanice to roll out.

Dashaun, the 19-year old corner boy I let live came through on his end. He contacted his lieutenant, a nigga by the name of Dro, and convinced son to link up with him. Telling him that he knew some shit about the hit on Ahmin. One of Dro's closest homies and a lieutenant like himself. Dro met with Dashaun at a chick's projects apartment and youngin' got the drop on his boss. When Shanice and I arrived, Dro was still unconscious. Taped up and lying face down on the bedroom floor. I nodded my head as I removed a wad of cash from my pocket and handed it to the chick that helped Shaun with the ambush. Judging by how shorty was dressed, I didn't have to ask how the move went down so cleanly. Ma was wearing one of those tight spaghetti string white tops and cut off jean shorts. Given the fact that she pretty as fuck and mostly tits & ass; it was clear as day. Dro was too busy eye fuckin' her when he entered her place. That was how Shaun was able to blind side him and knock his ass the fuck out. Smoothly.

I sent Neecy and shorty outside to smoke while Dashaun and I dealt with Dro. We woke the nigga up and I gave him a choice. Work for me, or die right here. To show him that I was dead ass serious, I cocked my .45 and put the barrel against his forehead as he lied on the floor. I saw fear in his eyes as he gave up a name. Hanif. I kept the gun to Dro's head as I looked up at Shaun and asked him if he knew Hanif. Son stood there near the door with his arms cross and nodded his head yeah. I had him help me get Dro to his feet and we left the bedroom. I made the nigga sit on the couch while I sent Shaun outside to tell Shanice to start the car. Cautiously, we took Dro outside and in the darkness behind shorty apartment, we put him in the trunk. Before me and Neecy drove off, I told Shaun to lay low in the chicks crib until I hit his phone.

Before going to see Mr. Hanif, we took Dro for a ride outside the city. I had Shanice drive back to North Philly and together, we escorted son from the trunk of her car and into an abandoned row house. Which was in the middle of an entire block of vacant homes. In the second-floor main bedroom, while Neecy held my gun to son's head, I set up the scene. There was an old bed in the room and I prepped a heroin syringe. I put more than the normal amount of dope in the tube, then went to Dro and Shanice. I took my .45 back from her and made the begging through the tape nigga move towards the bed. Son was struggling to walk and trying to plead with me as I forced his ass to move. I holstered my gun and put him in the sleeper choke hold to control him. Just before he passed out, I let him go and lied him on the bed. After cutting and removing the tape around his wrists, I pulled his belt off and tied it around his right bicep. Son was pretty much out of it and offering no resistance as I tapped his arm to make his vein pop. Once I found a good one, Shanice handed me the needle and I injected it.

We waited until Dro started convulsing & thrashing around on the bed and began to bounced off it before making our exit. I shot son up with enough H to cause an OD, but I added something else to it to make sure that he had zero chance of survival. Rat poison. A hot shot. Right after I injected the lethal dope into his vein, I put the syringe in his hand. Both Neecy and I had on dark blue latex gloves. All was quiet as we casually left the area. We drove back to Newark and parked half a block down from Hanif's apartment. I found son's number in Dro's phone and texted him. Fifteen minutes later, he exited his third-floor apartment. Instead of taking the elevator to the ground floor, he took the stairs. Neece and I watched him walk through the front door, down the stairs, and to his Expedition. We followed for about ten minutes before we made our move. Son stopped at a red light and Ma pulled up right behind him. I quickly pulled down my ski mask and climbed out of the car.

Neecy moved her car forward and bumped the back of the SUV. I heard son open the driver side door at the same time my home girl opened hers. From the other side of the Expedition, I heard him loudly ask her, *"What the fuck, yo??!"* Neece repeatedly told him how sorry she was, that she was a little tipsy and yada yada yada as I crept around the front of the SUV and approached Hanif from his blindside. He must have sensed something behind him and began to turn around. The moment I saw the side of his face, I rocked his jaw with a vicious leather glove covered fist. Son hit the ground and was out cold. We went right to work. Moving fast, shorty and I put him in the backseat of his ride and I hoped into the driver seat. The light was turning yellow as I pulled off with Neecy following me. A few blocks away, we rolled into an alleyway. Neece ran up to me with a roll of duct tape. Quickly, I wrapped Hanif's wrists behind him and his ankles together, then we broke out. I drove off in one direction and Ma went home. Son and I were going somewhere isolated and quiet to have a talk about a few things.

****

I had a gut feeling that Hanif wasn't going to be one of those bitch made motherfuckers. Was I ever right. The nigga didn't just have the look of a real street nigga; he definitely had the heart. I took son to an abandoned warehouse just outside the city. Unlike other dudes, I didn't have to drag or force Hanif to walk when I pulled him out of the Expedition. He walked on his own and wasn't shaking like a pussy. Inside the warehouse, being that it was starting to get light, it was easy to find an old metal chair for him to sit on. I had long since removed my ski mask. I stood back from son and lit a Newport with my .45 in hand before I asked my first question. Who in his crew ran the main stash for Na'jae and Kareem? Hanif sat there staring up at me with hard, cold eyes. Saying nothing. I took a pull on my port before repeating my question. Once more, the niggas voice was stuck on mute. I nodded my head and finished my cigarette. I crushed it out and put the butt in my cargo pocket. Before reaching into my back pocket to bring a silent friend of mine into the conversation.

Hanif watched as I pulled out a dark matte gray four-inch suppressor. Commonly referred to as a silencer. I screwed it into the barrel of my .45, made sure it was tight, moved closer to Hanif and repeated my question for a third time. Again, Hanif gave me the cold eyes and ice grill, but he finally spoke. Telling me that I might as well go on and kill him, because he wasn't telling me shit. Nothing! I flashed him a grin as I put my gun to use. POP! Hanif growled and roared in pain as a hot .45 caliber round nose penetrated the flesh of his right thigh. He was trying to endure the pain as I reached out and grabbed his throat with a latex gloved hand, held him still, and calmly asked him who was on the main stash? Son was breathing hard as fuck and starting sweat with glazing eyes. I could see that his teeth were clenched as he emphatically shook his head no. I stared into Hanif's eyes and gave him credit. Son was no pussy. There was no punk in him at all. I respected that. Respect or not though, I had to break him. I was a thug on a mission.

Five bullets, a lot of yelling, drool, tears, and blood later; Hanif told me what I wanted to know. He gave me a name, identified son's coded contact and number in his phone, and also gave up the location of the main stash. By the time Hanif's spirit broke he had a bullet in both thighs, shoulders, and he had a hole in his left knee cap. Son was lying on the dirty ass floor with his eyes closed, covered in sweat, his white T was mostly red, and shivering. He was going into shock from blood loss. I had the information I needed, so his purpose has been served. I aimed the silencer end of the Smith & Wesson at his head and pulled the trigger twice. As I made my departure, I unscrewed the silencer and left Hanif there to hopefully be found and properly buried. I drove straight to South Philly and into an auto junk yard. I paid the bearded white dude $2,000 to make the Expedition vanish. I leaned against a broke down van, watching Hanif's ride loaded into the compactor and crushed down to nothing. By the end of the day, the SUV will be shipped out as scrap metal.

Later that day, after almost nine hours of sleep, I woke up on Shanice's couch. Ma was sitting in her recliner chair smoking an L and watching TV. I got up to use the bathroom, but stopped near her as she passed the blunt to me. I hit a few times before handing it to back to her. Once I took a piss and washed my hands, I got my day started. Neecy and I finished off the blunt, I smoked a port, shorty left to get some food from a nearby diner, and I called Meek. I told him to scoop up Cannon, stop by the spot to grab some firepower, and then roll over to Newark. By the time my goons arrived, me and Shanice had eaten and discussed a few things. Now that my wolves were there, we sat around the living room and I broke down the next move. The streets were talking about the sudden misfortune hittin' the Matthew's brothers. Word was niggas were locking down their territory and on the watch for another assault. Which was exactly what I wanted them to do. Now, it was time to turn the heat up. That was where Meek and Cannon came in. I was letting my dogs off the chain to do what they do best. Attack.

Neecy, my goons, and I chilled for the rest of the day. There wasn't much in the way of conversation though. We smoked, watched a movie, got it in on NBA2K, Shanice made a run for KFC, and both of my goons caught some sleep throughout the afternoon. As the sun was going down, we watched the news before Meek & Cannon left Neecy's apartment. An hour after they bounced, we left and picked up Dashaun. The three of us rolled around the city, waiting to hear from my soldiers. It was just before ten when Meek hit my phone. He and Cannon were rolling solo in different cars. His text confirmed that he hit his target first. A couple of dealers from the Matthew's brothers camp were in body bags after son caught them on their corner and lit there asses up. He confirmed the kills, but we already knew. The whole time Neecy was driving around town, I had an ear bud in. Listening to the Newark police radio traffic on a scanner. Not five minutes after Meek did his thing, again, a call of shots fired went out over the police dispatch frequency.

I paid rapt attention as the police called in to report two victims. Both young black males. Code-187. D.O.A. Dead On Arrival. Patrol, Homicide, and a supervisor were talking back and forth when another report came in from dispatch. A second Code-10 (shots fired) less than an hour after the first. As I was listening to the dispatcher relay the location of the second shooting, Cannon hit my phone. Confirming that his job was done. Just like Meek, he didn't have to provide details of his kill in his text. I was listening to them over the police scanner. He opened fire on a crew of niggas in front of a row house. According to the Newark City Police, there were four victims. Three were seriously injured, one was DOA. All of them worked for the Matthew's brothers as a dope spot crew. The fire was lit. Na'jae and Kareem were well aware of their reality now. They were under assault. War has been declared on them. It was on now. Being that those two snake motherfuckers fancied themselves as two Kings, they have to do what every King must do when war has been imposed on them. Respond.

****

While Meek and Cannon we laying low in a motel over in Wilmington, I was keeping a low profile in Neecy apartment with Dashaun. Most of the day, we tuned into the news. All day long they were talking about the shootings and the police investigating. Shaun kept his eye on Facebook. Clocking the stupid motherfuckers talking about shit they shouldn't be on social media. Niggas and chicks posting RIP pictures and hashtags for the dudes that got dropped and posting their street conspiracy theories about the murders. Niggas that worked for the Matthew's brothers were online running their mouth about payback, reppin' their fallen homies, holdin' it down, and so on. Dashaun informed me about every post and we just let everything play out. We stayed down during the daylight hours, but as soon as it started getting dark, I left Shanice's apartment with Shaun. We took her car and met up with Meek and Cannon. Behind an abandoned building, youngin' and I put on Kevlar vests, I gave him a ski mask, and my niggas had black hoodies for us.

Cannon had the wheel of an old Explorer they copped in Wilmington. I was in the shotgun seat while Meek and Shaun rode in the back. There was no conversation between us and only sound was Power 99 on the radio. Set to a low volume. I smoked a cigarette as I gripped my .45 resting on my lap. Shit got tense a few times as we cruised through the streets. Police cruisers past by us and we were ready to bang it out with the cops if they pulled us over. But, the cruisers passed us by and never took notice of our ride. It was almost 10:30 when we pulled over and parked in the middle of a neighborhood. Cannon killed the lights first, then shut off the engine. Without looking back, I told Dashaun to do his thing. Son took out his phone and sent a text. To a nigga by the name of Anthony Mills. He went by Tone and dude was high up in the Matthew's organization. Ol' boy was in charge of the main stash of product for Na'jae and Kareem.

One of things I got out of Hanif before I sent him on his way was the codes. Being that son was a lieutenant, at that rank, he was in position to know the codes used by the organization. He told me every code they used and I planned to put only one in play. The shutdown code in the event that they law was coming after the main stash. Using Hanif's phone, Shaun sent the code "999" to Tone's. Within ten minutes of the text being sent, Tone rapidly exited his house. We were parked half way down the block, silently watching him make his way to his Lexus, climb in, start it up, and quickly pull off. By the time he was about to hit the turn at the end of the block, we were on his ass. Tone led us a few miles outside of Newark to a house on its own property. We stayed back and watched as he parked in the driveway and exited his car. A few minutes later, another car arrived and parked behind his Lex. Two niggas climbed out and quickly made their way into the house. When no other vehicles came through after five minutes of watching and waiting, I told my crew lets go.

All four of us concealed ourselves in the shadows on both the side of the house and waited. Almost ten minutes went by before I heard the front door open. When I saw Tone and his two niggas approaching his ride, all of them carrying a gym bag strap in both hands, me and Dashaun stayed right where we were. Just they reached the car, gun shots started cappin' off. Meek and Cannon rained .40 caliber rounds on Tone and his homies as I ran around the front of the house and up the stairs of the porch with Shaun right on my heels. I kicked open the door and scared a pretty ass red bone chick half to death. She was about to call someone on her cell when I burst into the room. Ma dropped her phone and was in mid-scream as she turned to run for the dining room. I caught up to her, grabbed her by her hair, pulled her back to me, and locked my arm around her neck. She was kicking and fighting until I put my gun to her head and barked at her to, *"Shut her ass the fuck up!"* Ma went silent, but was shaking like a motherfucker and whimpering. Now that I had her relatively calm, it was time to handle my end. I looked at Shaun through my ski mask as he stood a few feet away in his. Without a moment of hesitation, I raised my .45 and pulled the trigger. BOOM! BOOM!

The rounds hit Dashaun's vest and knocked him backwards. He fell on his back and I dragged shorty with me as I crossed the room and took aim again. Shaun was gasping for air as I put one into the side of his head through the black ski mask. Ma was crying and weak kneed as I took a fistful of her hair and forced her to leave with me. Meek and Cannon had loaded up the back of our SUV with the gym bags and were waiting for me in the driveway. I quickly forced shorty past the bodies of Tone, his two homies, their shot-up cars, and into the back seat of the Explorer. Cannon pulled off as soon as we were in. The whole drive back to Newark, shorty sat next to me hugging herself, shaking, and silently crying. She was wearing only a black tank top and satin pajama pants. At first, I was going to off her too, but seeing her super pretty ass sitting there terrified to the core of her bones, I decided to go a different route with her.

Once back at Neecy's apartment, while shorty sat in the living room with Meek and Cannon, Shanice and I had a conversation in the kitchen. When we were done, Neece took Ma into her bedroom for them to have a woman-to-woman, heart-to-heart conversation. Half an hour later, they came back out and my home girl gave me the nod. Miss Tamia was on board. She was scared to death and out of fear for her life and a strong sense of self-preservation, she agreed to keep her mouth shut about what happen at her house. The house her boyfriend Tone had bought for her as a smokescreen to stash their product in her basement. Neecy made it clear to her that in exchange for a large sum of cash and her life to start over somewhere, she will never speak on what happened. What took place at her home, never happened. I sent Meek and Cannon on their way. Tamia took a shower, Neece gave her something to wear, and once she was out in the bedroom, Neecy told me that Ma was in the clear. She had no record, so her prints weren't in the system. She was also a former foster kid, so she had no family, and the house was in someone else's name. I nodded my head. Luck was on our side for sure.

****

Shit got hot in Newark after we set it on fire. The cops were all over the place. Locking down drug corners, raiding dope houses, making arrests, and trying to stop what they believed was a drug war in the streets. We kept Tamia with us for almost a week. She wasn't much of a talker, but she was docile and didn't try any slick shit. Ma smoked, ate, drank, and watched TV with us. I had Meek deliver the money for her. $80,000. I gave her the cash that night and the next morning, Shanice drove Tamia to 30th street Station and waited as Ma boarded a train for North Carolina. She had a cousin down there that she was close with. Neece reminded her of our arrangement before leaving the station. When she got back, it was time to watch from the shadows as shit unfolded. Days went by and when things on the street began to cool down, I turned the temperature back up. By using Hanif, Dashaun, and Tone's phones to cause rumors on social media. Which sparked speculation. Which in turn created havoc, mayhem, and chaos.

By using those niggas phones, I turned the shit upside down. I posted shit on social media accusing certain niggas of snitching, some of playing both sides of the fence, and others of being traitors. I tagged females that I saw liked to run their mouth and were nothing but drama. Once the social media battles began, I had Meek and Cannon stoke the flames of anarchy. By shooting at niggas connected to the Matthew's brothers, they jumped another one, me and Neecy robbed a nigga that sold a lot of weed for them, and then we fell back and watched the city burn from a far. Friends were turning on friends, allies became enemies, niggas that once hustled on the streets together started beefing, and the lies we put out caused Na'jae and Kareem to make critical mistakes. They came out of the cocoon of their dope rich lifestyles to regain control. Exposing themselves. With their business drying up from a lack of product and their dealers beefin', other niggas started trying to move in on their territory. Which started a whole new wave of conflict and confrontation.

After weeks of moving everything into place, Newark, Delaware was now engaged into an all-out ghetto drug war. Niggas were banging it out on sight, running up in houses, fighting in the county jail, bodies were blood staining the streets, and the police had to quell all of the madness. From the relative safety of Philadelphia and with Neecy acting as my eyes in Newark, I watched as the law did my job for me. My 22nd birthday came and went as the FBI and DEA teamed up with Newark PD with a target in mind. The Matthew's brothers. My home girl kept her eyes open and ear to the ground like a spy. She reported to me that from the rumors and all signs, motherfuckers were cooperating with the law. They put the spotlight on Na'jae and Kareem. In which the police and Feds went after them. Hard. Two weeks later, their connect was arrested and indicted. A few days after that, Kareem went down. Son was found naked with his throat cut in a dumpster. Word on the street was that the connect had put a hit out on the Matthew's brothers. Believing that they had ratted them out. I expected Na'jae to be next, but the nigga pulled a bitch move and turned himself in. Neecy sent word back that he walked into police headquarters with a high-priced defense attorney to speak for him. And that was that. He was either getting indicted, or going into witness protection.

Either way, those snake motherfuckers were no more.

I did what I had sworn to do.

End them.

CHAPTER TWELVE

"Never trust anyone. Even your shadow leaves you in the darkness."

For two years after crushing the empire that Na'jae and Kareem stole from their pops, I was a King with an invisible crown. We let shit cool down and stabilize before building our own network. Over the course of two months, I had Meek & Cannon recruit niggas from all over Philly and they worked with Neecy to put on dudes from Newark. As for myself, I decided to play the unseen hand in it all. I didn't meet face-to-face with a single person other than Meek, Cannon, and Shanice. They reported to me and I issued orders. With the format of the operation I was planning, I wanted as few people as possible to even know I was the nigga calling the shots. I did however take on a right hand. A female hustler and thug by the name of Rasheeda, but went by Dutches. I met her at a North Philli pool hall. I knew within a few minutes of meeting her that she was something special. Something unique. A whole different breed of female.

Most niggas are and will always be taken by how a woman look. How pretty she is, how big her titties are, and how fat her ass is. The sexier a female is, the more power she will have over thirsty and weak-minded ass niggas. Meek and Cannon had more discipline than the average dude in the streets, but they too fall for bad ass chicks harder than they should. Not me. One, I know how attractive I am to women. So, nine times out of ten, I basically have my pick when it comes to women. Two, a beautiful face and a bangin' body doesn't move me like it always does to a tender dicked motherfucker. And three, I'm a stick & move type of dude. Once I fuck, it's a wrap. I don't call back or repeat. The more my life goes on, the less I trust. The less I trust, the less I require certain things from people. Things such as female companionship, affection, conversation, and love. What I love is the life. The life of crime. The life of an outlaw. I'm married to the game. I'm a thug and perfectly cool with that.

Dutches was exactly the same way. When I showed up at the pool hall on a Thursday night, she was there solo like me. Ma had a table by herself and was enjoying an evening of shooting pool and sipping on some beer without having to share her time and space with anyone. I set up at an open table next to hers and got to it. Both of us did own thing for a while, until shorty challenged me to shoot against her. After rejecting every other offer from niggas trying to get at her. I accepted, we got ourselves some more beer, and got to it. Dutches and I were silent competitors for a minute, but after a few matches, we loosened up and started talking a little shit as we shot. We ended up playing five back-to-back games before we put our sticks back up on the rack and left the pool hall. Ma and I were clickin', so we decided to go grab a cheesesteak and keep the night going.

Though the Italian's in Philly were well known for their cheesesteaks, it was black owned shops that were the best. Bernard's Sub's on 52nd street in Southwest was #1 in my book and Dutches agreed. We both ordered large Cheesesteaks, fries, two Pepsi's and took a corner booth to wait for our food. We continued our convo, verbally sparring about a few things, and feeling each other out before moving off into some real shit about one another. It wasn't often that I spoke about my mother & father, or about anything that hurt; but with Dutches, I did. And vice versa. I sensed that she wasn't the chatty or emotional type from the second I met her, but I felt her vibe. Just as she was feeling mine. I was looking at her the same way she was looking at me. Two lone wolves seeing and understanding one another. Dutches and I were the same. Exactly the same. It wasn't sexual either. Our vibe and connection were purely mutual. Kindred spirits type of shit.

She was 23-years old, been on her own since she 12, and both parents were dead. Pops died in prison and moms was a junkie that got picked up by the wrong trick. They found her dead behind a dumpster. Dutches was taken in by grandma at nine, but three years later, she was done with her grandmother's bullshit. Tired of being hit in the head with Bible talk and getting beaten with a leather belt all the time. Thus, she ran away at 12 and been on her own ever since. It was on the streets of Philly that she became who and what she is now. A 5'9, 150lb, dark brown skinned, beautiful wolf in disguise. To survive out there so young, she had to do questionable shit to get buy, and it was the ugliness of both men and women in the hood that killed something in her. She didn't fuck with anyone on a sexual level, but Ma didn't have to say it for me to hear it loud and clear. She was violated as a youngster and both genders tore something out of her. Thus, she wanted nothing from men, or women. Her life was armed robbery, drug dealing, money, and to whatever the fuck she wanted to do.

Normally, I didn't bring anyone to my spot, but I made an exception. Dutches and I fell back to my loft and continued chillin' with each other. I got the weed out, she started rollin', I fired a up a Newport, and once the Dutch was lit, we kept bonding. Keith was the last, and pretty much the only person I ever had this kind of vibe with. The only true homie I ever had in my life. I had only known Dutches for a few hours and I had to keep it real. Shorty's aura was too powerful to ignore. I sensed that she was feeling the same way. By the time the sun was coming up, we were high as fuck, relaxed, and laughing like lifelong friends as we sat in my living room playing Madden on my Xbox. She had her beloved Eagles and I had my Giants. We talked shit through two back-to-back games before we switched to regular TV and crashed out. Me in the recliner chair and her on the couch.

Days turned into weeks and as my domain was built from a foundation, Dutches and I became damn near inseparable. I started bringing her with me when I met up with Meek, Cannon, and Neecy. They thought that she was my chick and I let them believe that. Ma never spoke when I met with my people and she always played the background; further giving off the illusion that she was just a chick I was throwing dick up in. In reality, Dutches quickly became my silent partner and best friend. She and I spent nearly every day together. Ma was big into boxing and nice with her hands, so we hit the gym to work out and spar with one another. While I preferred a .45 caliber, she favored a 40. Packing a Taurus PT semi-auto. She liked to hit the shooting range as much as I did, so we went at least twice a week to keep our marksmanship skills sharp. Our time was split between her apartment in Southwest Philly and mine in West. When we weren't firing weed, getting down on Chinese, or playing Xbox; we discussed business.

Dutches dropped ideas on me that I had my crew put into play. Unlike damn near every nigga that sold dope and put in work on the streets; I didn't want my name to ring out in the hood. I wasn't in it for the fame and recognition as a drug lord or some kind of Kingpin. Save all that kind of infamous gangster bullshit for the movies. I established my operation as a narcotics trafficking pipeline with no central point or established level leadership. Meek and Cannon recruited hustlers and thugs in Philly to operate independently of each other in various spots that didn't overlap. They became the product supply and collectors of their crews in both Philly and Delaware. Shanice ran point in Newark. She put on a few niggas and chicks she knew and they mostly pushed weed, but they sold coke too. Being that the law and technology were now lovers, the cops were making cases spying on cell phone-social media traffic, narc raids, and by posting cameras all over the place. Corner level drug action and dope houses were dying, so Dutches suggested that go strictly old school.

My dealers worked off their phones, but it was stick & move only. All clientele hit one of my workers phones with a code for what they wanted and the dealer met with them face-to-face to make the transaction. In an alley, abandoned house, and for their weed customers, inside their homes. Niggas still pushed work on the corners and in the projects, but none of them were my people. I made it clear to Meek, Cannon, and Shanice to instill discipline their crews. To keep business off of social media, don't talk about shit over the phone or in text, and to avoid gunplay & drama. To hold down our dealers, Dutches and I put on trigger niggas. Soldiers. Motherfuckers that were about that murder shit. Every crew under my rule had a couple of goons as security and just like my lieutenants, the goons reported Meek, Cannon, and Neece. Never to me. They didn't even know the motherfucker that put them on. As the first year went by, with the amount of product we had amassed, green was flowing in constantly and consistently. Every one under my flag was making money and shit was good.

****

Rasheeda and I developed a true brother and sister, best friend, ride till we die bond. She and I were together all the time and we shared shit with each other that we revealed to no one else. It was a normal thing for us to be smoking weed or drinking as we talked about shit. She told me about killing one of the dudes that raped her when she was 14. She was playing niggas to get by, and at the time, she was willing to suck & fuck a hustler for money. A lot of young chicks in Philly were on that pay-to-play shit back then and there were plenty of pedophile ass drug dealing niggas to choose from. One night, she met a nigga in a bar, did the flirt and drink thing, and when she presented her offer; son was with it. However, as they entered the motel room, she caught a bad vibe from the nigga. An aura of violence from him that scared her and she wanted out of the arrangement. Son wasn't feeling that. Needless to say, Dutches got the shit beat out of her and raped. Repeatedly. When dude was done with her, he tossed a dollar bill on the bed with her bruised and bloody body before departing.

Ma caught up with him three years later. When he flirted with her in a club. Not recognizing her. By then, she was a far more cold and violent individual than she was at 14. She told me that she flirted with dude hard and left the club with him. Heading back to his place to get their fuck on. They never made it. I listened in silence as she revealed that as soon as he parked on the side street around the corner from his apartment, karma came to visit son. In the form of two .380 caliber bullets. The first one to his dick & balls, then #2 to the side of his head after she let him scream for a while as he held the bloody mush that used to be his genitals. After blowing his brains all over the driver side window, she calmly opened her door and walked away. Dutches told me about every body she caught. The nigga that raped her was the first, a dude that tried to rob her was the second, and a chick she was in love with was number three. Her lover at 20. I asked Dutches why she murked out her girl, and her answer was simple? Betrayal.

Her girl, the first person she trusted, believed in, and loved since her own mother; tried to have her killed. At the time, they had been together for almost three years. Nearly three years of love, passion, fun, and getting money together. Dutches and her girl sold weed, boosted designer clothes that they stole in NYC, and were on some real Thelma & Louise shit. That is until Dutches hit a big lick. By luck. She was meeting with her weed guy when son was shot and killed. She was using his bathroom when niggas hit his spot and murdered him, without robbing him. Why? She had no clue. But they didn't know that she was in the house. After they were gone, she came out and seized upon the opportunity. Her supplier had left his safe open. Thus, she bagged his pounds of high grade weed and cash, then got the fuck out of there. Dutches said that her girl was all excited about the come up, but seeing so much money and product, her true nature revealed itself. A week later, Dutchie girl saw something on her girls' phone as her lover took a shower.

A text message came though, and on impulse, Dutches took a look. The text convo between her girl and some nigga revealed that they were going to kill her and take the product & money. Dutches didn't waist a second. When her girl came out of the shower, she got dressed, and the two of them went out to dinner. Then to the movies. But on their way home, Dutches made a stop. On a dark South Philly street. She told her girl that she had to make a drop to a customer before going into an apartment building. Exiting the back door, pulling out her gun, and cutting through an alley. She then approached her girl's car from the rear and her chick was too occupied with her phone to notice her stroll up, aim her 9mm at the passenger side widow, and then put six rounds through it. Dutches then went home, packed up her money & product, then left Philly for the next year. The cops never identified her as a suspect, so her girls' case had long since gone cold by the time she returned.

The same as I asked her specific questions about certain kills, she asked me the same thing. About Dionne and Dashaun. The Dionne situation was simple mathematics. I couldn't buy her silence. There was no amount of money I could offer her or threat I could make to keep her quiet about me. I used her heart to infiltrate and Ma had fallen deeply in love with me. I broke her heart, ruined her family, and killed her people to make a move. The fact that she was so in love with me was why I had to consider her a loose end. She was a woman with a broken heart and a dead cousin. A cousin that she adored. That scorn and hatred for me couldn't be bought and any threat would have been futile. So, she had to die. When Dutches asked why did I used a poison laced cigarette, my answer was simple. I didn't regret my choice to end her life, but I couldn't shoot her. In a way, that was only act of mercy. Quick and painless. Dashaun was a different story.

In my eyes, son was a pussy ass coward. I would have more respect for him if he had chosen to die rather than turn on his crew. He would have done anything to survive. He also believed that he was going to be apart of my crew once the war was over. How could I ever trust a motherfucker without a spine and had no code? Nah! Son could be bought or threatened into betrayal. The nigga had no heart or loyalty. So, once he served his purpose, I bodied him at Tone's stash house to achieve two things. One, to clip another loose end. Two, to throw off the investigation. Dutches inquired about Tone's girl. Tamia. Why did I let her live? My response was simple again. I knew that she wouldn't talk, if she had a good enough reason not to. Ma was the cover disguise for major narcotics. She was well aware of what snitching would get her. I used that fact and the promise of money and being allowed to live as motivation to assure that she took what she knew to the grave. In retrospect, Tamia had more heart than Shaun ever had in his entire life.

****

Year one as the unseen King was smooth and we saw very little issues that couldn't be fixed. Our dope got sold, money stacked up, we dealt with niggas that were problems, and we held shit down. Halfway through year two, I started to see cracks in the foundation. Unknown to anyone other than Dutches and myself, we had eyes & ears on the streets. Carefully selected niggas and chicks reported back to us the ebb & flow of our people out there. What they did, who they were doing it with, where they went, and what they were up to. 18-months into our reign, the bullshit began. Niggas that dealt for us were playing games. Side hustles, flashing money like big ballers, getting into dumb shit with baby mama's, and some started breaking the rules. Dealing out in the open, acting wild in the bars, and getting involved in beef's with outside niggas. Beef's that often resulted in fights and gunplay. We had to keep bailing niggas out, paying lawyer fees, disappearing dudes out of town, and fix what dumb niggas broke.

Meek & Cannon were on some bullshit too. I noticed that like Zay, they were feeling themselves too. They made crazy money with me and that shit went to their heads. They were living in nice spots, fucking with bad bitches, they stayed fresh, and the more comfortable they were, the more arrogant they were. They had become cocky, lazy, and were rapidly losing control of their crews on the street. I grew tired of meeting with them, only to get the same reports from my eyes & ears. Niggas were still fucking up out there and I felt that at any moment, the law was going to get to me. Yet, it wasn't the cops or feds that put me on high alert. My own niggas did. I decided to follow Meek one day. I tracked her to a park in Camden that night. Cannon showed up as well. The two of them met with five other niggas and just by the look of the meet, I knew what was up. I decided to verify my gut feeling. I called Dutches, we rapped about the situation, and then she set off to put a plan in motion.

Between the two of them, Cannon was the weakest one. When it came to a pretty face and a fat ass. Dutches went out and found one of the sexiest, nastiest, and morally bankrupt strippers in Philly. Miss Deja Hill. Five feet, eight inches of light skinned, juicy assed venom. Dutchie girl paid Ma a grip of cash, explained what she wanted her to do, and shorty went out to get it done. 72-hours later, Dutches got the text from Deja. We were sitting in my SUV outside of Deja's apartment in Germantown. Ma let us in and then went to her kitchen to fix herself a drink. Less than five minutes later, we came down stair with Cannon. Who was high, out of semen, and wearing only his boxers. With duct tape over his mouth and his wrists taped behind him. Deja received the second half of her payment and went up to bed with her glass of wine as I sent Dutches to bring my ride around back. I escorted Cannon out of the house through the dark yard and into my SUV.

I expected son to hold it down like a warrior when we got him to a quiet and secluded spot. But no. Money and privilege killed the gangster in him. Cannon quickly revealed that he and Meek had formed an alliance with a coalition of dope dealing niggas to takeover my shit. The plan was to body me, Dutches, Shanice, and anyone else in the way. Take what I had built, then go on with business as usual. Meek and Cannon were making moves to position themselves as the next Kingpins in Philly. When son finished talking, I nodded my head. I had nothing to say, but my gun did. I put my .45 to his forehead and pulled the trigger. Blowing out the back of his skull and dropping his snake ass to the floor of a basement in an abandoned house. As I unscrewed the suppressor from the barrel, Dutches led the way out. I dropped her off at her place, told her to call Shanice, and I went to handle Meek. It only took me an hour and a half to set something up, then I hit Meek's phone. Telling him that we needed to meet and where to link up at. Five minutes later, he hit me back to tell me that he was on his way.

I watched from my SUV as Meek's Denali rounded the corner. I knew he was coming from blocks away. It was almost five in the morning and the nigga was banging music as he drove. I calmly smoked a cigarette from the opposite block as he pulled up in front of the row house I told him I was at and parked. The music cut off when he killed the engine. Son exited his ride, rounded the front of it, and was approaching the house when a female fiend suddenly appeared out of nowhere and started asking him if he had anything on him. Ma was begging him for a fix. Meek kept telling her to get the fuck out of his face, but she persisted. I watched with cold eyes. Son was good and distracted. As he grabbed the dope head by her arm and pushed her away from him, the door to the row house had opened. Meek had just turned around, when he froze. An ol' head dope addict with a black heart by the name of Melvin stood on the porch with a sawed-off shotgun. I watched as he blasted Meek with both barrels. Both junkies took off running in different direction as that snake ass motherfucker lied there twitching and shit with most of his face missing. As calm as the breeze, I put my gear in park and pulled off.

I was halfway to my spot when I got pulled over. I drove on for a minute though. Just enough time to factory reset my phone. When I stopped for the cops, another cruiser pulled up in front of me. Four patrol men did the surround the car with their guns out, ordering me to turn the engine off and whatnot. They snatched me out of my SUV, had me put my hands on the hood, searched me, and as one officer was informing me that my ride matched a stolen vehicle, another called out to his partners. He found a gun under the driver seat. I was handcuffed, all of my possessions were taken, and I was read my rights. Most niggas would be worried about getting popped with gun, but I wasn't. The pistol they found was clean. Illegal, but it had no bodies on it. The gun I used on Cannon was gone, along with the silencer. There were no drugs and I had about $2,500 in cash on me. The cops took me to the precinct, I gave nothing to the illegal weapons detectives, asked for a lawyer, and then I was processed. I had to wait a few hours to see a judge, and that gave me time to call Dutches and she got to work.

I met with my lawyer before my arraignment. She was certain that I'd be granted bail. Wishful motherfuckin' thinking. Normally, a bond would be set on a low felony gun charge, but not for me. Due to fact that I refused to cooperate with the police on where I got the illegal firearm and that I was arrested with it in a school zone; the judge denied bond and I was sent to the county jail. I caught Dutches eye as I was escorted out of the court room. I knew I could count on her and my lawyer told me that she will see to it that I don't get hit with anything crazy. However, she did tell me to get ready. I was going to do some time. The Mayor was cracking down on guns and gun violence, so the District Attorney's office wasn't going to let me slide off with a bullshit sentence or probation. My attorney advised me to think of a number of years that I can live with, and that's what she'll fight to get me on a deal.

Along with six other dudes, I was transported from the courthouse to the county jail. Curran-Fromhold Correctional Facility. The infamous CF-CF. I went through the bullshit intake process, cold shower, uniform-linens-hygiene bag issue, then over to medical with the other new inmates for an evaluation. After that, we were escorted to a housing unit. Once on my cell block, I was assigned to a cell. With a husky, dark skinned nigga with happy cornrows and a bushy Muslim beard. The guards slammed the cell door and that was that. My first time in prison had begun. Day one went by slowly. I kept to myself, watched everything moving, interacted with no one, and stayed inside my head. I called Dutches that evening during day room. Ma told me that she was in my corner, to not worry about my shit, and she was going to hold me down. Though I was skeptical, I didn't say anything to her about it. Before my fifteen minutes was up, she assured me that I wasn't going to worry about shit while I was inside, money was already on its way for my commissary, and that she will stay in touch with my lawyer.

Days, weeks, and a few months went by. As my hair and beard grew out and I did thousands upon thousands of pushups, situps, and dips in my cell; my attorney declared war with the prosecutor handling my case. Their first plea offer was six to twelve years. My number was no more than five to my lawyer. I could live with a nickel. My lawyer held the line for me for almost five months until the DA gave in. They wanted the stat for their conviction rate, city elections were coming up, so they relented and agreed to our terms. Two and a half to five years. I signed the deal at the county, my lawyer submitted it, I plead guilty to a felony possession of an illegal firearms charge in open court, and the judge banged his gavel. Nine days after that, at four am, I was woken up by the guards, told to pack my shit, they took me to reception, and I changed into a yellow D.O.C. jumpsuit. I was served a nasty ass jailhouse breakfast at 4:40 am, and at 5:10 in the morning, me and two other dudes were loaded onto a PA DOC van and we hit the road. I was the first prisoner to be dropped off that day. At SCI-Rockview in Bellefonte, Pennsylvania. 192 miles from Philly.

I went through in-processing, paperwork, cell block assignment, medical screening, and I was issued my sets of maroon colored uniforms. State prison looked more like college campus, within days I settled into my cell, and I formulated a plan for myself. Don't worry about shit other than the time I have to do. Workout, hit the weights, read, watch TV, and stay on my lone wolf shit more than ever now. Other than Dutches, I trusted no one. Trust in the criminal life is what got me here. Trust almost got me killed. Trust is going to cost me five years of my life. Fuck parole. I was giving the state all sixty months of this sentence. As niggas around me were playing cards, running ball in the yard, developing their rap skills, fighting over bullshit, engaging in homosexuality, and telling lying ass war stories from the streets; I disconnected myself. I needed nothing from anyone. I fucked with absolutely no one. Not even my cellmates. I did everything alone. Dutches was my only connection to the outside world. Other than that, I lived on a isolated plane of existence.

I reached a new level in my personality. Fuck the world and everyone in it.

CHAPTER THIRTEEN

"Mind of a Cobra, Heart of a Lion, Soul of a Wolf."

Prison does two things to a man without any kind of interference or influence of another person. Being incarcerated can turn a man into a fear consumed individual that relinquishes his life of crime, seeking to never return to prison. Out of fear of the physical structure of prison itself. When a man is locked up in a cell, especially the cut off from reality isolation of the hole; just being in prison can tear a man's mind and spirit to pieces. Everything in prison is based on power, domination, & subjugation. When man does time, he is in control of almost nothing in regards to his very own motherfuckin' existence. He is told when & where he can eat, where he is allowed to sleeps, what he can do, where he can do it, and when he can do it. There is no such thing as civil rights, freedom of speech, regard for physical safety, or a concern for human life. Mostly all prison guards are poorly trained, heartless ass cowards that provide a constant presence of intimidation, and they will not hesitate to stomp a man's skull and push his brains in to establish their state sponsored authority.

Most men inside become meek & weak ass conformists that develop an irreversible fear of prison. Whether they get fucked up or not. The opposite reaction is that a certain breed of men find out something about themselves within the walls of a correctional facility. They find out what they truly are. A werewolf. A savage. Its just like Star Wars. Niggas like me discover the dark side within themselves. The physical reality of a prison becomes a training ground for a nigga that embraces his darkness. That truly cold core within his heart. Time becomes irrelevant. Their sentence, especially if it's a short one, becomes a reason to prepare themselves. Their workouts become a means to transform their bodies into weapons. Time to sharpen the blade within their soul. And time to ready their minds to be far more dangerous than they were before they were incarcerated. That's exactly what happened to me over the course of sixty months in a Pennsylvania State Prison. I firmly accepted what I was and my only focus was to prepare for my release.

Dutches kept her word and held me down. I received a $300 money order from her every two weeks, she sent smut pics of porn stars, she kept me with a subscription for the Philly newspaper and several magazines, and once a month, she made the drive to visit me. Showing up to grace the visiting room as the baddest chick in attendance. As the months and years went by, she watched my transformation. From a just over six feet tall nigga with an athletic welterweight frame; to a wave haired-thick bearded-muscled out convict. I hit weights hard and worked out daily, but I didn't look like those goofy looking niggas on the cover of muscle magazines. I was ripped, solid, and diesel AF; but not overly stocky. Dutches loved how I looked and I felt the same way. By my third year, my partner developed into a full-blown grown woman herself. She kept herself in shape, took care of her hair & skin, and when she came to see me, niggas couldn't help by steal multiple looks at her ass. Even the guards were checkin' her out.

Her loyalty to me was etched in stone. Just as her commitment to our plan when I was released. Dutches was truly my kindred spirit. My mirror image. She was the same way on the outside, as I was on the inside. A lone wolf. She didn't fuck with anyone. No home girls or even one friend. Other than me. The only person either of us cared about or had love for, was each other. We were mutually on some real fuck the world shit. No love or mercy for anyone. I did my time quietly, a few niggas tried me and got their shit pushed in, I was sent to the hole three times, and other than that, my sentence went by smoothly. Niggas and CO's left me alone, I did the same, sixty months went by on the calendar, and the day of my release arrived. Five years ago, I arrived in a one-piece yellow D.O.C. inmate transport jumpsuit. On release day, I walked out of the main building in my typical uniform. Brand new Timbs, dark blue-faded front denim jeans, a crisp white 3XL T-shirt and a Navy blue Rocawear track jacket.

As expected, Dutches was waiting for me in the parking lot. Standing next to her ride. A silver Lexus LX SUV. It looked new and had smoke tints. Dutchie and I did the hug thing before we climbed into her whip and got the fuck out of there. About five minutes away from the prison, my wolf sister told me to look in the glove box. I opened it up and inside was a perfectly rolled Dutch Master blunt. We cracked the windows, I sparked the L, took a hit, choked a little, toked two more times, then passed the blunt to her as she drove. We had been on the road for almost an hour, when Dutches took an exit off the interstate. In Lewistown. We drove on for another ten minutes before she pulled into a Motel 6. Ma parked and told me to follow her as she opened her door. We walked up the stairs to the second level and up to room #24. She pulled out a keycard from her jacket pocket, handed it to me, and as she went to walk back the way we came, she hit me in the chest. Telling me to have fun as she bounced.

****

Forty-five minutes later, I busted my another nut into a condom inside shorty pussy. Nut #2 was much more satisfying than my first one. When I had entered the room, waiting for me was my welcome home gift from my sis. A chick whose name I didn't know or care to know. Ma was watching TV while lying on her side on the bed when I entered. She was in just her panties, dark milk chocolate skin, big heavy tits, hips, curves, and ass like a stallion. Shorty had long brown hair, bedroom eyes, juicy lips, and was on point. She sat up with the motion of a panther, locked eyes with me, and indicated with one manicured finger for me to come to her. Indeed, I did. Me and shorty did a little kissing, she sucked and licked on my neck, I sucked and licked on her titties, and as my mojo started bubbling; I threw her on her back and ate her pussy. Until my beard was drenched in her juices. She didn't even care when fingered her anus and pussy at the same time as I ate her out.

I've gotten my dick sucked at least a thousand times, but none felt as good as when shorty did it. I can't even front. She had me groaning like a motherfucker, unable to open my eyes, gripping her hair-guiding her head, and my toes curled more than once. Ma was an elite champion dick sucker. Zero gag reflex, lots of saliva, ball licking, and deep throat action. She moaned as she sucked my dick, stared up at me, and her slurping was wet & loud. I almost came, but I held on for the pussy. Ma used her mouth to roll the condom on my dick, lied back, and I slid in. I was two and half minutes into her wet, warm, and tight tunnel before I growled like a Rottweiler. Busting a hard and loud nut. Ma dug her nails into my lower back, raised her knees, met my strokes with her hips, and whispered in my ear, *"Keep going, baby!...Keep stroking!"* I did for like, ten more pumps before I dropped on top of her. Sweating and out of breath.

I fucked shorty again, but I beat the pussy up this time. I fucked her all over the room, in multiple positions, filling up two more condoms before we were done. Ma gave a wet kiss on the lips and a bright smile before leaving the bed and heading for the bathroom with fucked up hair and the bruised pussy strut. I took the time to smoke one of her Newports before I started getting dressed. Shorty was singing to herself in the shower as I exited her room. I found Dutches sitting in her SUV. Watching a battle rap video on her phone. As soon as I climbed in, she started the engine, put the gear in reverse and backed out of the parking spot. After stopping at a restaurant to get some real food in me, we were back on the PA Interstate. Two and a half hours later, we were home. Philadelphia. Immediately, she drove to Diamond street in North Philly. To Rakim's barbershop. A little over an hour later, I exited with a razor-sharp low cut that accentuated my waves with perfectly lined shape up and beard trim. Son that cut my shit was nice as fuck with those clippers.

Dutches took me on a shopping trip for clothes, we stopped by a Chinese spot so that I could eat again, then we went back to my spot. Sis held down my loft and kept it the way it was for the last five years. While I took a long ass hot shower, Dutches rolled up another blunt as she chilled in the living room. I came back out in a fresh tank top and basketball shorts. She playfully admired my muscled-out physique as we set up to play the latest Madden on my new PS4. We got in a few games and I lost each one. I was rusty as fuck, but once I get used to the next generation system, I'll bust her ass again. Now that we were done gaming, I was sharp again, got my dick wet, ate real food, and smoke some fire green; chill time was over. As I got dressed, Dutches reacquainted me with me with an old friend of mine. A brand new matte black Taurus 1911 .45 caliber semi-automatic. Ma handed me the gun case and I removed the gun itself from the foam lining. I ejected the clip, checked it, re-inserted it, pulled the slide back, racked a round into the pipe, and then placed it into the inside the pants holster after placing it on my right hip. Now, we were ready to roll out.

****

I rode shotgun as Dutches drove into Newark, Delaware. It was just after nine, but it was a Friday night. Motherfuckers were flowing towards the bars and shit. In the years that I been gone, the city was booming more than ever. A lot of business came to Newark, more niggas from Philly and NYC-Jersey had relocated there, the drug game was a bit more fierce, and we had a score to settle. During my second year upstate, Shanice met her end. At the hands of a nigga that was supposed to love her. Dutches got word to me that Neecy got out of the game after that shit with Meek & Cannon, but she got wifed up by a nigga that was deep in the streets. Dutchie kept an eye on Neece from afar though. Just to make sure that she was good. She was. For a while. Then, she was murdered. Shot dead in an apartment complex along with a nigga that she was fuckin' with. Her side dude. D found out that her main nigga was a notorious liar and cheater that had more than a few issues.

Son was insecure, possessive of Shanice, controlling, suspicious of her every move, and he was a woman beater. Neecy got tired of the bullshit and decided to fuck with a nigga that, according to Dutches, treated her like a Queen. Shanice's man found out that she was fuckin' with another nigga and bugged the fuck out. Dude rolled up on Neecy and her side piece with 9mm and shot both of them dead. No arrest was made because the cops had no witnesses and no one came forward. The case went cold, but the streets will always talk. Apparently, Neecy's boyfriend, a nigga by the name of Asad, had a serious rep in the hood. He was high ranking member in a Bloods & Crips type of gang that ran dope, terrorized, and were well known to body anyone even suspected of snitching. Word on the streets was that Asad and his crew were seriously feared. Niggas were scared as fuck of them. Well, I was back now. The nigga murdered someone I cared about, and I was miles past a shook ass bitch nigga.

Dutches and I sat in the bar under the camouflage that we were a nigga and chick out for a night on the town. We smoked cigs as we sipped on drinks, keepin' our eye on Asad, a few members of his crew, and a couple of bad ass shorties as they occupied a booth. Turning up, doin' their thing. Poppin' bottles and all that hood fabulous shit. Asad looked to be about six-two, kind stocky, light brown skinned, with a fade and waves, rockin' corner boy attire. White T, jeans, fresh J's, and jewels. Son was sportin' a chain, a shiny watch, and from a distance I could see silver colored grills in his mouth. I watched him like a sniper. The nigga was a cocky, smiling, animated, and obnoxious ass motherfucker. He had kept his arm around this pretty as fuck Rican looking chick. Whispering in her ear, being subtly sexual with her as they got their drink on. Dutches and I waited until we saw the sign that he was about to bounce. That time came about at 1:40 am. When we saw that he was getting ready to leave, we exited first.

Asad led us from the bar to a Waffle House. He and that Rican chick went in and had themselves a meal as they got to know each other. From a shopping centers' parking lot across the street, Dutches and I watched them as they ate. Son and mami were doing all that late night-after the bar-I'm feeling you kind of shit. Talking as they sat across from one another, smiling at each other, and making it clear that they were fuckin' before the sun came up. From the Waffle House, we followed Asad's black Infiniti Q50 to a hotel. The nigga parked, he and shorty went inside, and we waited again. Two and a half hours later, Asad exited the hotel. By himself. He was on the phone as he climbed into his ride and drove off. We followed him across Newark to an apartment complex. As soon as the nigga parked, Dutches pulled in behind his ride stopped. I quickly hopped out of the SUV, gun in hand, and ran up on Asad as he climbing out of his car.

I grabbed the nigga by his throat and pressed my .45 into his chest. I stared into his eyes as I told the motherfucker that if I made a sound, I was going to empty my clip in heart. He was church mouse quiet as I began to move backwards. Taking him with me. I made him open the door to the backseat and we climbed in. Dutches casually pulled off and into the night we went. After ten minutes of silence, Asad tried to talk his way out of the situation. He offered me money and dope to live. He altered his attention from me to the back of Dutches head as he bargained for his life. The more I sat there with my burner resting on my thigh, staring at him and saying nothing; the more I could hear fear creeping into his voice as he kept on trying to negotiate his way out of this shit. I shut him the fuck up by raising my .45, placing the barrel against his cheek, and turning his head forward as I quietly ordered him not to say another fuckin' word!

Dutches waited in the SUV while Asad and I went for a little night time stroll. Into a closed construction site. It was the perfect spot. Dark, quiet, and isolated. They were building an apartment complex and all that was up was the empty frame of buildings. Bulldozers and shit were all over the place. It was going to be day light soon, so once I got Asad deep into the site, I ordered him to stop walking. I moved around him, aimed my gun at his face, and revealed to him why he was here. The second I informed him that Shanice was like a sister to me and I was here to get even for what he did to her; the nigga went from thug to pussy nigga in the blink of an eye. Son started coppin' pleas with tears forming his eyes as he apologized. Begged for his life. Offered all the cash he had with a promise of more if I didn't kill him. The motherfucker had tears rolling down his cheeks as he pleaded for me not to do him like this. I was both amused and disgusted by his bitch ass performance. Which I let go on for a minute or so before I closed the curtain on it.

POP!! I put a hot one in the motherfucker. Right under his left eye. Asad dropped to the dirt and started twitching like a fish as I put two more rounds in his cranium and he stopped floppin' around as I walked away. Dutches handed me a half smoked blunt as I climbed into the SUV and she pulled off. We got rid of the gun in a river a few miles away before heading back to Philly. Sis and I first stopped by my spot to pack some shit, then by hers, and last, we dropped by the storage garage. We packed a bunch of cash into two suit cases, along with a nice load of guns and ammo. We rolled out in a clean vehicle, stopped for some breakfast, filled up the gas tank, and then hit the highway. Dutches and I decided to blaze a new path in our quest for money and the privilege to do whatever the fuck we wanted to do. No more running with a bunch of niggas, no more drug empires, or any of that typical Kingpin-Gangster bullshit. We were done with that. It was about living the life of a real outlaw. Now that I handled that personal shit with Asad, it was back to it.

Back to business.

CHAPTER FOURTEEN

*"You can be a King or a Street Sweeper, but everyone
dances with the Grim Reaper."*

-Robert Alton Harris

O ur first stop was New York City. Before we got to work, first things first. We rented a nice sized, furnished, two-bedroom apartment in St. Albans Queens from a Haitian couple. They were all formal and nosey until we put up six months rent, plus an extra thousand in cash to dispense with all the bullshit. They were quick to give Dutchie the keys when she whipped out that brick of Ben Franklins. Once our spot set up, we got busy. Our plan was simple. Find a major drug trafficker on the streets, hit em', take their shit, flip it, and then like Casper; turn into Ghosts. Though I was born in NYC and I'm native New Yorker, I didn't really know the borough's like that. Dutches and I spent a little over two weeks doing a lot of driving around the five boroughs, riding the subway, studying maps, and hopping on city buses to get familiar with the Big Apple. We also had a little fun in between.

Though I'm an unapologetic thug & criminal, life is still about living. Dutches was the same way. We both lived our best lives outside of what we do. My partner and I loved fire weed, sip quality liquor, eat good food, fresh clothing, hot sneakers, comfortable beds, and lit sexual satisfaction. In the five years I was locked up, D discovered her sexual nature and appetite. She fucked with men and women, but didn't even entertain the idea of an actual relationship. She didn't have that kind of love in her to give to another motherfucker. All she offered a nigga or chick was some interesting convo and fire sex. That's it. As we got to know New York City better, we also did our thing. Hit the bars and clubs. Every time we went out, D had no issue baggin' a horny ass dude or chick to take to a hotel room for a night of fun. I didn't have that problem neither. Females were on my dick no matter where we went. Dutches and I would even pull one-night stands together. She'd bag a playmate, I did the same, we hit the telly, and when we were finished fuckin' & suckin' in our rooms, we'd bounce on the motherfuckers that we got our nut off with.

The fun and games didn't deter us from our mission though. Being that we were staying in Queens, it was logical that we didn't target anyone or do any dirt in the borough. I had too much respect for Brooklyn to hit a nigga there, and on instinct, I wanted to make our flip in the Bronx. So, that left Manhattan for us to strike in. Harlem to be specific. D and I began cruising through Harlem World, using cash to dope fiends and hood rats as an incentive to give us the low on the niggas banking serious money in their hood. After a week of buying information on big names, we picked our mark. A Dominican crew run by a motherfucker known on the streets as Cruz. Full name: Marcos Eduardo Cruz. Son was 28, a life long hustler, a chick magnet, word was that papi's outfit was deep, but not made of wolves. His set was comprised of a few soldiers, but mostly motherfuckers that were more about making money. Not shedding blood. The perfect target for us.

While I played the eyes in the shadows, Dutches went into the valley by herself. As someone else. She went out and changed her hairstyle & color, got her nails done, bought a new & different kind of wardrobe, and then began leaving her scent for Cruz to get a whiff of. I did some research on son and found out that though he was Dominican, dude loved the sista's. Specifically, chocolate sista's with juicy asses. D was just right for him. It took two weeks for her pop on Cruz's radar. She pretended to move into the area by renting a furnished studio apartment in Harlem, she hit the stores, and every Friday and Saturday night, she showed up at the club that Cruz was known to drop by. The first weekend, he was a no show. The same as the following Friday night. But at 10:40 pm on the next Saturday, he walked into Sapphire. A hot spot night club on East 58th. D texted me as soon as she spotted Cruz rolling in with three members of his crew. Sis knew him the moment she laid eyes on him.

Son didn't have any kind of social media, so we didn't have a face to put to the name at first. We identified the motherfucker a different way. The modern way. Dutches got on her phone and did an internet search on him to see if he had a mugshot out there. Indeed, he did. Cruz was arrested two years ago for domestic violence against his baby mom and his booking photo was uploaded to a mugshot website linked to the NYPD. D followed the links until she found family members of Cruz that did have social media pages. A couple of his aunts, cousins, and his sister. The mugshot was from two years before, but on his sisters' Facebook, we found recent pics of his ass. One was taken only days before we found it. That's the one Dutches downloaded to mark him when he showed up at the club. Once she texted me that she had eyes on him, I waited for her to let me know that she was in. The next time she texted me was at 11:33 pm. A simple thumbs up emoji. I grinned as I started the engine to our New York vehicle, a Nissan Pathfinder, and pulled off. I cruised past the line in front of the club and was on my way.

When Dutches entered out third floor apartment in St. Alban's, it was almost five in the morning. I was still up, chillin' in the living room. Feet up on the table, .40 caliber Glock next to my feet, ashtray on the couch next to me, lit cigarette between my fingers as I played Call of Duty on our PS4. That's all I had been doing since I got back. I smoked and shot it out on Modern Warfare 3. This shit was lit as fuck! D came in with two orders of 18-hot wings, fries, and Pepsi. After changing out of her club outfit and into a pair of sweats and a T, she joined me in the living room. Ma picked up a blunt I had rolled for her, while I paused my game to dig into my wings. As I ate, she toked her L while filling me in on our target. Cruz was already walking into the honey she was out to trap him in. From the second he laid eyes on her at the club, he was on her. Sat next to her at the bar, bought drinks for her, and she smoothly drew him in by being flirtatious, but still reserved. D was getting down on her wings as she told me that Cruz definitely wanted a taste of her pussy. She had his number and made him a promise to hit him up in the near future.

That near future was two days later. When Cruz picked up Dutches at her Harlem studio apartment in a silver Benz. On his Rico Suave shit. D snuck a pic of him and sent it to me. Son showed up with a fresh cut, a straight razor shave, and his outfit was GQ. Black suit with a starched & pressed powder blue shirt, and no tie. I didn't know what kind of shoes he was rockin', nor did I give a fuck. Son took Dutches to dinner at an Italian restaurant, then they went for a stroll in one of the safe areas of Central Park. After a romantic horse & carriage ride, they ended date night at low key jazz themed type of lounge. Dutchie texted me a winking-smiling face emoji at 1:39 am. I didn't respond back. I simply put my phone back on the coffee table and resumed my online game of Madden. D's text was the sign that Cruz was about to get stuck in her honey trap. She was about to fuck his brains out and judging how the niggas & chicks she fucked acted after they got a taste of her; Cruz was about to get hit with the poison.

Dutches unlocked the door and came in a little after one in the afternoon.

I had only been up for like twenty minutes. She took a shower, threw on something comfortable, we sparked up a breakfast blunt, and instead of rehashing her night with Cruz, we smoked and ate big ass bowls of cereal while watching episodes of The Soprano's through HBO On-Demand. D fell asleep on the other end of the couch after an episode and a half. I kept on watching while ignoring her cellphone on the table. She got two calls and at six texts in the few hours that she was out. When she got up, she sent replies back to Cruz. Whom the calls and texts were from. They did the chit chat thing for a while, then son told her that he wanted to see her that night. D declined. Telling him that she had something to do and wasn't available. Cruz then asked her about the next night. Dutches looked at me and grinned. Before agreeing to meet up with him tomorrow night. I didn't say a woed, but I did flash a smirk at her. She had him. All in her web.

****

Twelve days, three dates, and some volcanic level sex had a so-called rising dope dealer falling the fuck in love. Dutches had Cruz wide open like Julio Jones. By the 10th day of their little affair, he had no idea that a stalker was on his ass. Early on the morning of day ten, as he drove away from D's studio, I was right on his heels. Following him in the Pathfinder. He led me to the projects where his 3rd baby mama lived. I guess he went in to get some sleep, because he arrived at 7 am, but didn't come back out until after two pm. I left and returned every 90 minutes just to put eyes on his car. At twenty after two, I watched him exit his BM's building and roll out. I shadowed him to another chicks' crib, then to a bodega, and then to a Brownstone. I was on him all day long and I took a bunch of pictures of everywhere he went and of every single person he met with. Three days of this and I pretty much figured out his routine and his operation. Dutches and I mapped out our plan, made the necessary arrangements, and then pulled the trigger on our target.

D surprised Cruz with a special night. She reserved a room for them in a Honeymoon suite at the Hilton. As she wined, dined, and made sweet love to him; I was handling my end. Securing the means of our leverage to guarantee one-hundred percent compliance. I quietly got it done and then waited until exactly midnight before I called Dutches. When she answered, I uttered the code to put her in play. Game time. She hung up and my wait was only three minutes before my phone screen lit up and started vibrating. I answered the video call and Cruz's bloody nosed face was staring at me. I could see the barrel of Dutches Glock to the side of his head as I told him how this shit was going to play out. First, he was going to clean himself up, then he was going to get dressed and leave the hotel. From there, he was going to bag up all of his cash, then collect his money on the street and bagged that too. Along the way, he was going to contact his people and have them bring him every bit of product he has. Son stared at the phone as I informed him that I knew he was sitting on a lot of dope and I wanted his entire inventory. Once he did what I told him to do, he was to text D, and she'll give him a location for the drop.

To make him understand how fuckin' serious we were, I climbed out of the Pathfinder. Which was parked in a darkness behind a vacant building in the Bronx. I walked to the back and opened the hatch. I switched my phones flashlight on and showed him what was inside. His mother, sister, baby mom, and his five-year old daughter. His moms and sister had their hands duct taped with a strip over their mouth, but I didn't tape up his BM. She held her sleeping daughter, but the look on the women's faces were all the same. Silently terrified and tear streaked. I let the camera linger on them for about ten seconds, then I switched off the flashlight, closed the hatch, put the camera back on me and told Cruz that he had until five am to get it done. If he fucked up, went to the cops, or tried to rally his crew to pull some Marine Corps shit; he had the money to buy four coffins. Then I ended the call before taking out my cigarettes and lighter.

Cruz must have moved at the speed of the Flash. Because he texted Dutches at 3:55 am. Telling her that he was ready with the money and product. Ma hit my phone and put me on notice. She then hit Cruz and told him where to go. At 4:47 am, I watched him from the shadows near the same building I was at most of the night. He slow rolled to a stop in front of the building. I stayed in the darkness near the trees and chain link fence, watching him take several gym bags out of the trunk. From behind him, an old Toyota Camry with the lights out slowly pulled in. Cruz turned to face it as the door opened. Dutches calmly walked up to him and with no hesitation, raised her Glock and popped him. Once. In the forehead. That was my cue. I emerged from the shadows, making my way towards Cruz's ride while Dutches jogged away. To cut his women and child loose. By the time she ran back around the building, I was behind the wheel and our score was in the trunk of her Camry. She hopped in, I hit a U-turn, and drove away.

First, we transitioned vehicles. Dutches and I moved the four gym bags from the trunk of the Camry to our new ride. A dark green

Excursion. The gym bags joined the rest of our shit in the back. After dousing the inside of the Camry with gasoline, we lit it up and bounced. At a motel, D and I checked out the product. We had three kilos of coke, a kilo and a half of heroin, and nine pounds of high-grade weed. We shaved off two pounds of the bud for ourselves, then texted a number that I saved in my phone. Informing the nigga on the other end of how much product I had and how much I wanted for it. I received a text agreeing to my price and we set a meet for one hour, along with a location, and then we departed from the motel. Dutches and I made a quick stop by McDonalds, ate in the parking lot, then made our way to the meeting location. A bar in the Bronx.

In the back of the bar, in the kitchen area, I handed off the gym bags, a nigga with dreads handed me a pouch with the money, and we verified that neither of us was being played. Son eye checked the product, I did a quick scan of the money, all was good, and we dapped each other before going our separate ways. A block away, I climbed into the Excursion and Dutches pulled off. We immediately left New York City. Heading south. With $285,000 in cash. $200,000 came from Cruz and the 85K came from the dread in the BX. Son came up. Four and half kilos of dope and seven pounds of top-grade bud for 85K. Yeah, it was his lucky day for sure. D and I drove back to Philly, got some sleep at her place, and by that evening, we were mobile again. On the highway heading for Georgia. We were going to have some fun, relax for a minute, then find a big time Atlanta hustler to grip & clip. That was what we do now. Run & Gun. Take what we want, from whomever had the misfortune of crossing our path.

****

We hit Atlanta, Houston, Tulsa, St. Louis, Kansas City, Chicago, and Indianapolis. Dutches and I robbed dope dealers and sold their shit to other dope dealers. We bar hopped, went clubbin', fucked, dined on top shelf food, hit up amusement parks, and had mad fun when we weren't on the job. Sis and I were smooth though. We planned all of our hits thoroughly, always had a backup plan, studied our targets, and cleaned up our tracks before ghosting the city. D and I also left a long line of broken hearts behind us. Which neither of us gave a fuck about. We cared about no one except for each other. I didn't expect to happen, and neither did Dutches, but while we were in Texas; we started fuckin'. One night we were smokin' and playing video games, then before we knew it, we were kissing on the couch. Then, we fucked. And on everything, it was best sex I ever had. Ma said the same thing. It became clear that we were going to keep doing it, but neither of us felt like we had to be all lovey-dovey about it.

Sex was now cool with us. Traditional love was not. Neither was having kids. Or getting married. We decided to always use protection after the first time, but now that we were fuckin', life became a bit more fun for us. D and I began having wild ass threesomes, often sharing that chicks that we pulled individually. There was a powerful form of love between us, but not like normal people. Neither of us said "I love you", we didn't cuddle, do any boo lovin', and if we slept in the same bed; it wasn't because of any romantic shit. We were tired from being high and fuckin' each other senseless. Dutches and I weren't intimately connected soul mates. We were violently unified kindred spirits. Mirror images of each other, Our energy was exactly the same. Aggressive, ruthless, and disconnected from normative society. D and I were outlaws. Werewolves in the skin of thugs, and the only love we possessed was for each other. We were the only friend, lover, partner, and blood we needed in this world. She and I were the only person on earth that we were loyal to. Incapable of hurting. Or betraying.

After almost a year of blazing a trail across America, Dutches and I took a break. We returned to Philly with ton of cash and our first priority was to secure our money. Half remained in physical currency that we stashed in storage and a few safety deposit boxes, while the rest was converted. D and I searched around until we found the right kind of criminal to wash our money. An Italian dope trafficker in South Philly played middle man to a Jewish defense attorney. We paid the Italiano 20K for the intro to the lawyer and Mr. Abraham Goldman's fee for the connection to his services cost us 50 G's. Dutches and I delivered $450,000 to Goldman at his office. A week later, he called us back to his firm for a private meet. With himself and a criminal minded financial consultant-accountant. A smooth looking brother by the name of Derek Walker. They provided us with two Platinum level bank cards, access codes to our new Manhattan based account, and an overview of our 400K on Goldman's laptop. Walker broke it down to us how he laundered our money.

The 50K that was sliced from the 400 bought us entrance into the world of legitimate currency in New York. Our cash was delivered to his contact in the Big Apple, 50 thousand paved the way, and his guy washed our money through several cash heavy businesses. Once the hard cash was absorbed into the legit cash flow, the owners wired the electronic returns back to Walker's guy on Wall Street. Who then transferred our $400,000 to a Chase Manhattan account set up by Walker and his dude in New York. Dutches and I shook hands with Goldman and Walker before leaving the law firm and going on with our life. A few weeks went by, and for the most part, D and I stayed indoors. We did lot of weed smokin', TV-movie watching, gaming, fuckin', and sleeping. It wasn't out of boredom that kept us in the crib. We just didn't feel the need, or have the desire to be out among regular society. D and I were rebels amongst the law-abiding population and it showed.

When we were out and about shopping, we just wanted to spend money. Buy new shit, relax, and do relatively normal shit. However, there were too many punk ass sheep in this world that believed that they were cold- hearted wolves. Niggas on that ice grill tough guy shit, and chicks on that ready to ride-baddest bitch on the block shit. Shit talkers that thought they were invincible. Coward motherfuckers that acted like they wanted that smoke. Dutches and I paid people no mind when we were out and about. We did us and were willing to let motherfuckers do them. Yet, both males and females wanted to tempt the beast with us. Stick their hands in the Lion's cage. At the mall on day, a nigga in Foot Locker kept giving me the ice grill. I guess I was taking too long looking at the new J's. I thought nothing of the nigga no until he got too close for comfort and passively, but still aggressively inquired if I was done? Without looking at son, I kept checking out the sneaker as I quietly informed him that I'll be done in a minute.

Dude decided to violate my personal space though. By reaching his arm across me, close to my face, to pick up a Jordan shoe on the shelf above me. I simply placed the sneaker I was holding back on the shelf, then humbled son the fuck up. I turned, gripped him up by his jaw and the top of his throat, looked him dead in the eyes, and calmly asked him did we have a fuckin' problem? Dude quickly turned into bitch. Though we were about the same height, I was about sixty pounds heavier, far more stockier, and he knew that from the power in my grip on his face that he'd get that ass brutalized if we squared up. Son looked deep into my cold eyes and started stuttering as he timidly replied that we didn't have a problem and apologized. I gave him the wolf stare for a few more seconds, nodded my head, let him go, and went back to checking out the new J's. I ended up buying two pairs in different colors. Dutches was sitting nearby the whole time, but never looked up from her phone as she sat with her legs crossed waiting for me.

A few days later, I was with her at the hair salon. We were out for a day to do our thing. I had gotten my hair cut next door while she waited to get her hair done. As normal, while in the salon, Dutches was the only silent chick in attendance. She was quiet among all the laughter, jokes, gossip, music, and shit talking. She either browsed the internet on her cell or read a magazine. By the time I was done getting my cut, I went inside the salon to wait for her. Females always gave me the eye when I was in there. Sometimes I entertained it and got their number, but most times I didn't. I wasn't moved by how sexy a chick looked or fat her ass was. My focus was a females' vibe and most women did absolutely nothing for me, so half of the time I acted like I didn't even see them. Normally, when D was done, it was simple. She paid her stylist, tipped her, then we left. This day though, the neighborhoods' bad bitch decided to let it be known that this was her territory.

On our way out of the salon, a raspy female voice called out, *"It's about time that bougie bitch got her nut ass the fuck out of here!"* A chorus of laughter erupted as Dutches and I stopped in the doorway. D looked back into the salon and handed her purse to me without looking. I took it and we let the door close as we went back inside. D looked around the salon, addressing everyone in attendance, calmly inquiring as to who it was that had something to say to her? I stood with my hands crossed in front of me with her purse, just as quiet as the salon now was. The only sound was the TV on the wall until the same raspy voice spoke up again. A caramel brown skinned chick with short hair stood up and replied with aggression that she said what she said, and what??! Dutches and the thick and hostile chick approached one another; but only the instigator was still talking recklessly. Getting hype, informing D that she didn't know who she was fuckin' with, she better ask about her, and yada, yada, yada.

Dutches finally responded just as they were about to be face-to-face. Ol'girl was in mid rant when she was sucker punched in the chest. Right between her titties. Hard AF! Ma's eyes bugged open and she clutched her chest as all the air in her lungs came rushing out. D then socked shorty in her nose with a crisp left, and followed it up with a nasty ass right hook to the jaw. Dropping Ma to the salon floor. D then turned and strolled past every chick in the salon that was stone silent. Eyes and heads following her as she walked up to me and retrieved her purse as we bounced. After that, we just decided to say fuck the bullshit and keep our distance. To avoid a confrontation with the police and to rid ourselves of the annoyance of punk ass motherfuckers.

We chilled for almost two months and were planning our next wave of licks. Our path was Detroit, Phoenix, Vegas, Los Angeles, and then come back across the country to hit Miami before taking a long vacation. D wanted to go to the islands, so that was the plan. Five more cities, wash more dirty money into legit cash, then disappear for a while. I liked the idea of fun in the sun in the Caribbean for a long get away. Just as we were getting set up, life threw a couple of curve balls at us. The first was a phone call from Goldman and Walker. They wanted to see Dutches and I on a matter that had nothing to do with laundering our money. We met with them, and what they offered was too good to pass up. They offered us a job that was right up our alley and we agreed to do it. So, we put our rampage towards the west coast on hold. The second curve ball happened when I was at a gas station in Southwest Philly and a chick called out my name from behind. When I turned around, a blast from the past hit me square in the face.

It was her.

CHAPTER FIFTEEN

"There is no such thing as coincidence.
Everything in life means something."

A'liyah's smile was just as pretty as it was when we were young. Her car was parked behind mine at the gas pump. After she called out my name and I turned around, she damn near ran at me. With no shame, she dashed into my arms. Wrapping hers around my neck. On impulse that was out of my control, I hugged her back. Her mouth was close to my ear and she kept whispering, *"Oh my God!"* I had long gotten over her, but from deep down inside, the love I had for my first started rising up again. A'liyah and I held each other for a while, then she stepped back holding on to my arms as I held her by her waist. Our eyes were locked and that hypnotizing smile was still on her face. It's been a little more than ten years since we last seen one another. Ma looked me up and down, liking what she saw of me as a man. She studied me as I did the same to her.

I could tell that she was feeling my beard and build, just as I was loving how she transformed as well. Liyah looked good! Black hair long & silky, her face had matured into the vision of a dark-skinned ebony queen, and though she only grew about two inches in height; her body drastically changed. Ma was pure thickness. She was all chest, hips, ass, and thighs. Coca cola bottle shaped, she worked out, and her Hershey Bar brown skin was smooth and flawless. A'liyah moved her hands down to mine, held them, and without unlocking her eyes from my own, asked me how have I been?? Unable to break eye contact with her, I gave her a vague response to how my life has been since we broke up. She flashed me that female smirk that told me she knew I was being vague, but she didn't confront it. Instead, she asked me was I busy? Would I liked to get something to eat with her and catch up on the last ten years?

She still liked Applebee's. We sat in a corner booth, and over an early dinner we caught up. A'liyah did most of the talking. She told me about her time in college, how her family were doing, earning her degree in business, and then moving to Chicago after graduation. Before she earned her Bachelor's, there was a job waiting for her in the Windy City. She told me that her professor had connections. Being that she was his favorite and brightest student, he did her a solid by calling in a favor with a friend of his. A'liyah spent five years in Chicago working first as an Administrative Personal Assistant for a corporate CEO, then she was transferred to the Strategy & Marketing Division as a team manager. Ma opened to me about her time in Chicago. She was there for seven years. She then let it go that she once had a husband. I asked her what happened with that, but she didn't answer right away. She looked away, stared off into the distance, and then focused on me again before she told me.

According to her, the motherfucker she married was a piece of shit. An arrogant, self-absorbed, a black fraternity-HBCU graduate dickhead. That cheated on her, played head games, and more than once put his hands on her. Though she couldn't see it, there was anger behind my eyes. It was fuckin' ironic that I, a thug, a street nigga, never did any of that shit to A'liyah. I never lied to her, cheated on her, or hit her. Yet, a straight-laced law-abiding citizen ass nigga did all of that to her. Liyah's eyes went from sad to happy again as she began to ask me something, but paused for a second as she changed directions and asked if I had a girlfriend? I replied, "Nah" as I shook my head. We held eyes again as she lightly bit the corner of her lip. I knew what that look meant. The same as it did when we were teenagers.

Liyah and I parted ways in the parking lot of Applebee's. We stood in between our vehicles and she held my hands low, looking into my eyes as she told me that it felt good to see me again. Now that I had her number, I better call her. I nodded my head as I returned her stare. For a minute, we just stood there staring at each other. I could tell that she wanted to kiss me, just as I knew she could tell that I wanted to kiss her. Unable to break eye contact with me, Liyah whispered, *"Call me, ok."* I nodded again as our hands unlocked and I opened the door of her car for her. I watched A'liyah drive off before climbing into my own ride. As I drove home, my mind was on memory lane. To the days when Liyah was my bae'. How she was the only trace beauty in my world. My only source of peace. The love in my life. To keep it real, there hasn't been anything beautiful or peaceful in my existence since she we broke up.

There was no reason to mention A'liyah to Dutches. Not that she would have been on any kind of jealous shit, but we didn't owe each other an explanation for shit. She didn't tell me everything about what she did when she was out and about solo, nor did I ask. It was vice versa and that's how we got down. When I arrived at the loft, D was smoking an L while playing PS4. I let her be until she finished her game and then got down to business. The job Goldman and Walker wanted us to do. The job we agreed to do. Hit certain players in a drug network on some Ninja shit. They wanted us to not only rob specific names on the list, but most of those motherfuckers were marked for death. At first, I wanted to decline. To be honest, what Goldman and Walker wanted sounded like it was above our pay grade, yo. The niggas they wanted us to hit were major players in the game. Some were street-hood level, more than a few weren't black, and a couple were seriously high risk. For a minute, it seemed to me that what they needed was a Denzel Washington in The Equalizer type of killer. A legit assassin. Dutches & I weren't strangers to the murder game, but what they wanted done felt like it was out of out league.

Goldman and Walker accepted our request to hold off for a day while we weighed our options. That was the day before. The lawyer and criminal money mover were waiting for our call. D and I spent a good hour & half talking about it together after spending a day thinking on it as individuals. Both of us spoke our mind, verbally sparring back & forth until we came to a conclusion. D & I were on the same page. Fuck it! Let's do it. It was a high risk-high payoff job. Living up to our predatory nature, as the true wolves we are, this job was a deer in the forest. Our next meal. I powered up our burner phone and called Walker. When he answered, I simply told him, "We're in." He told us to meet him in Goldman's office the next morning at 10 am. Then he ended the call and I powered the burner phone down. Dutches and I spent the rest of the day chillin'.

****

Our list had eight names on it, a specific order & manner to hit them in, and we were paid up front for the job. 250K to split two ways. That was $125,000 each. Dutches and I decided to go at the first target right away. Target #1 was a smooth operating dope boy in West Philly. Aaron Jamison was a former basketball player turned drug dealer and he was pushing both coke and weed in Philly and small towns outside the city. Son was paid out the ass, his name rang out in the streets, and he was sex addict type of nigga. AJ was one of those tall & handsome motherfuckers that loved pussy as much as he loved money. He had a two baby mama's and a long line of chicks that catered to his sexual need because he catered to their greed. We didn't know why Goldman & Walker wanted this dude robbed and clipped, nor did we care. His name was on the list, we were paid, and it was our job to cross his name out before moving on to the next one.

Just like many times before, Dutches lured a motherfucker to his end. She did her honey trap thing, the nigga took the bait, she drew him into a kill box, and I handled my part. Aaron Jamison thought that D was a high-class call girl. They met at a bar, it didn't take much for her to hook him, and 24-hours later, she arrived by cab at his apartment for their "date". Son really thought he was about slide dick up in a super bad ass chocolate toned call girl. Damn, yo. Pussy really is the most addictive drug on earth! He let D in at 12:05 am. She texted my phone at 12:25 am and I climbed out of my SUV. Parked behind his apartment building. D let me in and we got to work. Aaron woke up when I turned the cold water to the shower on. Not long after he opened his eyes, he froze in place. As he stared at me and the silenced 9mm in my latex gloved hands. He started bitchin' as I ordered him to stand up straight. He slowly did as I told him to, and once he was upright, I clapped him.

One shot to the face, to the left his nose, then four more to the chest. I left the shower on as his blood ran down the drain with the water. I joined Dutches in the bedroom as she on the bed next to the book bag full of money she had Aaron fill from his safe. After she ambushed him. I was unscrewing the silencer from my Glock as she was typing in text on Aaron's phone. The message was to his right-hand man. Issuing an order to be carried out in the next two hours. Once she received a response text telling Aaron that they were on it; we sanitized Aaron's apartment of D's presence and then bounced. Two hours later, I watched as Dutches walked up to a nigga in an old parking lot. He handed her the keys to the 2002 Corolla he climbed out of. As she climbed into the Toyota, he hopped into the shotgun seat of a Ford Expedition. D pulled off one way, the Ford in the opposite direction, and I drove off when both vehicles disappeared.

D and I met up at a closed Autobody garage in South Philly. Two dudes in expensive casual wear were waiting inside for us. One was Latino and the other was a brother. D handed off the book bag of cash as I opened the trunk and removed two Nike gym bags of dope from the trunk. I handed it to the brother and we watched as they both opened the bags. They checked the contents of them, then the brother looked at me. In a deep voice, he asked me was Mr. Jamison's insurance policy terminated? I nodded yeah and he nodded back. His Mexican partner stared at us with cold eyes as he handed the book in my direction as he nearly whispered, *"Mr. Goldman says this belongs to you."* I accepted the strap of the bag with a nod, he nodded in return, and the four of us exited the shop in two separate directions.

After stashing our money, Dutches informed me that she was going to blow off some steam. Meaning she was going to get some pussy. Or dick. She drove off into the early morning and I sat in my ride for a minute. Then I took out my phone and started typing a text to A'liyah. I asked her was she awake? Less than two minutes later, she replied yes. I hit call on her number. After small talk for a few minutes, I told her that I wanted to see her. Instead of saying yes, she gave me her address and told me that she'll see me soon. Liyah lived in the Wynnfield section of West Philly, which was one of the nicer and calmer parts of the city. Her house was nice too. She lived in one of those two-story stone homes with lots of front & back yard space, along with her own driveway and garage. I parked behind her silver Audi A6 and killed the engine. When I reached the door, before I could knock or ring the bell, she opened it up.

Liyah still took her time to get ready before I came to see her. She had combed her hair out and put on some lip gloss. Covering her thick and curvy frame was a tight white tank top and pink satin pajama pants. I caught a whiff of Chanel perfume, and she was barefoot. After inviting me in and closing the door, she told me to make myself at home. I sat down on her couch, looking up at her as she asked me would I want a drink? I nodded yeah and she moved off towards the kitchen. A few minutes later, she returned with a glass of what she knew I liked. Henny with two cubes of ice. For herself, she had a glass of white wine. Liyah sat down next me with her legs underneath her as we took our first sips. We were silent for a minute, then she moved her hair away from her face, licked her lips, then she spoke. *"I need to tell you something, Sha."* I gave her my full attention as she told me that she hasn't stopped thinking about me since we broke up. That I was always on her mind. Even when she married another dude.

The sun was coming up as she moaned. A'liyah had her legs around my waist, her nails in my back, and her expression was twisted in pleasure as I slowly stroked deep inside of her. We were face to face and her moans were the only sound in her bedroom. She bit her lip as she stared into my eyes with an expression of painful pleasure. Ma was so fuckin' wet & warm that I started stroking harder and deeper. As her moaning grew louder, she closed her eyes and turned her head to the side. Moving her hips to meet my strokes. Nails still in the skin of my back. As she moved her knees up higher, which lifted her pelvis up; I took a fistful of her hair and pulled her head back. Liyah kept her eyes closed with her head back and to the side, damn near screaming as I started goin' in on her. She had me growling like a bear and beads of sweat were drippin' off of my forehead and rolling down my back as I stroked. Ma gripped her sheet with one hand and my forearm with the other, repeatedly screaming that she was cumming as her body started trembling.

Just like back in the day, when she came, she came hard as fuck. Liyah was loud, she gripped me tight as a motherfucker, her eyes fluttered, and her legs locked up on her. I kept on stroking, pushing her legs open by her thighs, swimming in how wet her pussy was, and as she was pushing with one hand, trying to fight me; I busted a super big and loud nut. Growling like a Lion as I lost my grip on her hair and she pulled me down to her. My face in the crook of her neck and shoulder, her hand locked on the bac of my head. Moaning in my ear. When we were done, we stayed right where we were. My dick still inside of her, my face in her neck, our bodies all tangled up, and both of us sweating. Out of breath. Breathing hard. Liyah re-positioned herself underneath me and held me close to her. In my ear, she whispered for me not to move. To stay where I was and let her hold me. Like we used to do. I lied there on top of her and she caressed the back of my head and my back. Rubbing her cheek against my beard.

A'liyah and I ended up falling asleep all hugged up and shit. It had been a long time since I did that with a female. Dutches and I slept together all the time, but not like this. My ride or die partner was not at all the romantic type. After we fucked, she took her side of the bed and went to sleep. We Sometimes slept face-to-face, but mostly back-to-back. Never on some cuddled up, in love shit. A'liyah was different. Her showing back up in my world tapped into a part of my heart I had thought was buried. She was the only chick I ever genuinely loved. The night before, after she told me that she hadn't stopped thinking about me after we broke up, Ma went on tell me that no dude she got with ever measured up to me. The men she dated and the one she married were polar opposites of everything I was. They were college educated, sophisticated, successful brothers that she believed was the right kind of man for her. They were. On the surface.

None of them made her feel the way I did. Young or not, when we were together, she knew that I loved her. She told me that she could see it in my eyes when I looked at her. Here it in my voice when I told her. And feel it when I touched her. When I kissed her. When I was inside her. Liyah sat next to me on her couch, looked me in my eyes with tears in hers as she told me that not one of the motherfuckers she let into her life after we went our separate ways even came close to loving her like me or made her feel the way I did. I studied her face as tears rolled down her cheeks and just nodded my head. Normally, I wasn't the one for all that emotional shit, but for Liyah, I was patient. Understanding. If there was a single soft spot in me, she was it. Before I knew it, she sat her drink on her coffee table, took mine and sat it next to hers, then climbed into my lap. Wrapped her arms around my neck and kissed me. That's where how we got the fire started. A'liyah was the only female that I felt something deeper within her kiss.

****

Our second hit was two targets for the price of one. A couple of Italian mafia wannabe's that built themselves one of the hottest night clubs in Philly. Angelo Peretti & Giovanni Ricci were lifelong friends that hailed from South Philadelphia and both of their families had low-key ties to the old mafia. Though Angelo and Gio came from Italian lineage and were raised in an Italian part of the city; they were deeply immersed in Black culture. The file on them from Goldman and Walker described them as being avid hip-hop fans, they drove vehicles normally driven by Black hustlers & thugs in the hood, both of them dressed Black, talk Black, and dated Black. The pictures in the file showed them with Black women, but it was clear that the chicks they fucked with had to pass the paper bag test. Every female in the photos were either really light skinned or as dark as caramel. The Italian boys weren't into cocoa colored ebony sista's. They both liked the sweetness of blackberries, but not if the juice was too dark. Go fuckin' figure.

These two Gucci and Versace wearing motherfuckers were perfect for a honey trap lure to a body bag given their lust for women. However, they wouldn't go for Dutches lethally sweet self, and we didn't feel like going through the motions of recruiting some super sexy light skinned chick to bait & clip their ass. Besides, Goldman & Walker wanted these dudes hit publicly. D and I discussed how to clap these motherfuckers over Chinese at our spot and decided on an old school classic method. We set everything up and then separated. All day long, we stalked Angelo and Giovanni. Ma and I stayed in touch by text and when darkness fell over the city, we two wolves were amongst the shadows. I sat in an old busted Ford Focus I paid a junkie to use. Parked two blocks down from the Italian boys nightclub. There were mad people outside and the Friday Philly night life was lit. Dutches was on point and I was waiting for her signal. That wait was damn near all night. When the club shut down, D left with the crowd and climbed into the car with me. By the time she came out, I was in the passenger seat.

It wasn't until almost five am until Angelo and Giovanni were leaving their establishment. D got the text from her source inside the club that our targets were heading out and started the car. As she pulled off, I pulled my ski mask down and readied my firearm for the night. We made it around the building in time to see our targets standing behind Angelo's Benz and the two of them were talking. The lights in our ride were out as we slowly turned into the rear parking lot. Dutches sped up a little. As soon as the car was parallel to our targets, she stopped and I was up & out the whip. Angelo and Giovanni were just beginning their ebonics heavy rant of annoyance as I quickly rounded the front of the Focus and took aim on them. With an Ingram Mac-10 Submachine gun. They were frozen in shock as I opened up on their ass. Shattering the night with automatic gunfire. I swept the Mac back & forth, making them fugazi motherfuckers do the death dance and flail their arms as I hosed them down with a tornado of .45 caliber ACP rounds. I lit their asses up and got the fuck out of there. The second I was back in the car, D sped off.

We sanitized everything and got some sleep. The murders were all over the news when we woke up later on. D and I watched for all of five minutes before changing the channel and going on with our day. I got a text from A'liyah around seven that night. Dutches and I were kicked back and watching a movie, marinating our high with empty takeout cartons on the table. Liyah wanted me to come over, so I texted her back telling her that I was on my way. An hour later, my ex-shorty and I were chillin' on her back porch. She was sitting on my lap with a glass of wine, kissing me all passionate and shit as I palmed her ass cheek through her jeans. Its been almost a week since she seen me. Just like when we were together, Ma showered me with affection to show that she missed me. Lots of kissing, cuddling on me, touching my cheeks, running her fingers through my beard, and a smile on her face that couldn't be erased.

A few hours later, Liyah and I were naked on her bed. She was asleep with her head on my chest and her arm across my body. Hand on my face and her leg over mine. We fucked for almost two hours, going at it over and over until she had nothing left and passed out on me. Liyah really missed a nigga all these years. She was like a Lion in heat. To keep it a buck, I missed her too. Just as much as she missed me. Ever since we broke up, she was the one thing I couldn't erase from my mind. Like my parents' death. A'liyah was etched in my mind & heart. Neither of us have said I love you again, but we didn't have to. She never stopped loving me. I never stopped loving her. Liyah was the only person on earth that I truly loved like this. My love for D was different. That was my kindred wolf spirit. I'd kill for Dutches, but I'd die for A'liyah. The fact that she had suddenly reappeared in my life, out of nowhere, it couldn't have been chance or coincidence that I was at that gas station when she came back into my life. She had a nigga thinking.

Maybe after we complete the Goldman & Walker's kill list, it was time to get out of this bullshit. Maybe A'liyah was a sign to walk away and live differently. Before that night Liyah re-appeared in my world, I was content to be what I am. A thug. An outlaw. A predator. I was bred, trained, and conditioned for a life of crime. I am what I am, and I do what I do. I had no regrets about that shit. But now, with A'liyah back in my life and the love she still has for me got me thinking.

Maybe I can be different type of person in this world.

Maybe.

CHAPTER SIXTEEN

"It is double pleasure to deceive the deceiver"

-Niccolo Machiavelli

Target number four was a wolf in sheep's clothing. On the surface, son was a well known and respected North Philly hip-hop legend in the making. Once upon a time, he was a local football star that did his thing at Rutgers, but his name wasn't called on the night of the NFL draft. Rahim Johnson Jr came home from college, his football days over, and decided to make it in the music industry. It was too late in the game to learn how to rap, so he went a different route. The drug trafficking route. He hustled hard as a motherfucker with his cousins and niggas that he knew from his hood. With the proceeds of their dope dealing, they built Heavy Hittaz Productions. Rahim and his people established their first studio in a row house, developed a roster of local rhyme spitter's, cut a bangin' mixtape of niggas freestyling over well-known artist's beats, and with money from coke & weed being sold on the streets, The Hittaz became an underground hip-hop powerhouse.

Eight years later, as a strictly independent label, Rah Jay was a mogul in his own right. His artists put out quality mixtapes, solo albums, and hard-hitting compilations. Rahim's company turned down major deals from corporations out of New York City to own their shit and put out the type of hip-hop music that the hood loved to bang. They didn't care about awards, the Billboard charts, or sharing their wealth & success with anyone. For nearly a decade, Heavy Hittaz has owned and dominated the independent hip-hop scene on the East Coast and in many cities in the Midwest. Even niggas in Cali and down south fucked with their shit. Both with their music and via drug trafficking, Rahim Johnson was a rich ass motherfucker. The streets hailed him as the Jay-Z of Philadelphia. We didn't know why Goldman and Walker wanted son hit, nor did we concern ourselves with their reason why. His name was on the list, so it was our job to get it done. Simple as that. Dutches and I started stalking son, and it didn't take long to see that murkin' Rahim was not going to be a fuckin cake walk.

The nigga was surrounded by three goons at all times. Round the clock protection like he was the president or some shit. Dutches and I alternated running surveillance on son for three days straight and not once was the motherfucker without his shooters. With the way that Goldman & Walker wanted Rahim hit, we couldn't just roll up and let son and his goons catch a hailstorm of lead like I did the Italians. They wanted that move done in public. With Rahim, they wanted his murder to be violent, but committed in silence. With an additional measure thrown in. We had to figure out a way to get it done. Dutches hit that shit on the nose as we discussed how to make it happen. We weren't going to be able to touch the nigga by going through the front door on this one. The only option was to creep through the back door.

We shifted focus from Rahim to the niggas around him. Just liked I learned in school, the Roman Empire was destroyed from within. Dutches and I studied Rahim's goons and immediately crossed them off the list. All of those motherfuckers had the look. Loyal, fierce ass soldiers that were true believers in the code. Death Before Dishonor. We were cut from the same cloth, so I knew none of those niggas would turn. We bypassed sons' family too. Going at civilians to get to your target is always on the high side of risk of discovery and shit going bad. Quickly. Plus, we had to stay in the shadows on this move. That left us with one final option. Rahim's little secret. His side bitch. Son was fuckin' a sexy AF high maintenance chick that resided in a very expensive studio apartment in Center City. Rahim had a bad wife, they had three kids together, and though he played up that King in love with his Queen shit; dude had a girlfriend in the cut.

Shorty was bi-racial. Half black, half Rican. Just turned 24, an aspiring model, a college dropout, no kids, and Rah Jay was her sugar daddy. He kept her in a nice apartment, she drove a Mercedes CLK, Ma's attire was nothing but top of the line designer, and when she did all of that Diva shit. Daily session at the gym, reserved appointments at the hair & nail salon, and she had a crew of other beautiful chicks with money that she socialized with. Miss Davina Reyes was our way in. Dutches instincts led her to that conclusion and my partner went undercover to get it done. It took her four days, but she achieved what she set out to do. Turn Davina and get her to agree to shorten the kill chain on her benefactor. D was doing her with a chick she was feeling and I was with A'liyah when we got the signal that Rahim was heading for the kill box. Dutches hit my phone after receiving a text from Davina. Son was enroute to spend time with her. Liyah was asleep on the couch when I left. D and I linked up and rolled in one car as we went off into the night to carry out our mission.

A little over two hours later, Dutches and I waited with calm patience as Rahim took a shower. A few minutes before, Davina let us into her place, and like ninja's, we quietly moved into position. Once Rahim and his side piece were done smokin', drinkin', and fuckin'; after he was in the shower, she hit D's phone and we entered her building through the back door. Rahim entered Davina's bedroom, asking her something as he wrapped a long white towel around his waist. Only he froze where he stood and stopped talking when he saw what was in his side chicks' bedroom. Two people with black ski masks on, hands covered in latex gloves, and his girl lying on the bed with her wrists flex-cuffed together and duct tape over her mouth. Looking terrified. Dutches stood next to the bed with a silenced Glock 9mm to Davina's head. I held my suppressed burner low next to my leg as I told the nigga to come on. We ain't got all night, nigga. We on a schedule, yo.

D kept an eye on Davina as I got Rahim into character. Son and I went on a little trip to the kitchen and returned with a full bottle of liquor. Miss Reyes was a fan of Brandy. E&J to be specific. I made him pick up and carry the bottle. Once back in the bedroom, I made Rahim shit on the edge of the bed and start swiggin'. At my order, he guzzled a quarter of the bottle, then I made him stand up, and throw the bottle at the wall across the room. After it shattered, with my gun to his head, I whispered several instructions in his ear, then gave Dutches the signal. She started screaming and making crying noises, begging him to stop as she moved around the room breaking shit and Rahim joined her. He started barking at her. Both of them loud as fuck as she screamed *"I'm sorry!!"* and he hollered, *"Fuck you, bitch!!"* and a bunch of other shit. They kept it up as D cut Davina's flex cuff's off, gently removed the tape from her face, and I made Rahim shut the fuck up. Then I gave him something to wrap up this little act.

I made son snort coke off the dresser until he was completely fucked up and under my control. I moved the nigga to the center of the bedroom, and D handled her part. She had taken her silencer off of the Glock, moved to where Rahim was laid out, stood over him, looked at Davina sitting on the bed with a confused look on her pretty face, and with no hesitation, she clapped her. BOOM! One shot the chest, in her heart, dropped her back onto her bed. Dutches handed me the Glock and I placed it into Rahim's right hand. I pressed his fingers on the slide, grip, and trigger before I stood up and we made sure there was no trace of us in the bedroom. Then we became ghosts as we quietly left the building through the rear stairs. D and I were a few blocks away when a Philly PD squad car flew past us with it lights and siren going. Less than a minute later, two more raced by. Neither of us were nervous as we cruised off into the night.

After changing clothes, dumping our guns, and switching cars; it was on to the next job. Until this night, we were hitting our targets in isolated, separate waves. Now that Rahim was in the bag, #5 was given the green light. That was how Goldman & Walker wanted it done. Our fifth name on the list was a white dude named Sean Russell. An upper class, Ivy league educated, Philadelphia born-New York based money man. This rich, Republican ass motherfucker worked on Wall Street as a financial consultant and he handled investments for powerful people. This dude was living the true American dream. Mr. Russell wasn't married, he had no kids, he fucked with sexy ass, top shelf gold diggin' chicks, drove a platinum Audi R8 Spyder, and he resided in a half a million-dollar condo. Wall Street Sean was a coke snortin', champagne sippin', call girl fuckin', private jet flyin' pretty boy with a politician smile. Whose name was on a kill list for some reason. That's all that mattered to me and Dutches.

Unlike Rahim, we were going at Russell directly. Quietly, but right at his ass. D and I got into character, linked up with a white dude that was sent by Goldman, all of us went over the game plan, then we rolled out in one vehicle to get it done. We arrived at Russell's condo in a black Tahoe, climbed out, and the white dude led the way. He knocked on Mr. Sean's door like a cop until he answered. When the door opened, the Captain Wall Street was on his playboy shit. His normally well groomed and parted black hair was all fucked up, his eyes were red & glassy, he was shirtless, and only wearing a pair of black silk pajama pants. Playing our part, D and I silently stood back, allowing our subterfuge speak for us. My partner and I, along with our Caucasian roadie were on some real art of deception shit.

The white cat with us was about 40'something with a neat haircut, clean shaven face, and wearing a dark colored suit with a white shirt and a royal blue tie. Hanging from his neck on a ball chain in a black holder was a silver FBI badge. Dutches and I were in FBI shit too. The dark blue jacket, black Kevlar vest with big white FBI letters on the front, and both of had on black shirts, fatigue pants, and boots. We had one hand on our holstered guns like Federal security officers, while the "Special Agent" with us did all the talking. He identified himself as Agent Miller as he presented Sean with a real looking Federal warrant and calmly ordered him into his own spot. We followed them in and stood back as Miller handled business. As Sean read the warrant, he was informed that his name came up during the course of an FBI investigation in conjunction with the Department of Treasury. In regards to illegal trading activity and financial fraud related crimes.

Dude didn't argue or resist at all. He just went with the flow. Miller sent Dutches to escort Mr. Russell to his bedroom so that he could get dressed. Less than ten minutes later, we led our target to the Tahoe and he sat in the back with me as D drove off. The ride was quiet we took Russell to a dark and secluded area on the Jersey side of the Schuylkill river. Dutches parked the SUV in the closed industrial area close to a line of trailers. Sean looked around as Miller and D opened their doors. Son looked scared as fuck as he asked what was going on? I pulled my Glock 17 from the holster and ordered him to get the fuck out at the same time D opened his door. The motherfucker was too shook to move, so Ma had to pull him out. By his shirt collar, D made him walk. We stopped him in an open area and got him ready.

With his shoes off and shirt ripped open, I put on the last measure of his makeup. Dutches and Miller silently watched as I pummeled the white boy bloody, bruised, and damn near unconscious. With my latex gloves stained in Russell's blood, I pulled out a thick wad of hundred-dollar bills. As I removed the rubber band, making sure to stain the cash with his blood; D stepped up with a suppressor attached to her Glock. Sean was lying face down on the ground moaning as she put six shots in his back. I covered him with the cash and then we bounced. The white dude we knew as Miller dropped us off in a quiet neighborhood. Once he drove way, D and I climbed into our ride and went on our way. We got rid of everything before catching a cab, each of us carrying a large gym bag. To 30th Street Station. We claimed our reserved tickets for separate destinations. We split up without a word. Her heading for Florida, me on my way to New York City. Goldman told us to take a break before coming back to finish the list.

****

A'liyah joined me in NYC and we spent a week together. Going out, shopping, eating good, and re-building our foundation. Ma was mad happy to be spending time with me. On the real, I was too. She had that effect on me. No bullshit, I enjoyed seeing her smile, I liked having her close to me, and more and more I was thinking about stepping off the outlaw path I been on most of my life. When Liyah didn't occupy my attention or she was asleep; I kept an eye on the aftermath of our hits back in Philly. The picture became more as I read in between the lines. Aaron Jamison, Angelo Peretti, Giovanni Ricci, Rahim Johnson, and Sean Russell were all connected. The news reports didn't say it, there was nothing about it online, but when I went over the whole scenario in my mind; I saw the bigger picture. They were apart of a criminal conspiracy. Two major dope dealing niggas from the hood, two Italian boys with mafia family ties, and a Wall Street money guy. I came to the conclusion that they, along with the other names on the list were all apart of some kind of high-level organized crime network. That shit made sense.

Dutches was on the same page. When I ran my theory past her during a call, she agreed with me. It now felt like Goldman & Walker were cleaning house for someone. Mafia? Maybe. Drug Cartel? It was possible. We came to another conclusion that we were outsiders brought in to handle the dirty work because we weren't connected to anyone. Ghosts in the equation. D and I weren't worried about shit though. We figured that we were clean, only Goldman & Walker knew about us, that dude Miller didn't look like the snitchin' type, and if push came to shove, we had enough money and intellect to disappear. Dutches continued relaxing in Miami and I went on doing my thing in New York with A'liyah. Eight days after we hit Sean Russell, I got word from the lawyer. It was time to cross off the rest of the names on the kill list. However, Goldman wanted us to come to a meet before getting back to work. Hinting at paying us more money too.

A'liyah and I drove back to Philly in her car. I dropped her off at her spot and then headed for the meet. In a suite at the Ritz-Carlton Hotel. On instinct, I went to the meet solo. I advised Dutches to fall back on this one. She didn't trip either. Ma was that type. She knew that I was the lead wolf and played her part. I decided to dress down for this meet. Black sports jacket, white dress shirt, no tie, dark grey denim jeans, and black leather boots. I was strapped as always and other than my Driver's license, .45, and cash; I had my phone. When I arrived at the hotel, I walked past the front desk and hotel guests to the suite's elevator. I rode up to the 25th floor and got off. Walking into the Executive Luxury Suite. Walker greeted me with a handshake, before introducing me to three other dudes. A white guy that looked like a politician, a brother in a $4,000 three-piece suit, and a well-groomed Latino in a silk shirt with Versace shades on.

Though I accepted a drink, I wasn't going to take a single sip. I was hired to kill motherfuckers on some kind of silent, organized crime style assassination shit. I was put on as outside talent. Not an asset. At any time, these motherfuckers could see me as a loose end and clip my ass. If not by a bullet to the dome when I least expect it, the other way to do it was to assassinate my ass too. Poison in my drink while smiling in my face for example. So, a crystal glass of Remy with ice sat in front of me as Walker led the meet. He was speaking in coded language about the hits I pulled off, that those he reported to were pleased, and before we got down to the business of the remaining names on the list, he wanted to discuss money and future opportunities for me. I was focused on the nigga as he spoke, but I glanced at the other two motherfuckers as I thought about one thing. He never brought up Goldman or Dutches. Walker was going on and on about payment and other shit about money, when the meet was crashed.

By the Feds. The door bust open and in poured FBI agents in SWAT gear and automatic weapons. Yelling at us to put our hands up and don't move!! I raised my hands in the air and sat still as six agents in all black surrounded the table. Submachine gun barrels and lasers pointed at us. Two agents in suits strolled in and informed us that we were all under arrest. For criminal conspiracy to money laundering and affiliation with organized crime. One of the feds lied the warrant on the table as we were made to stand up. One by one. I stared at Walker as I was patted down. My gun and shit were taken, the cuffs were locked on my wrists, and then one of the FBI agents in SWAT gear led me out of the suite by my bicep. I didn't say shit, but it was clear as a motherfucker now. The agent taking me into custody was the white dude that helped us clip Russell. Miller didn't say shit, but when we locked eyes, he gave me a nod. I caught the message. *Keep my motherfuckin' mouth shut.* This shit was deep, and I wondered just how deep it was about to get.

****

I was transported to the Federal Building downtown, but kept separated from the other motherfuckers taken into custody with me. They put me in an interrogation room and left me there for almost three hours. I sat on the metal fold out chair at the rectangle shaped table with my arms crossed, waiting and mentally preparing myself. Thirty-years old and shit was about to get real for me. I got myself caught up in some dark shit, but I wasn't about to bitch up now. Live an outlaw life, deal with the outlaw consequences. My pops always told me that a man doesn't run from the bad shit. Because when shit was good, you weren't worried about nothing. My father taught me to be a man long before I became one. He put real man shit in my head and I stood tall on that my whole life. This was apart of the game. I was staring at the table when the door unlocked and I looked up to see who it was entering the room

Goldman walked over to the table and sat his briefcase on it as the door closed and locked again. He stared at me for a moment before turning his head and looking up at the security camera. I looked at it too as the red light went out. That's when he unbuttoned his suit jacket and sat down across from me. Goldman and I held eyes as he laid it out for me. No. He and Walker didn't burn me. They did burn a bunch of other motherfuckers though. The white dude at the Ritz-Carlton was the special advisor to a Senator. A Senator that was connected to high-level narcotics trafficking. The same narcotics that the cartel was moving into the country. The Latino at the meet was a member of a rival cartel. He was there to negotiate a deal with the Senator's advisor to outbid *(undercut)* the cartel his own was in competition with. I nodded my head as Goldman went on. Aaron Jamison, Rahim Johnson, Angelo Peretti, and Giovanni Ricci were the cartels main distributors for their East Coast-Philadelphia pipeline. And Sean Russell? He was the main investor and inside man for the cartel on Wall Street.

The lawyer gave it to me straight up. Revealing to me that he had a special relationship with the Feds and if it wasn't for him, "we" would be doing life in a federal prison. The FBI knew about what me and Dutches did for a living. It was our own good luck that we found him and Walker. A damn good stroke of luck. The feds wanted him to find a way to draw out the cartel and their American connections when I fell into his lap. He made a deal with them. Use Dutches and I to clip the heads of the cartel's Philadelphia network, take out their guy on Wall Street, and expose the Senator's advisor and the cartel representative for their alliance. Goldman told me that Dutches and I were the tools they put into play to keep the Feds hands clean, allowing them to cripple the flow of dope in this area of the pipeline. In exchange, D walks away clean, they agreed not to involve A'liyah, we keep our money, and it all came down to me. I asked what the fuck that meant? Goldman looked me in the eyes and answered.

If I accepted a plea agreement with the U.S. Attorney handling the case, I'd only be looking at ten years of federal incarceration. On a weapons and conspiracy charge. The deal was that I said nothing about anything, eat the charges, agree to the plea bargain, I'll be out in five, and my people walk away free. Especially Dutches. If I fell on my sword, the feds will not charge me or her with a laundry list of federal charges, which includes multiple counts of murder, that will see us behind bars for the rest of our natural lives. Ten-year plea deal, out in five, with a special bonus at the end. The remainder of my sentence will be secretly suspended upon my release. Goldman explained that this was a true, once in a lifetime, divine intervention gift for someone in my position. I did the Feds dirty work for them and they were willing to let me walk on countless bodies if I agreed to keep quiet and do a relatively short stretch inside. It took me all of two minutes to make my decision. Goldman removed several documents from his briefcase, went over them with me, and gave me a pen to start signing.

****

They allowed me to make a phone call before shit got complicated. I called A'liyah and explained the situation to her. I was preparing myself for her reaction. I anticipated her being done with me and moving on with her life without me again. She had a peaceful life, a good job, she was happy with me in her world again, and once more; walking the path of an outlaw thug was going to force her hand. Liyah listened without cutting me off as I explained as much as I could to her without going into detail. When I was done, as I hardened myself for her to verbally dismiss me from her world or simply hang up the phone; she did neither. Instead, she quietly told me that she loved me, she was with me no matter what, I was her everything, she wasn't going to abandon me a second time, and to watch my back in there. Also, to call her again when I can so that she will know where I am and she'll come visit me when she's able to. Ma shared her love with me again, I said it back, then we ended the call.

About an hour later, two Federal agents in suits and FBI windbreakers on escorted me down to the underground garage. Unlike others, they only cuffed my wrists in the front. No shackles and shit. They put me in a tinted sedan and then we hit the road. A little over two hours later, I was led into the Federal Detention center in Brooklyn. Before going through the intake process, another Fed took me to an interview room. The agent I knew as Miller reminded me of the arrangement. Don't talk about what I knew. To anyone. Ever! Keep my mouth shut, do the nickel, and then walk out of prison to my woman, my money, and my freedom. Miller reiterated what Goldman had said to me in Philly. This was truly divine intervention for me. If it wasn't for life throwing me a rope, I'd be done! Life in prison, or even the death penalty. Yet, because major indictments were on the way that were going to elevate a whole lot of careers; I was going to come out clean in the end. I nodded my head, Miller did the same, then he left the interview room so that I could be processed into Federal custody.

A'liyah came to see me a few days later. She told me that Dutches had reached out to her and sent word that she was good. She was far away and keeping a low profile. I told Liyah that she could trust D and my lady just nodded her head. I then asked her to get in contact with my former partner and tell her that when she gets a chance, deliver my end to her. The look on A'liyah's face clearly showed she had no idea what that meant, but when Dutches makes good on the delivery, she'll understand. Ma agreed to contact D and we spent the rest of our visit talking. I was at the detention center for just over two months. Then, I was transported to the Federal courthouse. In a private-closed door hearing, Goldman submitted my plea deal. There was no discussion or normal proceedings. Three federal judges penned their signatures on the document without a word, and that was that. I was taken back to the detention center.

Two days later, a Federal plane flew me out of New York City and I began my ten-year sentence that I was only going to serve five of. It didn't take me long to settle in and establish a routine. I worked out twice a day, most of my time was spent reading books that elevated my intellect, I watched my sports teams on TV, listened to music at night, and I worked in the library. I still didn't fuck with niggas like that, but there was an ol' head that reminded me of my pops that I rocked with. OG was six years in on a twelve-year bid when he arrived and was assigned to my cell block. We sat in the yard together, I made sure that he had plenty of commissary because he had no people for income, we watched sports together, and at every week, we played multiple games of chess. Time went by and days-weeks-and-months were scratched off the calendar. The only person I spoke to outside the walls of the prison was my lady.

A'liyah stayed true to her word and was riding this sentence out. She wrote me at least once a week, we talked on the phone every few days, and she sent me pictures a few times a month. The further I moved away from a thugs' state of mind and heart; the more she breathed life into me. She always kept it real with me, spoke & wrote words of encouragement, expressed how much she believed in me, and always expressed her love for my ass. Though we had enough money to build a life with, her concern was for me to be the person she saw in me when I was 16. Liyah wanted more and better for me, but she kept it 100. She couldn't do it for me. I had to become the man she knew I could be, for myself. Leave all that outlaw shit in the past, enjoy life with her, and finally have peace in this world. The closer time moved towards this five year bid being over, the more I believed in her words. The more I believed it myself. By the time I had four years and eight months in, I was ready to get out. The prison informed me of my release date and I was ready to go.

Until a face that I haven't seen in years was transferred in.

EPILOGUE

This motherfucker awakened the sleeping wolf in me the moment I saw his motherfuckin' face! Almost five-years of walking the path of a calm, quiet, and trying to change man started to detour with his arrival. On the real, I had forgot about this nigga over the years. He had fallen so deep into my sub-conscious mind, that I had forgotten how much hate I had for his ass. The first time son saw me and my OG in the yard, it was as if he saw a fuckin' ghost. Na'jae Matthews was almost 40-years old now. Back in the day, son was on that pretty boy, smooth player shit. Always kept his hair cut low and faded, his dress style was sharp, he always had on the latest expensive sneakers or Timbs, and he was always dipped in shine. When he was slingin' dope in Newark, he was that hustlin' nigga with diamond studs in his ears, a blinging chain around his neck, and the nicest watch on his wrist. Na'jae was all about money, power, respect, bitches, and being that nigga on the streets.

All these years later, he was a shell of his former self. He looked much older than he was. His hairline was mad receded, his face was wrinkling, eyes permanently bagged, and he was skinny as fuck. The moment I saw his snake ass, I immediately started to see red. The hatred I had for him began to course through my veins. Na'jae spoke to me, saying what up? All nervous and shit. I gave him the wolf stare as I held my fire in check and responded to him. Telling him that he was good. We good. He got the message. In code from our hood, telling an enemy that we were good meant that though there was no beef between us anymore; we ain't cool. *I ain't goin' to come at you, but we ain't friends. Keep ya motherfuckin' distance and I'll do the same.* OG and I walked past Na'jae and that was that. Or, so I thought.

For the next two weeks, that nigga consumed my thought process. All day, every day. I saw the nigga in the chow hall, in the library, the yard, or going to and from our cell blocks. Every time I saw his face, I saw my brothers'. I saw Keith. The hate I had for Na'jae was just as strong as the love I had for K. The red in my eyes kept getting brighter, and the longer I didn't act on it, the more it fucked with my mind. It got harder and harder to push my blood lust down. A'liyah could detect it in my voice when we talked on the phone, but I never told her what was bothering me. My lady did her best to comfort me without knowing what had gotten to me and I was holding the beast at bay. Just to finish my time and be done with all of it. At less than months out from my release, I had all but put the animal in me back in its cave. I believed I had let it go with Na'jae. Seeing him didn't turn my heart cold and I was just about there to my release date. Then, it happened.

I called A'liyah and she told me the last fuckin' thing I wanted to hear. Dutches was dead. My old partner linked up with a chick from LA that was just like us and the two of them got money together. Buying large quantities of high-quality weed to sell off in the Midwest. D was actually in love with shorty, they did everything together, and my partner was in serious talks with her girl about them going legit. Dutches wrote me, and in her letter, she told me that she was getting tired and just wanted to live. She found someone to share life with and she desired to see what it was like to be happy and know some kind of peace. That is until a motherfucker ambushed her and her girl. D died from two gunshot wounds and her chick survived to get word to Liyah in Philly. When I learned of D's death, there was something in me that caught fire. Then it detonated in my soul.

All of the repressed pain, anger, and anguish in me ignited at once. My mother, father, Mr. Marvin, Miss. Shanda, and Keith. I sat in my cell alone and began to drown in all the blood in my spirit. I thought about Dionne. That look in her eyes when she realized my betrayal. I cried for the first time in years as I sat there. Suddenly consumed by guilt. Regret. Shame. And rage. Dutches was supposed to be there when I got out! My fuckin' parents shouldn't have fuckin' died on me! I wished I had never met Keith, because I truly had a brother in him and when he died, apart of me did too! My emotions became a toxic volcano in me and I hated it. I paced my cell and smoked, crying my eyes out. Wishing I had never been born. I hated how I felt and this shit had to go. Na'jae's face popped into my mind and the blood pact of vengeance I pledged to him returned. I spent the next hour making a shank. I didn't give a fuck no more!

I didn't give a fuck about going home. I didn't give a fuck about life, freedom, or that niggas life. Na'jae was about to get all this hate! I owed his ass anyway. He was going to get what he deserved! Everything I felt was his now. Fuck him! It was almost yard time and I was going out to handle that nigga. I tucked my shank in my waist band and went to the sink in my cell to clean myself up. In about five minutes, they gonna announce yard activities over the loud speaker. As I looked at myself in the mirror, a face took over my thoughts. I stared into my own eyes as every single one of those toxic emotions began to scale back. I stood there looking at my reflection, my mind taken over by the beautiful image of my son. Hakim. My five-year old son with A'liyah. I sat down on my bunk and took out my little man's most recent picture. I stared at it as yard was called and I ignored it. Hakim was smiling at his mother as she took the pic.

Our son looked exactly like me. My twin. Liyah got his hair cut like me, he was quiet like me, and a natural born athlete too. My son was smart, funny, he was going to be tall like me, and his mother told me that he took after me in so many ways. She told me of her pregnancy while I was at the detention center in New York. I had pictures of Hakim from birth to now, and I saw him multiple times a year when he and his mother flew out here to visit me. My child was the true reason I decided to leave the outlaw life in the past. It's why I had a second chance. As I stared at my son's smiling face, a quote ran through my mind. When plotting revenge, always dig two graves. One for enemy, and one for yourself. Hakim and I stared at one another as I finally let it all go. If I killed Na'jae, if I took out what I felt on him and ended his life; I'd be ending my own. I'd never get out and my son will become me. A young black boy without a father to guide and lead him away from all the things in life and society that turns black boys into monsters. I got rid of the shank and went on with my day.

I was going home soon. A'liyah and Hakim needed me. My pops wasn't there to save me from the streets, and though I can't save every black boy in America from becoming a thug, I can stop the cycle with one.

My son.

THE END

Thank you for your support, it is truly appreciated, and if you haven't read any of my other books, here is the full list of my titles:
(All available on Amazon)

Black Reign Publishing (Independent releases): **Ty Robinson**

-Hood Royalty Series
  (Queen of Diamondz, Queen of Diamondz II,
  King of Spadez, Royal Reign: The Finale)

-Power & Justice
-Power & Justice: Backlash
-Power & Justice: Backlash II
-Power & Justice IV: N.J.N.P
-Power & Justice: Final Solution
-Brother's & King's
-Natural Born Ryderz
-Natural Born Ryderz II: Death Before Dishonor
-Legacy of the Master
-Let It Burn
-Venomous Fruit
-Legacy of a Champion: PART ONE
-Legacy of a Champion: PART TWO
-Loving This Woman Right
-Rise of the Warrior Queen's: a Domestic Violence novel
-A'shani: The Black Angel of Death
-Loving my Man Right: Kazim & Mekena II
-Black Ice: Chronicles of a Hitta

Soulja-Choc Presents (Publisher releases): **Ty'Son**

-Mr. Inferno
-Mr. Incredible
-Safire: The fall of an angel
-Safire II: The Rise of a Fallen Angel
-Jaguar: Memoirs of a Bad Girl
-When a King Loves a Queen
-You Belong to Me
-Seductive Flavors: An interracial erotica love story
-Naughty Girls
-Touching Fire
-Pain & Pleasure: a Story of Sex, Money, & Misery

Novel's can be purchased on:
www.amazon.com

Author can contacted at:
E-mail: tylegend365@gmail.com
Instagram: tyrob3428
Facebook: Ty Robinson / e-mail search: tylegend365@gmail.com
Twitter: @authorTyRob

Coming Soon

Soulja-Choc Presents
Do You Feel Me?
a Black Romance novel

Black Reign Publishing
PERFECT REFLECTIONS
in a BROKEN MIRROR

"The two most important days in your life is the day you were born, and the day you find out why."

"Greatness is achieved when skill meets drive, and then coupled with humility and belief"

"Hard work beats talent, when talent doesn't work hard."

CPSIA information can be obtained
at www.ICGtesting.com
Printed in the USA
LVHW081451281220
675097LV00004B/144

9 798686 917873